DON'T

Breathe

A

Word

ALSO BY JORDYN TAYLOR

The Paper Girl of Paris

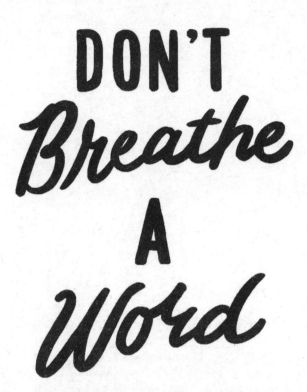

DON'T

Breathe

A

Word

JORDYN TAYLOR

An Imprint of HarperCollins*Publishers*

HarperTeen is an imprint of HarperCollins Publishers.

Don't Breathe a Word
Copyright © 2021 by Jordyn Taylor
www.epicreads.com

ISBN 978-0-06-303888-2

Typography by Corina Lupp
21 22 23 24 25   PC/LSCH   10 9 8 7 6 5 4 3 2 1
❖

First Edition

For my parents

ONE

Eva, present day

I swear to god, sometimes the harder I try to do the right thing, the more spectacularly I end up failing. I was right on time for French, but when I get to the classroom and open the door, the desks are completely empty.

Time to pull out the trusty ol' schedule and see where I messed up—again. On Monday, I sat in the wrong room and gradually realized the teacher was speaking Spanish, not French, which I probably should have deduced earlier from the red-and-yellow flag tacked to the wall. When her back was turned, I seized the opportunity to stand up, whisper *"lo siento"* to my confused classmates, and tiptoe to the door.

Strangely enough, I seem to be in the right place. Maybe I'm just the first one here.

Oh, shoot.

It's Friday, which means there's an assembly in between first and second periods. I swing my open backpack onto my shoulder and run full speed down the hall, which is empty—*obviously.* That should have been my first clue. Breathless, I burst onto the quad, and to my relief, there's still a small crowd of navy-blue blazers shuffling up the steps of the auditorium next door. I join the back of the line all casually, as if sprinting is my go-to mode of transportation. I feel beads of sweat poking out beneath my thick, dark curls.

I'd love to snag a seat next to someone I can introduce myself to. Even as an outgoing person, it's been harder than expected to meet people. Well, let me clarify: I *technically* meet people all the time—group discussions in class; meals in the dining hall where I plop myself down in whatever open seat I can find; the line for the communal showers that inevitably stretches down the third-floor hallway in the half hour before curfew—but it's hard to *actually* meet people. Like, in a "let's hang out and not talk about school stuff" way.

Most students at Hardwick are "lifers," meaning they start in the fifth grade and go all the way through; by eleventh grade, social groups are calcified like bone. Despite being the same Eva Storm who could strike up a conversation with literally anyone in New York City—a talent that came in handy when my friends asked me to charm corner store cashiers into selling me beer with my fake ID—I've felt more or less invisible since Mom and Caleb dropped me off here last weekend. At Tuesday's assembly, I sat down beside a girl from my English class who'd seemed kinda nice when we'd gotten into groups to read scenes from *Macbeth.* I said, "Howdy, 'tis me, Banquo"—my delivery was funny, I swear—and she said, "Sorry, do you mind going over there? I'm saving a spot for someone else."

Shocked at her dismissal, not to mention her failure to appreciate high comedy, I had to move across the aisle to a seat beside my math teacher, Mr. Richterman, who smelled like a blend of coffee and chalk and didn't seem to recognize me.

At the top of the stairs to the auditorium, an exasperated teacher in a no-nonsense pantsuit shouts at people to tighten their ties and fold down their collars. "Margot and Cassidy, *please* unroll your skirts," she calls to a pair of girls with their arms linked. They giggle and cry, "Sorry, Ms. Pell!" as their fingers fly to the fabric at their waists.

"You there, with the curls! Stop!"

Oh no. My foot is on the final step, and Ms. Pell's laser-beam gaze is pointed at me. The other people weave around me, rubbernecking like they're rolling by a car crash.

"You can't go in there dressed like that."

Is this a prank? Some kind of Hardwick initiation? I'm wearing the same black loafers, same white knee socks, and same gray kilt as every other girl who's walked through those doors. But then she reaches out, pinches the corner of my cardigan, and holds it up like the tail of a dead mouse.

"Friday is formal assembly," she snaps. "You need your blazer."

Ah. I figure this rule is printed somewhere in the student handbook I got on my first day, but there are a *lot* of rules at

Hardwick (like, sixty-something pages of them), and it isn't exactly easy to keep track of them all. I know the biggies—like the aggressive nine o'clock curfew every night except Saturday—but I'm hardly an expert in formal assembly regulations. Right now, my blazer is hanging off the chair in my dorm room, conveniently located on the opposite end of campus.

"I, um, don't suppose you'll take pity on the tragic new kid?" I venture. You know, the only new student in the whole eleventh grade—the one whose mom and terrible stepdad sent her away to boarding school like a character in some depressing fairy tale.

Ms. Pell's mouth forms a thin, wrinkled line. "I don't take pity on students for things they can control, such as remembering a mandatory clothing item. This is how we've done things for over a century, and I'm afraid you won't be the exception. You'll have to sit out on the steps today."

"But—"

"*Sit*, please."

There doesn't seem to be any other option, so I sit on the steps, facing the last few arrivals like a fool in a dunce cap. Finally, I hear the door shut, and I'm alone: one tiny speck on a quad surrounded by the ancient stone buildings of Hardwick Preparatory Academy. I picture my loneliness multiplying, like cell division. What I could really use right now, besides a blazer, is a friend.

Maybe my problem is that I just can't summon the Hardwick spirit that everyone else seems to have. You've got the eager beavers, who dash to the front row of every class; the student council members, who make enthusiastic announcements about upcoming social and charity events; the athletes, who strut around campus in their special team jackets; the ultra-rich kids, whose last names sound familiar during attendance because they're also the names of buildings around campus. They all have their own deep, meaningful connection to this place—not like where I used to go in Manhattan, where everyone had their own shit going on outside school. At Hardwick, it's like they're one big happy family, and I'm an intruder barging into the living room with mud on my shoes.

Well, wouldn't be the first time.

Okay, positive thoughts, please! I won't always be an outsider. I'll find someone to hang out with eventually—right? Like . . . uh . . . that redheaded girl in math class, maybe. Jenny something.

Jenny actually seems kind of promising.

I don't have anything to go on, really. It's just a hunch. But compared to the other people I've encountered in my first week at Hardwick, the girl with the pin-straight, waist-length red hair who sits behind me in math doesn't seem quite so—I don't know—*indoctrinated* by this historic boarding school of ours. The other day, as Mr. Richterman went on about the point of intersection of something or other, I was staring out the window directly beside my desk when I caught her gaze in the reflection of the glass. At first, I wasn't sure if she could see me too, but then she jerked her head in the direction of the chalkboard and rolled her eyes. The moment the bell rang, she gathered her things and marched out of class, but I'm certain we had a connection of some kind. Maybe I'll see if I can talk to her today.

When I walk into the room for fifth-period math, Jenny's sitting in the same seat as last time. I get a better chance to look at her now: pale porcelain skin; long, lanky limbs; fuchsia lipstick that clashes with her hair, but somehow—maybe it's how she leans back confidently in her chair, arm resting on the windowsill—she makes it all look so cool. Even the blazer and kilt. She looks at me without any expression on her face.

"Hey," she says.

"Hey."

She acknowledged my existence. After a week of invisibility, it feels like a drug. I slide into the empty desk in front of her.

Mr. Richterman takes his position at the front of the room. His voice is dry and robotic, like he's been teaching this stuff since the school's founding in 1906. "Okay, class, let's start by reviewing quadratic equations . . ."

Across the room, two dozen mechanical pencils click into action. I try my best to follow along and take notes, but twenty minutes in, I'm having a hard time keeping my grip on the lecture.

Finally, Mr. Richterman puts down the chalk and wipes his fingers on a handkerchief he plucks from his breast pocket. "Now, for the next few minutes, I'd like you to break off into pairs and work through the questions on page forty-nine. If you finish early, feel free to test your knowledge with . . ."

There's already chatter brewing as people lay claim to their partners, so I twist around, ready to shoot my shot with Jenny. Sweet—she hasn't paired off with anyone. Better yet, she nods at me.

"You wanna do this, or what?" Her voice is deep. A little husky.

I drag my binder into my lap and flip my chair to face her desk. "Okay, but I feel like I should warn you: I haven't fully grasped anything math related since, like, *Sesame Street*."

She cocks her head and purses her fuchsia lips, like she's analyzing me. There's an awkward pause where I'm certain I just Banquo'd myself again.

Then she laughs—loudly. It's a full-on cackle.

"Quiet, please!" Mr. Richterman shouts.

Jenny downgrades to a giggle and leans over the desk. "Guess what?"

"What?"

"You could put a gun to my head, and I would not be able to confidently tell you what a parabola is."

We both snort and try to hold in our laughs, which is always next to impossible when you're not supposed to be laughing. Jenny and I do our best to focus on the math problems, but they're also next to impossible, so we end up playing tic-tac-toe in the margin of the textbook. She beats me in the first two rounds, but in the third, I draw a triumphant line through my three diagonal Os.

Putting down her pencil, Jenny abandons the game and peers out the window. "It's so nice out," she says longingly, twirling a lock of coppery hair around her finger. I didn't notice it before, but her nails are painted the palest of pinks, even though nail polish is forbidden (according to a page of the student handbook I actually remember).

I follow her gaze out the window, down to the main quad, where two groundskeepers snip at a manicured garden. Inside the rectangular edges, yellow flowers are arranged on a green background to spell out "HPA," for Hardwick Preparatory Academy. A bronze plaque at the front notes which wealthy alum donated funds for such a thing. There are a *lot* of those plaques around Hardwick, dating from the early 1900s to now. Again: people really love it here.

"I wanna be *outside*," Jenny whispers. "Don't you?"

She stares at me with those huge gray eyes flecked with gold, a smirk playing on her lips. She isn't like the other people at Hardwick. She *sees* me. Maybe I'm not thinking straight, but her last question almost sounds like . . . a challenge. My heart thumps like I'm boarding a roller coaster.

"Okay, back to your desks so we can go through the answers as a class!" Mr. Richterman calls out.

Damn. I turn back to my desk, but my pulse still pounds as I consider my next move. I have an idea—something that worked one time at my old school, when my friends made a pact to skip class and go lie out in the sun on Randall's Island. But do I dare?

I find Jenny's reflection in the window.

She's looking right back me.

That's it. I'm doing it. I scribble three words in the corner of a piece of paper, tear it off, and crumple it into a ball. I flick the ball along the windowsill with just the right amount of force, so that it rolls to a stop near Jenny's shoulder.

Through the window, I watch her notice it. Then she looks at me. I give her a small nod. She grabs the ball of paper and unfolds it in her lap, reading my simple message:

COME WITH ME.

Once again, our eyes find each other's in the glass. Baby, we are *doing this*! The next part is up to me. I close my eyes and steel myself for pain. Three . . . Two . . . One . . .

Smack.

I fling my upper body onto my desk, letting my chair legs scrape against the floor for added effect. People gasp. Mr. Richterman stops talking, and everyone turns to the source of the noise. Slowly, I push myself up, blinking and looking around like I'm in a daze.

"Miss Storm, are you okay?"

I pretend to sway dangerously in my seat. "I—I don't know," I reply. "Low b-blood sugar, maybe . . ."

Mr. Richterman pinches the bridge of his nose and scans the room. "Can someone please accompany Miss Storm to the infirmary? I don't know if I want her walking there on her own in this state."

Yes. This is exactly what I was banking on—but will Jenny get the message?

Before anyone else can volunteer, her gravelly voice comes to the rescue. "I'll take her, Mr. Richterman."

"Thank you, Miss Price."

"It's no problem at all."

"All right. Off you two go."

The next thing I know, Jenny is helping me from my seat and shepherding my fake-stumbling body out the door. We keep up the act as we descend the wide wooden staircase and step outside onto the quad. I'm delirious with excitement that we pulled this off. Hopefully I don't *actually* faint now.

"This way," Jenny whispers, because we're still in earshot of classrooms with open windows. She turns sharply to the right, down a shady path that snakes behind the library. I follow her across an empty parking lot, because she seems to know what she's doing and where she's going. She leads me into the sprawling glen that surrounds the campus, home to a network of twisting trails that ramble for miles through the trees.

I'm no stranger to this part of campus: every morning, I've been sneaking out the back door of Ainsley House to go jogging through the woods. I'm actually a pretty strong runner; I did cross-country all throughout middle school, back when I still wanted to prove I was good at stuff. I was definitely one of the best on the team, but still, Mom and Caleb never came to my meets, which were often in Jersey or Connecticut. In high school, I gave it up—gave it all up, really. But running still makes me feel happy, especially this past week, when I've been stressed about not fitting in here.

When we're deep enough in the trees that I can't see any school through the gaps between trunks, Jenny finally speaks.

"Nice performance in there, lady. I'm impressed."

"Hey, you gave a nice performance, too. You seemed *very* concerned."

"But your final stumble into the doorframe!" She mimes a chef's kiss. "Brava."

I laugh. "Why thank you."

"Seriously, you were so smooth."

"I tried my best."

Jenny tosses her hair over her shoulder, then takes off her blazer and ties it around her waist. For some reason, I'm hyper-aware of the way I'm walking, my body just behind her left shoulder. Should I stay in back and let her lead? Or should I move to her side, like we're friends? My solution is to stay at a perfect diagonal, tracking my position in relation to hers with every step.

"So. You're new, right?" Jenny asks bluntly.

Oh, great. I can feel myself deflating faster by the second. Do we really have to focus on what an outsider I am? "Yes, ma'am. How long have you been here?"

"I started last year," she says, "so I know what it's like. Everyone's friends already, and you're basically this invisible blob drifting around campus. Like, *Hello?! Does anybody want to talk to me?*"

Wait. Jenny was new last year? Jenny actually *gets it*? Oh my god, I want to hug her. "Yeah, that's exactly how I feel."

"You managing okay?"

"It's a little lonely." An understatement. "But I go for these long runs every morning to try and clear my head. That helps."

"Oh, cool. You're a runner?"

"Yeah. Just for fun. Not, like, marathons or anything."

"I *hate* working out. Did you try out for cross-country?"

"Nah—I didn't even know there had been tryouts until they emailed out the sports schedules the other day."

"Damn. Sorry, dude."

I shrug. "It's whatever." In reality, I'd been a little disappointed.

Jenny suddenly stops in the middle of the path, tilting up her face to catch a narrow ray of sunshine that somehow made it through the crisscrossing branches. "Hold up. The lighting here is really great." She pulls out her phone and opens the camera app with the fastest thumbs I've ever seen. "Just a quick pic. This might be feed-worthy." She slips her backpack off her shoulders and holds it out to me. "Do you mind?"

I take it from her immediately. "No. Of course not."

"Thanks." She shakes out her hair so it hangs all over the place—but in a cool way—and ever so slightly purses her lips. She takes about twenty rapid-fire selfies, swipes through them, and hearts a few. Others make her recoil in disgust.

"For Instagram?" I ask.

12

"Yeah. I'm getting five hundred bucks to post a photo with this lipstick on, so . . ."

"Whoa. Did I just witness you . . . *influencing*?"

"Oh my god, stop. That word is horrifying." But she smiles to herself as she puts her phone away, and we start walking again. She forgets to reclaim her backpack, and for some reason, I don't say anything. I just keep on carrying it.

"So, how did you end up here anyway?" Jenny asks.

Oh, good. A chance to revisit the memory of the night they told me I was enrolled—the four of us sitting around the table in our Upper West Side apartment eating takeout sushi. The way Mom leaned over and squeezed my shoulder with her polished talons, like she was telling me something good; that smug look on Caleb's face that made me want to hurl my dinner at him. When I found out my half sister Ella, who's in ninth grade, wasn't going to boarding school—it was just me, the *other* daughter, being sent away—I really *did* pick up a cucumber roll and throw it at Caleb's chest, which unfortunately only bolstered their argument that I needed a stricter academic environment.

But I give Jenny the sanitized version—the one that doesn't hurt as much: "My mom and her husband want me to get my grades up before college applications. I was kind of slacking off, I guess. But they didn't tell me I was going to Hardwick until, like, right before we left. So . . . surprise! I'm here."

"Jeez. That is *seriously* harsh."

"It wasn't amazing! How'd you end up here?"

"Well, I'm from Philly, but my parents bought this major brewery in Albany, so we moved up there. Hardwick's like two hours away, but it's by *far* the best private school upstate, so I was like, 'Yes. Let's do this.'"

"Ah. Less harsh."

"Yeah. Your story is rough, dude. And I take it you weren't at another boarding school before?"

"Nah, it was a public school in Manhattan. It's, um, super weird having my *school* tell me when I need to be in bed with the lights out. I'm surprised they don't supervise teeth brushing."

Jenny laughs again. Every time it happens, I feel like Mario collecting coins in a Nintendo game. "Yeah, the curfew was hard to get used to," she admits. "And the Saturday classes— super rough." She pauses and then her voice changes. It's softer and sharper at the same time, like she's telling me a secret. "Eva, I know everything feels like absolute garbage right now. But I promise, Hardwick is a great place. And it gets better as soon as you find the right people to hang out with. Listen . . . I know we, like, *just* met, but you seem really fucking cool."

Oh my god.

I was right.

Jenny and I were destined to be friends.

And then all of a sudden, without my express permission, my brain is picturing me and Jenny doing *everything* together. I'm coming up with questions I can ask her parents about beer making when I visit their brewery: How do you add the different flavors? Who makes the designs that go on the labels?

A tiny warning bell goes off in my head. I'm doing what I did with Jeffrey Chung last fall, when I was all-in from the moment he took me to the roof at Alicia Barney's Halloween party and kissed me against the railing, even though I was legitimately concerned about us both falling over, and even though he was wearing one of those awful Scream masks, which he'd pushed up onto the top of his head, and the strings were cutting into the sides of his face. *We'll be a couple*, I told myself as I stroked the back of his neck, *and we'll go to winter formal in color-coordinated outfits*. The next weekend he hooked up with Alicia at Nina Brown's party, and I felt like a rug had been ripped out from under me.

But that was different. Jeffrey was a boy, and everything is more complicated where boys are concerned.

All I need is for Jenny Price to be my friend.

And she just told me I'm *really fucking cool*.

"Aww. Thank you." I don't know what the right response is.

Jenny lifts up the side of her blazer and pulls out her phone again. When she looks at the screen, she stops in her tracks. "Oh, *snap*."

"What is it?" I figure we might have to go back and retake the selfies.

"My friend Heather just texted me. She has a free period right now and wants to know if I can hang out." Jenny looks back at me over her shoulder, biting her fuchsia bottom lip. "I'd obviously invite you, but, like, it's Heather's room, and she's kind of particular about us inviting people over who she doesn't know, so . . ."

"No, no, it's totally cool!" But my stomach drops. I was the one who MacGyvered us out of class! I had imagined the two of us spending the rest of the afternoon together wandering through the woods and then maybe drifting to the dining hall for dinner.

"Okay, cool. Sorry about that. I mean . . . at least you're not in math anymore." She looks at my hand. "Wait, are you still carrying my bag?"

"Oh—I—um—yeah. I guess I am."

"Why didn't you say something?"

"I don't know." I hold it out to her. "Here."

"Thanks." She takes it and slings it over her shoulder, then starts walking faster than before. Apparently, Jenny doesn't want to keep Heather waiting. We get to a spot where a smaller path splits off to the left, up a hill and toward another opening in the trees. Beyond, there's a stone building that looks like a dorm; I see a window with a navy-blue Hardwick pendant stuck to the glass.

Jenny turns to face me. "I have to run. Heather's letting me in through the back door." Before she leaves, she shoves her phone in my hand. "Give me your number. There's a party tomorrow night, and if Heather's okay with it, I'll text you the info."

Oh my god oh my god oh my god oh my god. I put my number in Jenny's phone and hand it back to her.

"Thanks."

"No problem."

"Well, see ya."

"See ya. It was really nice meeting you."

It was really nice meeting you?! What did I think it was, an internship interview? She hurries up the hill, backpack bouncing heavily against her side—not quite running, but almost. From the trees, I can just make out the back door opening and Jenny disappearing inside. I wish more than anything that she could have stayed—or better yet, that I could have gone with her to Heather's.

Which is silly, because I don't even know these people.

And at least I didn't have to sit through the rest of that math class.

But I can't deny the crackle of electricity in my chest when I look at my phone half an hour later and there are two text messages from a number I don't recognize:

Hey it's Jenny. Heather says it's cool if
you come to the party tomorrow. Meet in
the parking lot behind the library at 10.

And don't bring anyone else.

TWO

Connie, 1962

I only see two ways to cope with the current state of affairs: either get on with your life like a normal person, or spend every waking hour imagining the world being blasted to smithereens—like me. In my sixteen years of existence, I've only ever managed to think about the bomb, or actively try *not* to think about the bomb; either way, I'm technically thinking about the bomb.

"You're thinking about the bomb again, aren't you?" Betty asks.

"What? How did you know?"

"Because you were doing that thing where you stare into the distance like an old frontier woman who's about to succumb to diphtheria."

"Really?" I frown. "I was going for dysentery."

"Connie."

"Sorry, Bets. I'm here now."

It's a sunny April afternoon, just warm enough that we can

finally wear our knee socks instead of tights, and we're lounging on a blanket in the corner of the quad. Betty looks at me through her red cat-eye glasses, which match the color of the giant bows holding her pigtails in place. She asks pointedly, "Is this about the assembly?"

This is what happens when you've been best friends since the fifth grade: you learn to read each other's minds. She knows I'm thinking back to this morning, when we were leaving Ainsley House for breakfast and there was a notice on the bulletin board for a special assembly on "nuclear preparedness" tomorrow during fifth period.

The last time we had one of these, it was right after we got back from winter break. They brought us into the auditorium and played a recording of President Kennedy's inauguration speech from last year: the one where he talks about the "dark powers of destruction"—the "deadly atom" that could destroy all humanity should our enemies not make peace with us. *Ask not what your country can do for you—ask what you can do for your country.* Then the dean of students got onstage and explained that on government orders, a large basement room had been converted into a public fallout shelter for the community. The underground shelter could apparently hold hundreds of people, with walls thick enough to shield us from the harmful radiation that follows a nuclear blast. It had food and water and beds so we could live down there for weeks, if need be. I was so light-headed when I left the auditorium, I tripped and fell into a waist-high snowbank.

"Yes, it's about the assembly," I tell Betty.

She sighs and scoots closer to me on the blanket. "I know all the bomb stuff scares you, but think about it: There hasn't been a nuclear attack anywhere on Earth for what, seventeen years? Why would it randomly happen now? They just have to do this stuff as a precaution. The assembly will probably be some stupid duck and cover drill."

"Stuff has happened since Hiroshima and Nagasaki, Bets. They've tested all kinds of bombs and missiles."

"Okay, but have the tests *amounted* to anything?"

"I don't know, but if we're all being told we should build fallout shelters, that must mean the situation is *kind* of serious, don't you think?"

"Connie, you need to calm down. No fallout shelter is *ever* gonna be used."

I lie down on my back, like a starfish. Sometimes I feel so flattened by the threat of nuclear war, this invisible sense of doom that's been hanging over me since the day I was born. I'm not even sure I fully understand who the Communists *are*, or what a nuclear weapon looks like, which means my thoughts can spiral to an infinite number of terrifying places. I've never been able to rein them in; even if I'm distracted by something else—like class, or a book, or Betty, or the complicated world of boys—they're always there, in some capacity, chugging along in the back of my brain.

I roll over into the fetal position, facing Betty. A lock of sandy-colored hair falls in my face and I blow it away, only to have it fall right back where it was. "Bets, how do you not dwell on scary stuff? What do you think about instead?"

When she doesn't answer immediately, I look up to find her gazing off to the left. I follow her eyes to a window on the first floor of the nearest building, through which I can clearly see the interior of our social studies teacher's office. I can also see our teacher, Mr. Kraus, entering the room, sitting down at his desk, and pulling out a notepad and pen.

"Oh god, Bets, have you memorized his schedule?"

"I have no comment on the matter."

"And is that why you insisted we sit in this very specific corner of the quad, which is in no way different than any other section of grass?"

"I think you know the answer."

"Fine." I push myself up and poke her playfully on the shoulder. "But I don't understand why you're so in love with him."

Betty tilts her head to one side, her eyes never leaving the window. "I'm not in love with him," she muses. "I'm just . . . *intrigued* by him."

So is everyone at Hardwick, boys and girls alike. In class, they scramble to sit in the front row, the better to catch the attention of the handsome twenty-four-year-old prodigy from Yale. Mr. Kraus is full of stories from his college years—not just about studying under some famous social scientist, but also about his wild exploits outside class, like the time he spent a summer backpacking around Europe, or when he and his ex-girlfriend rented a car and set out to drive all the way from Connecticut to Alaska without a map. Everybody is jealous of his grown-up adventures except for me; I like things that are familiar—things that feel safe. Why would you go on a road trip to Alaska and not bring an atlas? What's there to gain by doing that?

"Andy's had all this amazing life experience," Betty continues.

"I still think it's weird that everybody calls him Andy. He's a teacher—he's not supposed to have a first name."

"He *told* us to call him that," she says defensively.

All of a sudden, Betty bites her bottom lip and opens her eyes really wide at the exact same time.

"I know that look, Bets."

"I have an idea," she says. (I can always recognize her idea face.) "Let's go tap on his window and say hello."

"Seriously? We'd have to walk through that flower bed to get there."

"It'll be spontaneous. He'll like it."

"I don't know . . . I don't really want to."

Now *she* pokes *me* on the shoulder. "Don't be a chicken. We can ask him what the special assembly is about. He's probably the only teacher who would tell us."

She has a point—not that it would really matter either way, because I've always been happy to let Betty take the lead. The next thing I know, Betty and I are delicately stepping around the yellow tulips spelling out "HPA" for Hardwick Preparatory

Academy. I let her walk a few feet in front of me, just so it's abundantly clear to Mr. Kraus that Betty is the ringleader of the operation. I'm in it for the information he can offer to quell my nerves—not for him.

Tap, tap, tap.

At the noise, Mr. Kraus jerks his face toward the window. For a second, he seems startled at the sight of us, but he regains his composure and flashes a rakish grin. Most teachers at Hardwick would probably wave us away or shout at us to get out of the flowers, but Mr. Kraus puts down his notepad, saunters over, rolls up his sleeves, and wrenches open the window.

"Hi, Andy," Betty chirps.

"What the heck are you two doing here?" Mr. Kraus asks. "And did you just walk through the tulip garden?"

"We wanted to come say hi."

She nudges me with her elbow. "Uh, hi," I mumble.

Mr. Kraus shakes his head, but he's still smiling. He has a heavy brow and distinct dimples, an expressive face with lots of nooks and crannies. I've heard people compare him to Clint Eastwood.

"Well then. How do you do, ladies?"

"We're good. We were just catching some rays."

Another elbow. "It's nice out," I chime in, gesturing vaguely at the air. Can't we just get our information and get out of here?

"It *is* nice out, isn't it? Early this morning I jogged all the way to Burk Creek and back. Beautiful."

"That's a long way, isn't it?"

"Oh, it's gotta be around six or eight—actually, it might even be ten miles, when you factor in the curves."

"Wow!"

"I used to run even farther in my high school cross-country days. It's all about pacing yourself correctly."

"*Totally*," Betty says. I know for a fact that she hates exercise more than anything else in the world.

"Anyway, girls, I'd love to keep chatting, but you two should probably jet before someone sees you in the flower bed. The gardeners are always outside my window tending to it."

"Wait," I cut in. "Mr. Kraus, we were also wondering if you knew anything about the special assembly tomorrow—the, um, the 'nuclear preparedness' thing? There was a notice on our bulletin board this morning . . ."

"Of course!" He claps his hands. "The whole thing was actually my idea."

"It *was*?" asks Betty.

"Yes, ma'am," he replies. "You'll see what it's all about tomorrow."

"You can't tell us anything?"

"I'm afraid not."

"Sh-should we be worried?" I ask, unable to keep my voice from faltering.

"Worried? No way," Mr. Kraus says. He gestures with his chin toward the garden we've just trodden through. "This is Hardwick. You're in good hands."

Talking to Mr. Kraus doesn't entirely ease my concern about the assembly. I mean, I'm relieved there isn't some international emergency going on, but I wish it were a run-of-the-mill safety drill instead of something *he* planned. In class, he always makes us play these weird games he dreamed up the night before. Yesterday, half of us had to be blindfolded and follow verbal directions from our partners to find a series of random objects hidden around the room. It was bedlam, with people constantly bumping into each other. I tripped over a chair and hit a desk when Betty accidentally said "right" instead of "left," and now there's a bluish-purple bruise sprouting over my hip bone. Despite the chaos, people were thrilled not to have to sit at their desks for the whole period, but I couldn't help wondering what the exercise was meant to teach us, other than "maybe we should just stick to the textbook before more of us get hurt."

I never thought I'd say this, but I spend the whole next day wishing they would just show us that *Duck and Cover* cartoon from the first grade—the one where Bert the Turtle disappears inside his shell when an evil monkey drops a stick of dynamite from a tree. The song was so pleasant.

There was a turtle by the name of Bert,
and Bert the Turtle was very alert;
when danger threatened him, he never got hurt.
He knew just what to do.

When fourth-period math is over, I hurry to the arts building and join the throng of students filtering into the auditorium. Betty, who had French class right next door, is saving me a seat inside. The lobby feels like the inside of a beehive, except it's hundreds of students buzzing with questions about why we've been summoned here out of the blue.

As the crowd gets denser, something collides with my back and I stumble forward. The next thing I know, two large hands are wrapped around my shoulders, steadying me.

"Sorry, Connie. It's friggin' packed in here. Are you okay?"

It turns out, the hands belong to Craig Allenby: class president, star midfielder on the soccer team, and ridiculously handsome person whose blue eyes and long lashes make my knees go all wobbly every time I see them, which is often. By some stroke of luck, Craig and I were randomly assigned to be lab partners in chemistry this semester, which means I've gotten to spend a *lot* more time in his presence than ever before—a relief, because I've kind of been in love with him since he came to Hardwick in ninth grade.

Then again, so has everyone. At Hardwick, he might be more popular than the Beatles. He's handsome, smart, outgoing, and singlehandedly—or singlefootedly?—responsible for making the school's soccer team the best in the league. Girls stare when he passes in the halls or on the paths around campus, and boys practically trip over their own feet rushing over to give him a high five or a pat on the back and talk about some big play from his latest game. Every issue of the *Hardwick Herald* seems

26

to have at least one story on Craig's latest accomplishment, be it a winning goal, a Model United Nations victory, or a successful student council election campaign. There was even that time he rescued an injured barred owl from a tree branch in the glen, patiently coaxing it to safety over the course of three and a half hours. You would think the constant fanfare might go to his head, but that's the other thing about Craig Allenby. He's humble—a true man of the people. Case in point: he pays attention to quiet nobodies like me.

"Yeah, I'm okay. Thanks, Craig." You should probably keep your hands on my shoulders—my knees are still wobbly.

With people pressing in on us from all sides, we have no choice but to stay next to each other as we shuffle toward the door. Other kids keep bumping into Craig and then sheepishly saying hi to him, and after the third or fourth time this happens, I'm absolutely certain they're doing it on purpose. Craig, as usual, is a human magnet.

"You have any idea what this is about?" he asks, turning away from the doe-eyed senior girl who just stepped on his foot.

"Nope, but I do know that it was Mr. Kraus's idea. He told Betty and me yesterday."

"Andy planned the assembly?" Craig's face lights up. "Outta sight. That guy's the best, isn't he?"

He looks so handsome when he smiles, and I can't help but feel proud of myself for making it happen. "Yeah," I reply. "He is."

As soon as we make it into the auditorium, a high-pitched voice calls out Craig's name. I look to my right, where a few rows up, Helen Honeyman is waving to him. She has a blond flipped bob parted off to the side, the ends curling softly around her smooth, rosy cheeks.

Helen is one of the prettiest people I've ever seen, and she's wealthier than just about anyone at Hardwick, which is saying something. Her father's apparently some famous lawyer in New York City, and her mother owns seven horses, which she keeps at a farm in Connecticut. It's proof of how superior Helen is that I know these things about her, despite us never having spoken one-on-one in all the years we've been at school together. Meanwhile, I can almost guarantee she doesn't know what my father does for work—accounting—or anything else about my life, for that matter. If Craig is a man of the people, Helen is, well, a *normal* popular person. She spends most of her time in the center of an exclusive group of girlfriends and doesn't seem to notice anyone else.

"Looks like I gotta go," Craig says with a quick wave, and he hurries up the aisle to where Helen is sitting. The two of them must be an item again; I can usually get a read on their ever-changing relationship status by how hard Craig slams his books down when he arrives in chemistry. Just last Monday, the sheer force almost sent an Erlenmeyer flask flying off the table.

I find Betty sitting a few rows behind Helen, wrinkling her nose at the school's most volatile couple as their mouths collide in a hungry kiss. The way Craig's hand grasps the back of Helen's neck—how he draws her into him, like he wants to breathe her in—makes me ache with jealousy and longing at the same time.

"Why do they keep getting back together?" Betty asks as I take my seat. "We all know how it's going to end."

"Beats me," I reply.

Betty scratches her chin. "I mean, *she* must be the problem, 'cause it wouldn't be him, obviously. She's probably *so* high maintenance in a relationship, don't you think?"

"Yeah. I can't even imagine." Really, I can't. If I were lucky enough to date Craig Allenby, I wouldn't ask him for a single thing. I'd probably follow him around like a golden retriever, tongue lolling out, just happy to be in his presence.

Once I'm settled, I realize my brief conversation with Craig helped distract me from the mysterious presentation ahead of us. Anything remotely related to Mr. Kraus makes me apprehensive. I think it stems from this look he gets on his face during every one of his social experiments, as we careen around the room acting ridiculous. His eyes go wide and his jaw drops, but with a hint of a smile. It's almost like he's reveling in the power he has over us, and I don't like it at all.

Finally, the stream of students entering the auditorium starts to thin, until each one of the red velvet chairs has a uniformed body in it.

A hush settles over the room as the dean of students walks

onstage and takes his place behind the podium.

"Good afternoon, students."

"Good afternoon, Dean Denton," say hundreds of voices in unison.

"Thank you all for being here. I'll make sure this doesn't last too long, so you can still get to the latter half of your fifth-period classes."

In the seat directly in front of me, Bobby Tackett boos at the prospect of going back to class; a few people laugh, but most of us are focused on Dean Denton, who continues.

"Now, I'm sure you all saw on your bulletin boards that the purpose of this assembly is nuclear preparedness. Needless to say, we are living in very dangerous times, and the school is doing everything it can to keep you safe, such as constructing a fallout shelter on campus—which you already know. But since then, I've been wondering about the best way to *acquaint* you with this shelter, so you know what to do should the worst-case scenario transpire."

As soon as the dean says "worst-case scenario," my thoughts go back to the president's terrifying speech. *Dark powers of destruction. The deadly atom.* I'm scared I might be sick on Bobby Tackett's head.

While I try my best to take deep breaths, Dean Denton motions for Mr. Kraus to join him onstage.

Some of the students whoop loudly—Betty included—when the young teacher comes jogging into view. Mr. Kraus waves to the crowd like a movie star, and when he reaches the podium, he accepts a hearty handshake and a clap on the back from the dean.

"Andy Kraus has been a wonderful addition to our staff this year," Dean Denton says, "and the other day, he came to me with an excellent proposal regarding our underground shelter. Mr. Kraus, would you like to take over?"

The two men trade places. When Mr. Kraus steps up to the microphone, he grins at the room one last time before transitioning to a more serious expression. "Good afternoon, students. I, like your dean of students here, want to make sure you're prepared in case *you-know-what* hits the fan. And so I said to Dean Denton, 'I think the only way to *fully* prepare people is to have them live in the shelter for a short period of time—the same way they would in the event of a nuclear attack.'"

Wait—what?

A current of gasps and murmurs travels around the room as people piece together what Mr. Kraus seems to be proposing. Students living inside the shelter? By themselves? For how long?

"Settle down," Dean Denton says, taking back the microphone. "*Settle down.* Mr. Tackett, get back in your seat, please. The plan is to test a group of six students. That group will stay in the fallout shelter for a period of four days, communicating with Mr. Kraus via radio. If everyone agrees it was a good learning experience, then we'll open the training program to the rest of the student body."

This time the auditorium explodes with noise: people asking questions; people insisting *they* want to be among the first group locked inside the shelter. I feel dizzy—a bit detached—like the pressure from above is finally starting to suffocate me.

"A week from today," Dean Denton says, "Mr. Kraus will put a sign-up sheet on the door of his office. Take some time to think about whether you'd be interested. It'll be first come, first serve."

Betty grabs my wrist, and by the look on her face, I know exactly what's about to come out of her mouth—and I am *not* going to like it.

"You're not going to like this . . . ," Betty begins.

"Just say it, Bets."

My friend takes a deep breath. "I know you're freaked out . . ."

"I am *very* freaked out."

"But I think we should do it."

THREE

Eva

I wrap my flannel shirt around me like a robe as I wait for Jenny in the dark parking lot. I don't normally get nervous about stuff, so it must be the cool September air that's making the hair stand up on the back of my neck.

Okay, fine. I'm nervous. And not because I'm out after curfew. I just really want Jenny to like me, and I want her friends to like me, too. Tonight, I had three hours to kill in between dinner and sneaking out the back door of Ainsley House, and I spent them alone in my room sending emoji reactions to Instagram stories posted by my friends from home and listening to other girls' laughter through the cinder-block walls. Depressing, right?

Back in the city, Alicia, Nina, and Celeste Bernardo were drinking vodka Red Bulls on Alicia's roof, according to their Instagram stories. It sorta sucked that none of them replied to my messages, but at the same time, I'm not shocked. The four of us met at the start of high school, and our friendships were purely situational; none of us felt like caring about anything, and that made us apathetic allies in everything from gym class to field trips. At the time, it felt good to be surrounded by other aggressively indifferent people, but naturally, they probably didn't care that I wasn't there anymore.

At one point, I texted Ella to say hi. She's actually pretty cool, considering she's the spawn of Caleb, but we've never been super close. It's hard to say why, exactly. Different interests? The fact that Mom and Caleb *love* her and *resent* me? It's probably a little bit of column A and a little bit of column B.

In any case, she responded right away, which made me feel good—even if our conversation was a little on the formal side for two people who lived under the same roof until recently.

Ella! Miss you! What's up?

Eva! Hey! So good to hear from you.
I'm actually getting ready for a date.

OMG! With??

Benji from my grade.
We're seeing the new Marvel movie.

Cute! Be safe! Make good decisions!

I promise I will! What are you up to?

Oh, you know.

Trying to increase my friend count from

zero to not zero.

I hear footsteps coming from the side of the library. Peering over my shoulder, I spot the outlines of two girls moving toward me. It's dead quiet up here in Middle of Nowhere, New York, so even from a distance, I can pick up what they're saying.

"Is that yours?" one of them asks.

I have no idea what they're talking about. The parking lot is empty—unless they're talking about *me*?

"Yeah, I think that's her," the other one answers.

As they pass through the glow of an emergency blue light box, I recognize Jenny—and I feel like I'm in the presence of a celebrity. During my downtime, I also decided to lightly stalk her Instagram, and I couldn't believe what I found: Her account, @jennypriceless, had a hundred and eighty thousand followers. She had, like, *fans*—no wonder she could charge five hundred bucks for a lipstick photo. Her aesthetic was basically "hot woodland nymph who doesn't know she's hot"; every photo was Jenny surrounded by nature, looking slightly dazed but very stylish.

The other girl walking toward me is taller and curvier, with dark-brown skin and shoulder-length twists. My stomach does a flip-floppy thing. What if I'm seconds away from meeting Heather? And why are they talking about me like I belong to Jenny?

"What's up?" Jenny says when we're close enough to talk. There's a canvas tote bag slung over her shoulder that clinks as she walks.

"Hey!" I let go of my shirt and slide my hands into my back pockets. Like a cool person who's casually hanging out in a parking lot alone at 9:57 p.m.

"Eva, this is Niah. Niah, Eva." Jenny gestures between me and her friend.

The girl I thought was Heather gives me a curt nod. She's wearing long beaded earrings that swing as she scans our surroundings.

"Mine isn't here yet," she mutters to Jenny. "Not off to a good start, is he? Probably thinks he's entitled to special treatment."

Jenny checks her phone. "It's nine fifty-eight. If he's not here at ten, we'll leave without him."

"What time is Heather expecting us again?"

"Ten fifteen. We have time."

"He's going to make us look bad. Jackson and Xavier texted and said they're already there with their people."

Jenny and Niah are talking like I'm not even here. I desperately want to know what's going on, but I don't want to say the wrong thing and ruin the moment.

"Look, there he is," Jenny says.

A pale, skinny boy in a thick turtleneck sweater strides across the lot and gives us a wave. "Hope I didn't keep you waiting long," he calls out. Jenny and Niah exchange apprehensive looks. When he gets closer, I recognize his blond hair and pointy, mouse-like features from around campus. "Simon Banbury," he announces to the group. "I'm really excited about this. I knew it was going to happen, obviously, but I didn't know—"

"Let's get a move on, shall we?" Niah says.

Down the pitch-black trail we go, navigating by the flashlight on Niah's iPhone. It's Niah and Jenny in front, and Simon and me in back. Nobody says a word—not even Simon, although I can tell by the bounce in his step that he's looking forward to whatever's about to happen. I want to ask him, but I feel like I'm not supposed to talk right now. My heartbeat thuds in my ears. Finally, I notice an orangey glow coming through the trees to our right. I hear voices and . . . is that live violin music?

The path twists sharply, and at last I'm standing at the edge of a small clearing, and . . . wow. It's the feeling I got when Celeste brought us to her cousin's speakeasy in Bushwick— when we slipped down the dark alleyway, pressed the buzzer next to the unmarked door, and the next thing we knew, we were swept into a packed basement with pink-neon lights and a glittery burlesque show happening on a stage at the back.

I've stumbled into another magical world—without the sequined bras this time, but just as mysterious and exhilarating. There's a roaring bonfire surrounded by a ring of colorful quilts, and the quilts are surrounded by a ring of lanterns, like some kind of forest séance situation. Sprawled across the blankets are maybe a dozen kids, their limbs all crisscrossing like they couldn't be more comfortable with each other: elbows on shoulders and heads in laps and hands passing beer bottles to other outstretched hands. Some of them are talking and laughing, and some are listening to a beautiful dark-haired girl as she kneels and plays the violin by the light of the flames. Her name's Raven—she's one of the seniors in my French class. I'm not a musician, but to my untrained ear, her playing sounds incredible—and she's not even reading off any sheet music.

And there's that guy from gym, Xavier. He's, like, a world-champion badminton player, which has been serving him well in our first unit of the semester: badminton. At our last gym class, Mr. Hind had him play against four of us at once, just to see what would happen. Xavier crushed us.

What is this, a party for ridiculously talented people? And if so, what am I doing here? Jenny thinks you're "fucking cool," I remind myself. And Jenny has a hundred and eighty thousand followers on Instagram.

Jenny pulls two more beers from her bag, twists off the tops, and hands one each to Simon and me. "Courtesy of Mama and Papa Price," she says. I didn't know it until right this moment, but there's something about a person opening a drink for you that makes you feel like you belong.

As I accept the bottle from Jenny, my eyes catch on a cluster of people I didn't see at first, because I was busy checking out the crowd around the fire. There are seven of them hovering just outside the ring of lanterns, all of them around Simon's age, except for one: another eleventh grader named Westley, who keeps taking huge gulps of his beer. They *could* just be standing to watch Raven's performance, but something about their body language makes them seem kind of anxious, like they're debating whether or not they should cross the lantern line to sit with the others.

"You guys should totally feel free to mingle," Jenny says, before following Niah around to the other side of the fire and leaving me standing there with Simon.

"Simon, what's going on right now?" I whisper out the side of my mouth.

"You don't know?" he replies. I think he's trying to look sophisticated as he takes a teensy sip of beer, but he wrinkles his nose as he swallows.

"No, I don't. That's why I'm asking you. Quick, before she stops playing and they can hear us."

"They're recruiting us," he whispers back.

"*Who's* recruiting us?"

He rolls his eyes as though it should be obvious. "The Fives."

"The *who*?"

"The Fives. Hardwick's secret society. It's been a thing since the 1960s."

I fight the urge to let my jaw drop open. I take a sip of beer and try to act casual, but I have to remind myself how to swallow.

"Are you being serious right now?" I ask.

"My mom was a Five. She told me everything. They take a maximum of five people per class, grades nine through twelve. See those people over there?" Simon nods at the awkward group lingering outside the circle. "They're all in my grade except for Westley."

"He's in mine."

"Right. So that's seven of us going for the five ninth-grade spots. There must be an eleventh-grade spot open, too."

"Simon, are you sure you're not drunk?"

"This is *real*. Why do you think they told us not to bring anyone else to the party?" He raises his nearly full drink to his lips but thinks better of it and drops it to his side. "You must have passed some sort of test already, if they invited you here tonight."

I think back to math class and meeting Jenny for the first time. My Oscar-worthy performance. Our great escape. Had she really been challenging me, to see if the new girl could roll with people who were Instagram influencers, violin prodigies, and badminton champions? I guess it's possible. And to my credit, I knocked it out of the damn park. But I'm still in shock—I didn't know secret societies were actually a *thing*. And even if they were, I definitely didn't think they happened until college.

Raven stops playing, and everyone claps. She stands up, pirouettes, and curtsies, soaking in the applause. "Jackson, now you!" she cries.

An extremely hot guy with unruly black hair and model-level cheekbones picks up a banjo. "Only if you sing with me," he fires back with easygoing confidence.

"Ugh, *fine*," Raven groans, but she happily skips around the circle to sit closer to him. They launch into a plucky folk song, the two of them singing in perfect harmony. Some of the people sprawled across the quilts listen for a few moments before picking up their previous conversations.

Knowing what I now know, I have to get in there. I have to make them like me. I finally have a shot at being part of something—something where I'm not invisible—and I'm not going to hang back and let Westley the beer chugger take my place. Jenny told us to mingle. I can mingle. I'm a class-A mingler! Without a second thought, I roll back my shoulders, step across the lantern line, and squat next to Xavier.

"Hey, mind if I sit here?"

I hold out my beer, and he clinks his bottle against mine. "'Sup, Eva?"

I fake-wince as I sit down. "Still struggling to use my butt muscles after you destroyed us in gym."

Xavier laughs. Some people nearby notice me and scoot closer.

Success!

I wave Simon over to join us. It'd be a dick move to abandon him after mining him for information. And whaddaya know, now that Simon and I have made entry, the other recruits start to mingle, too. Hopefully everyone remembers that I broke the seal.

Xavier introduces me to Alyson and Nikki, two seniors who scrutinize me over the tops of their drinks.

"You're the new girl who fooled Richterman?" Alyson asks.

I'm walking a fine line: I want to charm them, but I also have to be careful not to sound *too* confident. "My forehead still hurts from hitting the desk, TBH."

Alyson smirks.

"That was bold of you," Nikki chimes in. "Richterman's strict. I'd be scared to mess with him."

"After playing Xavier in badminton, I don't think I'll be scared of anything else again."

They all laugh.

"Mind if I swoop in?"

Jackson, a.k.a. sexy banjo guy, is standing over us. He and Raven just finished their song, and a guy with a Bluetooth speaker put on a country playlist to give the musicians a break.

"No prob," Alyson replies as she and Nikki get to their feet. "We should go talk to the others, anyway."

They wander over to find seats near two nervous-looking ninth-grade recruits, and I steal a quick glance around the clearing. Westley's talking animatedly to Niah while chugging another beer; Raven and a couple of tenth-grade guys are talking to the four other ninth graders. Jenny's chatting with a girl on the other side of the fire, but I can't see her face—only the back of her blond bob. Could *that* be Heather?

Meanwhile, Xavier moves over to talk directly to Simon, which leaves me with Jackson.

"Howdy, little lady." He shakes a curtain of dark hair out of his face, and his beige skin glows orange in the firelight. I pretend not to notice how his eyes take a leisurely tour of my body, stopping wherever they please. I usually find it gross when guys check me out so transparently, but this time, I get a little spark of excitement.

"Howdy," I reply. "Your performance was great."

Jackson winks. He's the rare kind of person who can wink and have it *not* look totally pained. "Thanks. It's Eva, right? I'm Jackson. I heard your performance was pretty great, too."

"Jeez, Jenny really talked me up. All I did was strategically slam my face into a desk."

"Well, whatever you did, it was enough to get you noticed." He raises his drink to me. "Cheers."

"Cheers."

"So, you talk to Heather yet?"

I'm getting serious vibes that Heather is the leader of the Fives, and the one I should be most concerned about impressing. "No, not yet."

He lets out a long, low whistle. "Good luck. Not that I think you'll need it. You seem pretty chill."

His eyes, glinting from the flames, rove my body again.

My stomach does that flip-floppy thing, both at the prospect of meeting Heather, and Jackson's thinly veiled flirtation. "Is she over there talking to Jenny?" I nod to the girl with the blond bob.

"Yup, that's her."

"What's she like?"

"Heather's cool once you get to know her."

All of a sudden, there's a crash and a shatter of glass as Westley stumbles over a lantern. The conversations grind to a halt. I don't know what Westley was trying to do—maybe sneak off to pee in the woods—but he's clearly having trouble walking in a straight line after all those drinks. One of the sophomores sitting with Raven leaps up and grabs him by the shoulder before he does any more damage with his drunken swaying. The sophomore looks at Heather, who responds with a curt nod.

The next thing I know, Westley is being ushered out of the clearing the same way we came in. People watch him go, but soon their conversations resume, as though he were never even here.

I guess I should feel a little bit relieved, but if Westley's out of the running, it still doesn't mean I'm in the clear. Simon said the secret society takes on a *maximum* of five people per class, which means they technically don't have to fill the open junior spot with anyone. I still have to win them over.

"Hey, Eva!" I hear my name called out in Jenny's husky voice. "Can you come over here?"

I look at Jackson and bite my bottom lip. "I guess it's happening." I put down my drink and wipe my palms on my jeans. "I'll see ya later."

"Hope we get to hang again." Jackson holds up a two-fingered peace sign.

I feel eyes on me as I walk to the other side of the fire.

A dramatic plume of smoke blocks my view for a second, but when it finally clears, I lay my eyes on Heather for the very first time.

My first thought is that she looks . . . friendly? The girl seated on the quilt next to Jenny has white-blond hair framing her round face—her whole head is a circle, like the moon—and she's smiling at me with perfect teeth. It's only when I get close enough to smell her floral perfume that I notice her eyes are cold and sharp like shards of ice, and it occurs to me that her smile is just a shape she's making with her mouth. I come to a stop a few feet in front of where she's sitting.

"Hi, Eva," she says sweetly. "I'm Heather."

"It's nice to meet you."

"Thank you *so* much for coming tonight."

"Oh—um—of course." I look at Jenny, who nods encouragingly. "Thank you both for inviting me."

Heather cocks an eyebrow and giggles. No one said anything funny, so the giggle seems like a bad sign. "I thought you were supposed to be all brave," she fires at me.

I swallow hard. I can already tell Heather is dangerous—that she's prepared to use any observable weakness against me. I shouldn't have stammered or tried to exchange pleasantries.

"You can sit," Jenny translates.

Ah. Right. I plop to the ground faster than a falling acorn.

Heather needles me with her eyes as she leans back on her palms and crosses her outstretched legs. She's wearing tight black pants and black boots with a pointy toe. I'm wearing black-and-white-checkered Vans. Like a peasant.

"So, what makes you special?" Heather asks.

I can't help it: I hug my knees to my chest. Heather is intimidating as hell. "Special?" I ask. "What do you mean, exactly?"

She gestures to the group behind her. "You've had a chance to meet some of my friends tonight. I'm sure you can tell they're all fairly exceptional people. Why do you think you should get to hang out with us?"

How the hell do I answer that and not sound totally full of myself? Am I supposed to sound full of myself? What should I say right now? I'm about to blow this, big-time.

Jenny jumps in to help me—I guess because of our new-kid bond. "I told you, Eva's fucking fearless."

"Well, she'd better be," Heather replies. "She's the only new person in a class where everyone's known each other forever."

Yeah, no kidding, Heather. I'm this close to being so invisible I fade away to nothing. "I'm getting by," I reply with a shrug.

"Where do you think that fearlessness comes from, exactly?" Heather pries.

I let go of my knees, straighten my legs, and think about how best to answer. Why *had* I been so fearless in Richterman's class? And why didn't I care about consequences back home, either?

"I guess when you know you're at the bottom of the ladder, you have nothing to lose."

"Hmm." Heather nods slowly. "Interesting. That's a good answer."

I feel like I'm floating a foot off the ground.

"Eva," she continues, "can you keep a secret?"

I don't have to think twice. "Yes."

She leans forward. Even in the dark, I feel her eyes boring into me. "Are you sure?"

"Yes." I make sure my voice stays steady. "Absolutely."

"Okay." She shifts her weight back again and nods at Jenny. "You can take her."

Take me where? I figure there's no point in asking: if I were meant to know, she would have told me. And who really cares, as long as I just passed another test? I'd probably go with Jenny to drink battery acid if she asked me. Fine, not battery acid. But I really want them to accept me, and I'm probably not thinking straight. I follow Jenny into the dark woods behind the clearing, because that's apparently what's happening now. There's a light shining up ahead: another lantern, placed at a much smaller clearing where two trails intersect. We stop in its golden glow.

"I know you're probably confused right now," Jenny mutters. "It'll all make sense pretty soon, I promise."

Next comes Alyson, trailed by a ninth-grade recruit.

"She passed?" Jenny asks.

"Yup," Alyson answers.

Well, I'll be damned. That must mean I passed, too. Am I in the club now? Or do I still have to pass more tests?

Nikki, Xavier, and Raven come next, each with a wide-eyed ninth grader. The tiny crossroads is starting to get pretty crowded, and there's a sharp stench of sweat coming from one of the other recruits. After ten minutes, I start to wonder where Simon is. Did Heather send him home, like Westley?

Finally, I hear a boy's voice. "I *knew* I would nail the interview."

"You're not supposed to be talking right now."

Niah and Simon come marching through the trees, Niah with her arms crossed, and Simon grinning from ear to ear.

"Heather's going to text me in five to let me know if the last one makes it through," Niah murmurs to the other Fives, who nod solemnly.

We stand there in silence for what feels like forever. The branches creak in the autumn breeze, and the sweat smell gets stronger.

Bzzzzz. Niah looks at her phone, then at the other Fives. She shakes her head.

Another one bites the dust.

"Okay, you six," Jenny says, clearly addressing the recruits. "We're very sorry about this, but we're going to have to take your phones."

"Excuse me?" Simon demands.

"Those are the rules. Hand 'em over." She holds out her palm, and without a second of hesitation, I give mine up. The others do, too—even Simon, but first he makes a show of turning it off and polishing the screen on his sweater.

"Your Apple Watch, too," Niah tells him.

"What?" he cries. "Why?"

"We need anything that makes light," Jenny explains.

Begrudgingly, Simon takes off the watch and hands it over, and Jenny slides everything into her tote bag. "All right," she says, "here's what's going to happen. Right now, it's midnight. You have half an hour to get this done. We're going to pair you off and take you to different points along this second trail. Once you're at your spot, we're going to leave. You're each going to count to two hundred, and then you're going to find your way out of the glen. We'll be waiting for you at the spot where we came in. Got it?"

"Got it," I answer immediately, along with a couple of the recruits.

"But we won't be able to see anything," Simon says.

Niah groans. "That's the point, Banbury. You and Eva can come with me."

We follow her obediently, away from the other recruits, who are busy dividing up into pairs. We walk for another few minutes along a winding trail, until Niah tells us to stop.

"So, remember: Once I'm gone, you're going to count to two hundred," she explains. "Then you're going to find your way out. Make sense?"

"Yep," I reply. "You got it."

"Fab." Niah gives me a thumbs-up. "And please be safe. Don't put your hand in the hot coals, like one of our recruits did last year."

Simon gulps audibly. "We won't," I promise.

Niah claps. "Well, good luck, you two."

I nod. "Many thanks."

And then she leaves us in the trees. The moment her phone disappears around a corner, Simon and I are swimming in darkness.

Simon, who isn't nearly as confident as he was after his interview, grabs my upper arm with what feels like a claw.

"My mom never told me about this part," he whimpers.

I can see why not. "It'll be okay. Come on, let's count. *One . . . two . . . three . . .*" I try to go slowly to calm his nerves. "*Four . . . five . . . six . . .*"

"I want out of here."

"Just try counting with me. *Thirteen . . . fourteen . . . fifteen . . .*" At twenty, Simon joins in. We get through the thirties and forties, and his grip on my arm starts to loosen. We pass a hundred, and he manages to let go. Finally, we cross the finish line at two hundred. I can't hear any music or voices anymore, but I keep it to myself.

"Okay, Simon. Let's go."

"I can't move."

"Yes, you can. Watch me. Or—shoot, you can't see me—I'm crouching down and feeling for packed earth. That's where the path is."

"O-okay."

With Simon somewhere near my heels, we bear crawl in what I *think* is the direction of the bonfire. I wonder how the other recruits are making out. I can't hear them, either—they must have really spread us out.

"Argh!" Simon cries. "I think I just touched a slug."

"Don't worry, it won't hurt you."

"Why do you sound like you're not remotely freaked out?"

"Because I'm not."

"Well, good for you. I feel like I'm going to puke."

"Not on my Vans, please." He laughs, which is what I was hoping for. I can't just leave him here in the dark, but I also can't have him freezing up and ruining our chances of getting out in time—because if we fail, who knows if they'll ever even speak to us again, and if they never even speak to us again, how the hell will I survive at Hardwick, knowing I could have had a chance to *not* be completely invisible? And not just that, but to be friends with some really cool people. To lie around a bonfire talking, laughing, drinking, and listening to Jackson and Raven play their instruments . . .

When my forehead bumps into a tree stump and smoke hits my eyes and nostrils, I know we've made it back to the clearing. The rest of the group must have rushed to pack up and run away while the other Fives took us to our various starting points. "Grab on to my shoe and follow me," I tell Simon. "Remember what Niah said? We don't want you crawling into the hot coals by accident."

His hand is around my ankle before I can finish getting my sentence out. "This *really* is unnecessarily dangerous," he grumbles as I steer him in a wide circle around where I'm guessing the firepit is.

The next thing I feel for is a rock I remember seeing when we came in; I noticed it had an unusually flat top to it, like a table, and people had used it to store their bags and sweatshirts. By now, my eyes are getting used to the dark, enough that I can make out a big rectangle to my right. And there, next to it—

"I see the path! Come on, Simon. We can stand up now." He climbs me like a tree trunk to get to his feet, which is annoying, but at least he's moving. "Follow me," I say, "and be careful not to trip on any roots."

With my arms out in front of me to guard against hanging branches, I continue leading Simon on foot. One thing I've figured out on my early-morning runs is that the glen slopes downward away from the school, which means as long as Simon and I are walking uphill, we must be *sort of* heading in the right direction. It's slow going, but eventually the trees start to thin. And just when Simon says he thinks he has to pee (*can't it wait?*), I see the unmistakable glow of the emergency blue light box.

"We're almost there!"

I break out into a run. Simon starts to protest, but I don't care. He knows where he's going now, and he can take his sweet time if he wants to. I get to the end of the trail, and there's Heather standing with a candle in her hand. With her other hand, she makes a peace sign.

Jenny steps out from behind her and hands a candle to me, which Heather proceeds to light with her own candle. "Congratulations, Eva," Heather says. "You made it through your first trial. You're on your way to joining our secret society. We're called the Fives."

As Simon arrives behind me, panting, I hold the burning candle near my waist. If it lights up my face, they'll probably see I have tears in my eyes.

FOUR

Connie

The morning after the assembly, Betty and I come downstairs to find a gaggle of girls gathered around the Ainsley House bulletin board. "What do you think it is?" I ask Betty, knowing perfectly well that other than a surprise upcoming dance, there's only one thing that would generate this kind of crowd before eight a.m.

Betty grabs my wrist and uses her other elbow to part the sea of students in front of us, until we're standing face-to-face with a mimeographed announcement about the fallout shelter experiment. There are disappointed sighs as people read through the details listed on the sheet.

"I can't believe they're doing it over spring recess."

"It says here they needed four days in a row that didn't interfere with classes."

"But that's not fair! My grandparents are coming to visit, and I have to be home."

"I would have been *fine* to miss class for Andy."

The timing seems to be a deal-breaker for most people, which is why Betty practically skips the whole way to breakfast. "Less competition for spots," she says cheerfully.

"You sure you don't mind missing your family's lake house weekend? I don't know . . . I was kind of looking forward to going this year."

Betty rolls her eyes. "Nice try, Connie, but no one looks forward to sitting in a musty old cabin and playing cribbage with my grandpa. Not even *my grandpa*. We're totally free to stay here over the break, so stop being a downer and standing in the way of my dreams."

I try a different strategy. "Do we *really* need to test out the shelter, though? Just yesterday you were saying the likelihood of—"

"I could lie and say I did some reading on US-Soviet relations, but I think we both know my interests lie in another aspect of this experiment."

"You want to impress Mr. Kraus."

"*Andy*. And . . . yes."

Well, it was worth a shot. And I can't use my parents as an out, because they got married the same weekend as Hardwick's spring recess, and they always celebrate with an anniversary beach trip, just the two of them.

I still feel queasy about the thought of being locked inside the shelter, especially after the dream I had last night. Betty and I were pacing around the underground space, and then Mr. Kraus appeared out of nowhere and announced the bomb was hidden somewhere in the room with us. With that wide-eyed look on his face, he said I'd have to be blindfolded in order to find it. When I woke up, my sheets were a tangled mess and I was covered in sweat.

In the dining hall, the announcement is all anybody can talk about. The usual din beneath the vaulted ceilings and stained-glass windows is peppered with the words "fallout," "shelter," "Andy," and "spring recess." From the sounds of it, lots of people are struggling with whether to cancel their vacation plans for a shot at one of the six available spots.

Our plates of toast and scrambled eggs in hand, Betty and I weave around the tables in search of two free seats. My heart skips a beat as we pass by Craig, who's in the middle of telling some funny story to the rest of his soccer teammates. People at neighboring tables twist in their chairs to listen in, their own conversations apparently far less interesting. He's the sun at the center of a mini solar system, so I'm not surprised that he doesn't look my way. And it's okay, because I'll see him in chemistry this morning, anyway.

There's no room at the table where some of Betty's drama club friends are sitting, so we settle, as we often do, for a corner table with a hodgepodge of random characters who don't fit anywhere else—including Bobby Tackett, the class clown, who's flinging Cheerios at Mary Simpson as she seems to be cramming for a test.

Unlike Betty, I don't mind that we always sit at the "outsider table," as she calls it. One upside to my constant worrying about the end of the world is that it doesn't leave much time for fretting about my social status. The all-consuming dread puts everything into perspective, too. The things that Betty *agonizes* over—her hair, her glasses, whether she totally embarrassed herself in some random conversation—feel, to me, like tiny dust motes floating in the general vicinity of my head. It's been that way ever since I got to Hardwick.

As we take our seats, Betty's going on about her harebrained scheme to sleep outside Mr. Kraus's office the night before he posts the sign-up sheet.

"Andy probably wouldn't tell anyone," she muses.

"You girls planning on signing up, too?"

The question has barely left Bobby's lips before he lunges to catch—with his mouth—a Cheerio that Mary Simpson pelted back at him. "You're so weird," Mary groans, but when she looks back at her book, she's clearly smiling.

Somewhere around the seventh grade, I started noticing this coded flirting between boys and girls, but it's always seemed a bit foreign to me. Like a language I can recognize but not actually speak. Betty says that according to her magazines, when I meet the right guy, I'll just magically know how to do it. She said the same goes for making out and everything that comes after—stuff I *definitely* don't understand yet, either. Maybe if Craig got tired of being jerked around by Helen once and for all . . .

When I drift back into the conversation, Betty is saying to Bobby, "Gee, I really didn't peg you for a fallout shelter kind of guy."

"Oh yeah, *big-time*," he says, stuffing a spoonful of cereal into his mouth and continuing to talk as he chews. "My church showed us this video that explained everything. When a bomb goes off, there's the giant mushroom cloud, right?" He makes a big circle with his arms. "The mushroom cloud makes these radioactive particles rain down, and if they touch you, you're in trouble. In the hours after an explosion, those particles could be carried, like, hundreds of miles. That's what nuclear fallout is. It looks like dust. And if you're anywhere within two hundred miles of an attack, you're supposed to put a plate on the ground and check it every fifteen minutes to see if anything accumulates on it."

Suddenly, the pepper I sprinkled on my eggs doesn't look so appealing.

"Of course, that's assuming you're not dead," Bobby babbles on. "Fallout shelters work if you're far enough away from the blast site, but if the bomb lands on top of you . . ." He drags his hand across his throat and rolls his eyes back into his head.

Normally, I find Bobby's antics pretty entertaining—like the other week, when he snuck a whoopee cushion on Mr. Castellano's chair before the start of English class—but that's not the case today. In the center of the table, there's a copy of the *New York Times*, which someone left behind with ketchup splattered across it like blood. I pull it toward me, hoping to find something distracting enough that I don't have to listen to him ramble on anymore. Instead, I see the following headline:

US OPENS A-TESTS IN AIR WITH BLASTS OF MEDIUM YIELD

My toast becomes cardboard in my mouth, and it's a struggle to swallow. I start to read the story below:

WASHINGTON, April 25—The United States resumed nuclear testing in the atmosphere today by setting off an intermediate-size explosion near Christmas Island in the Pacific. The explosion took place at about 10:45 a.m. (Eastern Standard Time), just as dawn was beginning to light the overcast skies above the equatorial atoll in the Central Pacific. Rising through the overcast, the mushroom-shaped cloud symbolized a new competitive phase in the atomic arms race and the frustration of more than three years of effort to reach an international agreement to prohibit atomic testing.

At *new competitive phase in the atomic arms race,* I turn over the newspaper and slide it across the table, making a mess of the ketchup. I should really wipe it up, but all I can do right now is stare at the stained-glass windows and try not to vomit.

Betty pauses her conversation with Bobby and looks over at me. "Is it dysentery or diphtheria this time? I can't tell."

I know she's trying to make me laugh, but it isn't working. I swallow hard and nod at the *New York Times.* "Read that."

She and Bobby flip it over and scan the front page. Bobby's eyebrows go halfway up to his brown curls, and Betty places a hand on my arm. "This should make you *want* to do Andy's test, Connie. If something bad ever does happen, we'll be the best at surviving."

She has a point . . . but I just don't know. The thought of nuclear apocalypse scares me enough as it is. How could I handle four days locked in a shelter, pretending it's actually happening? And all of it under the supervision of Mr. Kraus, the same guy who doesn't believe in road maps for cross-continental travel? "I'm going to head to chemistry early, you guys. See you at lunch, Bets. Later, Bobby."

Chemistry will help me clear my head a bit, as long as I make a mess. I am the neatest person I know, besides my mother, who vacuums our carpets in a precise diamond pattern and gets agitated the first time someone walks across and ruins it. I singlehandedly clean the dorm room I share with Betty: sweeping the floor; taking out the trash; picking up the clothes strewn haphazardly across the floor and folding them neatly on her bed, because otherwise we might step on them. But when it comes to chemistry, I try to be as sloppy as possible; with Craig as my lab partner, I quickly realized the more there is to tidy up, the more time he and I will have to linger together after the bell rings.

At the start of the semester, during those five glorious clean-up minutes, we discussed neutral topics like the weather or what we were doing after class. But then, one morning, something miraculous happened. Craig tapped the end of his pencil on the front of his notebook—I remember the pencil was blue, with a pristine pink eraser—and said, "Connie, can I ask you a random question?"

"O-okay," I stammered.

He whispered, "You know Helen Honeyman and I are going steady, right?"

I nodded. In general, I barely paid attention to Hardwick's dating scene, but Craig was a different story. Plus, all that public kissing with Helen was impossible to ignore.

"Connie, why do you think Helen picks fights with me for no reason?"

I didn't have any idea what the right answer was, but I liked that he was confiding in me, so I made up something that *sounded* like a blurb from Betty's magazines, and he seemed to think it sounded good.

"You won't tell anyone we talked about this, right?" Craig looked concerned. "I wouldn't want Helen to know I was asking another girl for dating advice . . ."

"Of course not."

From then on, during those five minutes—ten, if I manage a *really* big catastrophe—Craig has opened up about his relationship problems, and I've tried to help him as best as I can. I wanted us to become friends, and I think we're on our way there. I mean, we're not at the point where we'd make plans or anything, but we're . . . something. Maybe one day we'll be something even more. But for now, it feels special to have a tradition no one else knows about—not even Betty.

During today's chemistry class, I intentionally squirt a jet of green food coloring across the table, and I don't warn Craig when I see his elbow about to knock over a bag of salt. The tiny crystals go everywhere, including the floor. Bingo.

Craig wets a yellow sponge under the sink. "So . . . Helen and I are going steady again."

"Yeah, I saw that." I feel the same tug of disappointment that I did hearing her call his name in the auditorium yesterday. "How are you, um, feeling about that?"

"Good. *Great*." He wrings out the sponge so it doesn't drip. "But I also have this weird kind of stress. It's kind of like . . . a constant feeling of fear. Because right now things are fine, but I know we could fall apart at any second. I just feel like no matter how hard I try with her, it's never enough. And the fear of disappointing her makes it hard to enjoy the good stuff." He sighs. "Am I making any sense? I'm probably not."

Jeez, Helen. I've never spent time with her, given that she doesn't seem aware of my existence, but the stress lines deepening in Craig's forehead tell me everything I need to know. If I were Craig's girlfriend, I would never pick fights with him, but I'm not brave enough to say that out loud.

"You're actually making perfect sense, Craig." Just saying his name, in his presence, makes a tiny firework go off in my chest. "I know what you mean with the constant dread, because I get it, too. About other stuff. It's like . . . this evil force humming in the background of everything you do. And if you try to convince yourself you're being irrational, then the bad thoughts only get worse."

"Yeah," he says, mulling it over. And then, more definitively, "*Yeah*. That's exactly it. You're friggin' smart, Connie."

I feel like I could run to Canada and back.

"So . . . what do I do about it?" he asks.

"Trust me, I wish I had a definite answer." As he drags the wet sponge across the table, I follow along in his wake with a towel. "Trying to analyze everything that scares me only makes me more scared, so I just do my best to ignore it. Which is also really hard. It's obviously not a perfect solution, but . . . I don't know."

I chew my bottom lip.

Should I say it?

I'm going to say it.

"At the very least, you can remind yourself that someone else on campus knows exactly how you feel."

He squeezes the last of the green-tinged water from the sponge and flashes me the most beautiful smile on Planet Earth. My goodness, I would do anything for Craig Allenby. Even coach him on his relationship with someone else. I just want to be significant to him in any way.

"Thanks, Connie," he says. "That means a lot."

I feel my cheeks getting hot. "Of course."

He dries his hands and picks up his backpack. "You sticking around?"

"Yeah, I have to finish some English homework," I lie. The truth is that most days, I secretly let him leave the room first and count to thirty before I follow, so I can spare him the awkwardness of having to walk down the hall with me. I know Craig would never openly object to us being seen together, but what if he felt embarrassed about it on the inside? I figure I'm doing him a favor, just in case.

"How are you feeling about this whole fallout shelter thing?" he asks. "You thinking about signing up?"

The shelter. I had almost stopped thinking about it for a full hour. "I'm not sure. Betty really wants us to do it . . . and I think it could be useful . . . but honestly, it also sounds . . . intense. What about you? You probably have plans for spring recess."

"Eh." He shrugs. "My mom has enough on her hands with my younger siblings, and the house is pretty crowded, so . . ." He lets the sentence trail off into nothingness. From what I've overheard of Helen and her friends' conversations in the common room, Craig's home life hasn't been easy. A few years ago, his father abandoned the family to go live with some other woman he'd been seeing, leaving his mother to support him and his three siblings on her own. They ended up moving from Ohio to live with his grandparents in New Jersey, who generously offered to send Craig to Hardwick. They wanted to keep him on the right path and nurture his athletic abilities. Plus, it would free up some room in their crowded house.

"Does that mean you're signing up?" I ask.

"If I can get a spot," he says. "It seems like the right thing for a class president to do. Also, Andy is boss."

I nod in fake agreement as I process this new information. *Craig Allenby could be in the shelter.* "What about Helen?"

He laughs. "She's not jazzed about the idea, but I'm trying to convince her."

"That'll be fun for you guys. If she says yes."

"It'll be fun if she can go the four days without fighting with me." He wanders over to the door, adjusting the straps on his backpack. Instead of walking out, he pauses on the threshold and drums his fingers on the doorframe. Then he looks back over his shoulder and runs his fingers through his golden-blond hair. "You know, Connie, you should listen to Betty and sign up. It would be good to have one fun person down there."

My breath catches in my throat, and I make a garbled noise that's somewhere between "sure" and "okay." It sounds like "sho-kay."

Real smooth, Connie.

When Craig leaves, instead of counting to thirty, I sit and stare at the blackboard for three whole minutes, wondering what I should do. Eventually the kids from the next class start to trickle in, and I realize I'd better get a move on, or else I'll be late for English.

The night before the sign-up sheet is posted, I manage to convince Betty to sleep in our dorm room and not on the hardwood floor outside Mr. Kraus's office. But at six o'clock the next morning, as soon as curfew lifts, she and I rush across campus to check and see if the paper is on the door.

I never told Betty about my conversation with Craig, and *she* never asked why I suddenly changed my mind about the test. She probably assumed I just gave in, which, to her credit, is normally what happens when she gets fixated on a new idea. For the record, my stomach is still in knots at the thought of being locked inside a fallout shelter as though a nuclear attack just happened, but I also see the value in preparation, and—well—I just *can't* turn down Craig's invitation. I've replayed it in my head a million times over, and I still get just as many butterflies at the thought of him wanting to spend all that time with me. All week I've been oscillating between utterly terrified and irresistibly excited.

"It's not there!" Betty wails as we round the final corner in the math and social studies building. As we both pace the hallway to catch our breath, she says, "I thought maybe he would put it up late last night, so it would be here first thing."

"What time does he get to school?"

"I think it depends if he goes running in the morning."

I sit down on the bench next to Mr. Kraus's door, where usually students are waiting to catch him when he returns to his office after class. "Let's wait thirty minutes, and if he doesn't show up, we'll come back after first period. The list won't fill up *that* fast."

"Okay," Betty says, plopping down beside me.

Thirty minutes go by, and there's no sign of Mr. Kraus. No other students show up either, but a lot of people have sports practice in the morning before class.

"I hate to leave," Betty says. "What if he comes the second after we go?"

"I know, but we have to get ready for class."

"As soon as first period is done—"

"We're sprinting. I know."

Betty and I have English class together, and it seems to move slower than any other English class in the history of English classes. When the bell rings and Mr. Castellano is *still* going on about what he's expecting from our essays due next week, Betty looks like she's going to shred her novel into pieces. I'm feeling antsy too, imagining Craig getting to the sheet before us, seeing that my name isn't there, and being disappointed in me.

"Seven extra minutes he rambled on!" Betty cries as we rush to the math and social studies building for the second time today. "It's not that hard to say, 'Write about the symbolism in *The Great Gatsby.*'"

I'm reaching for the door when it blasts open from the other side, nearly hitting me in the face. Betty yanks me to the side as Steve O'Leary barrels down the front steps, apparently oblivious to the fact that he almost just broke my nose. Steve is a senior on the football team—six-foot-five and wide as Betty and me put together, with a harsh buzz cut. A little dazed from the encounter, we stumble down the hall and around the corner and skid to a stop outside Mr. Kraus's door, where the sign-up sheet must have been up for a little while, because I already see a few names on it.

Craig Allenby
Helen Honeyman

Bobby Tackett
Steve O'Leary

And then, in a thick red marker she pulls from her pocket, Betty fills in the last remaining spots:

Betty Walker
Connie Abbott

Once we make it official, time disappears like water running down the drain. Things happen so quickly they barely register in my brain. At some point, I call my parents on the dorm pay phone to tell them the news, and they're excited to hear I'm doing something so uncharacteristically adventurous. At some other point, Betty and I tear through our wardrobes deciding what we should wear in the shelter. Since we're not going to be showering the whole time, we figure we should try to look at least halfway decent in all other respects. For clothing, Betty chooses a loud red-and-blue-polka-dot dress with a belted waist and wide skirt, while I opt for a rather quieter peach shift dress that's also easy to move around in. Betty says I can pack one of her short baby-doll nightgowns to sleep in. ("I love you, Connie, but we both know you look like a five-year-old in that long frilly thing you usually wear.")

I'm used to people's eyes skimming over me, but lately, they've been lingering a little longer. I'm not sure if they're jealous of me or just suddenly noticing me for the first time, but

I don't particularly like it. I feel like I'm under a microscope, and I get all sweaty and hyperaware of what I'm doing with my face.

"It's like we're celebrities," Betty gushes on our way to lunch, clutching her bookbag to her chest. We just had our last social studies period before spring recess, and at the end, Mr. Kraus told the class to have a good break. Then he winked at Betty and me. "I'll see *you two* soon."

As soon as the words left his lips, twenty faces whipped around and glared at us enviously.

"I'm learning how it feels to be you," I mutter to Craig at the start of chemistry class the next morning.

Every time someone new comes into the room, they glance at Craig *and* me before continuing on to their seat. Stephanie Maxwell, who almost always stops to flirt with Craig—regardless of his current relationship status—today plucks up the end of my braid and rolls my hair between her fingers. "Connie, your hair is the *prettiest* color," she gushes. "Ever tried curling it?"

"Er . . ."

"You could come by my room, and I could show you sometime."

I like my hair fine the way it is. "Er, yeah, maybe."

She drops my braid and waves to us both. "Craig, stop by my table at lunch today, will you? I have *such* a funny story to tell you."

He grins and salutes her. "Will do."

I slouch down in my seat as she bounces away. Craig chuckles and nudges me with his elbow. "Not a fan of the attention?"

I cross my arms over my chest. "Not really, no."

"Well, try to think on the bright side," he says. "Starting tomorrow, you get to be locked in a shelter for four days straight."

"I still don't know if I should consider that a 'bright side.'"

Before I know it, the day of the test has arrived, and the six of us are following Mr. Kraus down some narrow stairs, through a door, and into a dank basement hallway.

"Who's excited?" he asks.

Bobby, Craig, and Steve make whooping noises. Betty squeals, "Me!" I don't say anything, and neither does Helen. Craig must have worked extra-hard to convince his girlfriend to be here.

When we're all at the base of the stairs, Mr. Kraus instructs us to fan out against the cinder-block wall and face him. With his hands on his hips, he paces up and down our ranks like a general about to send his troops into battle. The yellowy bulbs on the ceiling cast dramatic shadows on his face.

"Before we begin, there's something I have to tell you," he announces.

I wish I'd showered one last time this afternoon; I can already feel my armpits prickling with sweat, and I hope the deodorant I packed in my one allotted toiletry bag is going to cut it for four days.

"When I first proposed this idea at a staff meeting, some of the teachers didn't like it. They said, 'Andy, it's too extreme,' or, 'Andy, the kids will be scared.' But I said, 'Bullshit. The country is in danger, and we can't keep treating our students like babies. They need to be informed. They need to be equipped.' I said, 'I don't know who *you're* teaching, but I know my students, and they sure as hell can handle it.'"

Steve laughs. "We can definitely handle it."

Even Betty stands up a little straighter, as if to show she can handle it, too.

Mr. Kraus continues pacing. "So then the teachers said to me, 'Four days? You're never going to get students to follow instructions for four days. They're going to disobey you. They're going to make their own rules. It'll be like *Lord of the Flies* down there.'"

"Did Mr. Castellano say that?" Betty asks.

"I'm a gentleman, so I won't name names," Mr. Kraus replies—but he winks at her. "So, you six." He comes to a stop front and center and clasps his hands behind his back. "Before you go in, I want you to know how hard I defended your right to be here, to take part in this very important test. I believe— rather, I know—that you are all intelligent and mature enough to succeed, even though some of my colleagues think otherwise. So, what I ask you in return is this: Prove me right. Do everything I say. Can you do that for me?"

Everybody nods.

"Phew. Good." He smiles and rubs his hands together. "Now that that's out of the way, let's begin, shall we?"

71

And then without another word, he marches down the hall and disappears through a door.

"Are we supposed to follow him?" Bobby asks. "Where do you think he—"

BOOM!

The earsplitting noise makes me drop my bag. Betty yelps. I miss seeing the others' reactions as I snatch up my bag again, but I hear Steve scream the F-word.

"What the hell was that?" Helen snaps.

I knew I shouldn't have agreed to this. Above ground, everyone else is heading off campus for spring recess. I could have been one of them—I could have gone home to my empty house. *You're fine, Connie.* My heart is hammering. *Try to breathe.* But this is scary!

Mr. Kraus comes barreling out of the room he just entered. "There's been an attack," he barks. "The Soviets bombed New York City." It takes me a second to remember this isn't real. "The fallout is in the air *right now.* You need to get someplace safe."

Nobody moves. Nobody's ever interacted with this version of Mr. Kraus.

"Let's go," he commands.

Because of the way we lined up before, I'm in the lead. I very much do not want to be in the lead. Maybe I'm visibly trembling, because Craig puts his hand on my shoulder and says, "Don't worry, Connie, I'll go first."

Craig Allenby. Perfect Craig Allenby. I let him go ahead of

me, and I focus on his broad shoulders. We file past the open door, where I catch sight of a cot and a desk laden with electrical equipment. That must be where Mr. Kraus is sleeping this weekend. We turn a corner and arrive at a heavy-looking door with a yellow-and-black sign on it. The sign has a circle with three triangles inside it, and the words "FALLOUT SHELTER" underneath.

Mr. Kraus yanks open the door with tremendous force, then stands aside to let us in. The room beyond is dark, and Craig enters first. He doesn't seem the least bit scared—*I can do this.* As I shuffle past Mr. Kraus, I search his face for some kind of reassurance, but instead I find a flicker of that expression I've seen in class.

We form a six-person clump a few feet inside the room and turn to face our teacher in the doorway.

"In a moment, I'm going to close and lock this door, and from then on, only I will be able to open it," he explains. "When I'm not here, we'll communicate through the radio, which you'll find on the table, along with instructions on how to use it. There's plenty of food and water to go around. Remember what you promised me. I believe you can do this."

"Groovy," Bobby says.

Is it, though? I have about a million more questions, but there isn't any time. Mr. Kraus salutes us, and then the door slams shut in our faces.

FIVE

Eva

Everything feels different—better, brighter, more exciting—after the night in the woods. Being chosen by the Fives feels like carrying around a shiny gold coin in my pocket, so even when I'm alone in the dining hall or languishing in line for the shower, I feel like the luckiest girl in all the land. Turns out, it's impossible to feel lonely and invisible when you know there's a secret society full of absurdly cool people who somehow think you're cool, too.

When I got back to Ainsley House that night, part of me wondered if it had all been a dream, even though I still had the candle wedged into the back pocket of my jeans. But as I slid into bed, I got a text from Jenny on my newly returned phone. It was a strict list of rules I had to follow, now that I'd passed my first Fives test.

RULES FOR ALL NEW RECRUITS:
☞ You will not breathe a word about the group to any nonmembers.

☞ You will not post anything about the group on social media.

☞ You will not take photos or videos at any group events.

☞ While your final confirmation is pending, you will not speak to group members or other recruits outside of class (unless at a group event, which you will be invited to via text message).

☞ You will follow all instructions handed down by group members.

Breaking any of these rules will result in your immediate removal from the group. There will be no exceptions.

Well, I sure as hell wasn't going to break any of the rules. Desperate for more details on my soon-to-be new friend group, I went to Jenny's Instagram page, clicked on her massive "followers" list, and searched the names of some of the Fives I'd met at the party.

First, I found Niah. Her mom was a New York City council member famous for her groundbreaking climate-change initiatives—I'd seen her name in the news. Niah seemed to be following in her footsteps: she sold handmade biodegradable beaded earrings and donated a hundred percent of the proceeds to environmental groups. Her one-woman company had been featured on *Teen-freaking-Vogue*.

Jackson, the sexy banjo guy, actually played a *lot* of instruments quite sexily. There was a video of him playing the harmonica shirtless that I may or may not have watched upward of ten times.

Alyson wrote short poems on a vintage typewriter and posted photos of them to her grid.

Nikki was a serious swimmer—a few years ago, at fifteen, she became the youngest person ever to swim around the island of Manhattan. (*I didn't know whether I should be impressed or grossed out.*)

And Heather, the leader of the group. Apparently, she was already doing full-time summer internships on Wall Street. In *high school*. She had headshots where she was dressed in a power suit and looked like she could star on *Shark Tank*.

I kept on sleuthing, and I managed to find a few more people I'd seen around the bonfire—and they were equally impressive. The Fives were all so *intriguing*, and I wondered if it meant I was intriguing, too. I had to admit I liked the sound of it—the idea that someone could meet me and sense that I was somehow special.

Since then, I've come to learn that some of them take the Fives rules more seriously than others. One evening, Niah and I are the only two people in the third-floor bathroom of Ainsley House; I obviously keep my mouth shut, seeing as we're not in class or at a Fives event, but I'm surprised that she won't even make eye contact with me in the mirror as we brush our teeth side by side. Another day, I hold open the door of Ainsley House for a sophomore Five named Jazmine and a few of her non-Fives friends, and she sneaks me a wink without missing a beat in the story she's telling them.

Then there's the intense lunch period with Heather. I'm minding my own business, eating a turkey sandwich and attempting to cram for a quiz on ancient Greece, when somebody yanks out a chair and slams down their tray across from me. I'm about to gently inform them I'm trying not to fail a test over here, but when I lift my head and recognize her pale face and blond bob, I immediately look back down at my history textbook.

Did Heather just try to trick me into breaking the rules?

In my peripheral vision, I watch her sit down, pick up her fork, and spear a leaf of spinach.

She pauses.

And coughs politely.

A throat-clearing, I'm-about-to-say-something cough.

I glance up and find Heather staring across the table, her blue eyes locked on me like laser beams. I was right. She's *absolutely* trying to test me—and I'm not about to take her bait. I keep my face expressionless and turn back to my textbook.

She clears her throat again.

I stare at the labeled photos of Doric, Ionic, and Corinthian columns, absorbing literally nothing. My blood pounds in my ears, a billion times louder than the hundreds of conversations taking place around us.

Heather drums her long fingernails on the lacquered wooden tabletop.

I keep on pretending she's not there.

This high-stakes game of chicken goes on for about ten minutes, until Heather, apparently *hopefully*—satisfied with my obedience, picks up her tray and marches off to join Alyson and Nikki on the other side of the room.

My heartbeat goes back down to normal.

Of course, I'm fully aware the no-talking rule makes no sense from a practical standpoint. It's not as though this test is training me for anything; eventually, I'll be able to talk to the other Fives as much as I want, the way Heather's chatting with Alyson and Nikki at the other table right now. And I'm *already* allowed to speak freely to them at group events. I'm guessing they're testing our loyalty—they're seeing how willingly we'll follow their rules, even the most ridiculous ones.

It all feels very exciting.

And then something completely unexpected happens before math one afternoon. I'm walking down the corridor when I notice a bald man waiting by the door, craning his neck to look over the clusters of students coming in and out of the classroom. He's dressed in a tracksuit, with a whistle hanging from around his neck.

"Eva Storm?"

I think I've seen this guy in the gym before, but I have no idea why he'd want to talk to me. I amble over to him, wondering if I'm in trouble for something.

"Eva, I'm Coach Rodriguez," he says. "I'm sorry to hold you up like this, but I wanted to talk to you about an opportunity."

What could he be talking about? In all my life, no teacher has ever singled me out to talk about an "opportunity," unless you counted my old school principal talking to me about detention.

"Okay," I say tentatively.

"I coach the varsity cross-country team, and I've heard through the grapevine that you're a damn good runner."

My breath catches in my throat. How could he possibly know that? The only person I've told about my running is Jenny, on the day we busted out of math class. Maybe someone saw me sneaking out of Ainsley House in the morning . . . but if that were the case, I would have been punished—not given some kind of opportunity.

"We lost a bunch of good runners when they graduated at the end of last year, particularly on the girls' side," he continues. "If you're interested in joining, we could definitely use you on the roster, Eva."

I stare blankly at Coach Rodriguez. "Didn't I miss tryouts, though?"

"Well, yes. You did. Normally I wouldn't make this kind of exception, but I'm desperate for new talent, and you come very highly recommended. What do you say?"

I say . . . Well, *I'm confused* is what first comes to mind. But then a wonderful sense of lightness floods my body, like I'm floating an inch off the ground. I've never been chosen for anything before, let alone a secret society and a varsity team in the same week. It's always been Ella who gets picked for academic awards and student council seats—always Ella who makes Mom and Caleb proud. A memory flashes through my head of being six years old and practicing my cartwheels in the spare bedroom of our apartment, which I could do for hours when I was little. I went to the kitchen for a drink of water, and as my vision adjusted to being right-side-up again, I overheard my mom catching up with an old friend on the phone in the dining room: "Well, you know I had Eva before I met Caleb—she was my *surprise* baby."

That's how I first found out she never really wanted me to begin with. From then on, I've been looking for people who do. Scooping them up like fistfuls of sand, even though they usually end up slipping through my fingers.

"I'm in," I tell Coach Rodriguez. "I'm—um—very flattered. Thank you so much."

"Great!" He claps me on the shoulder. "I'll email you this afternoon with all the details. Now go on and get to class. I'm looking forward to seeing you wow us at practice."

Dumbfounded, I glide into the classroom. I have no idea why Coach Rodriguez just offered me a spot on the cross-country team, or how he even found out I'm a runner, but now I feel like I have *two* shiny coins in my pocket.

When I steal a glance at Jenny before sliding into my seat, she smiles knowingly and makes a peace sign with her fingers.

A peace sign . . . Jackson also flashed me a peace sign in the woods that night. Why do all the Fives—

And then I get it. It isn't a peace sign at all.

It's a V . . . a Roman numeral V.

The run to Burk Creek is six miles there and back. We start at 6:15 a.m. with a stretching warm-up in the gym, and then we all take off—maybe thirty of us in total—down the quiet road that cuts through campus. At least, it's quiet until we pass through the stone archway at the entrance to the school, at which point one of the boys lets out an animalistic battle cry, and a screaming mob of gangly arms and hairy legs surges forward to race each other down the hill into town.

I stand by what I said about boys being strange and complicated.

Now it's just me, Coach Rodriguez, and a dozen girls who—surprise!—all know each other super well. During warm-up, they cackled at inside jokes from last season, and then right before we left the gym, they formed a circle, started jumping up and down as a unit, and belted out a cheer with coordinated arm movements. I stood off to the side, scared of getting knocked out by a flying elbow.

"You'll learn it eventually," the girls' team captain, Marissa, said to me afterward. On the word "eventually," she waved her hand as if she were brushing away a fly. Normally, the exclusion would have stung, but not this time, because I had the Fives.

The group of girls spreads out considerably along the road,

with me at the front. I'm the first one to pass through the stone archway.

"Eva, you're doing great. Don't feel like you need to hold back," Coach Rodriguez says. I've been matching him stride for stride this whole time, not wanting to blow past my coach on day one, but he must be able to tell I have way more gas in the tank. "I need to stay back with some of the stragglers," he says. "When you pass that post office up ahead, you're gonna hit a stop sign. That's where you turn right."

"And I follow the same road the rest of the way?"

"There's a turnoff at two and a half miles that's a bit hard to spot, but you'll catch up with some of the boys and they'll show you where to go. Those goons always gun it in the first mile and run out of steam before they even make it halfway. See if you can teach 'em how pacing works, while you're at it."

I power ahead, past the redbrick post office and the tiny shack that sells maple syrup on an honor system. ("Really smart business plan," Caleb joked sarcastically when we passed it in the car.) The changing leaves are incredible—reds so bright they don't even seem possible—and now I get why our eighty-year-old neighbors down the hall drive north for "leaf-peeping" in the fall.

I turn right at the stop sign, and sure enough, in the distance, I see boys in Hardwick gym uniforms walking with their hands on their hips. I swiftly close the gap between us, my legs taking on a life of their own, but when the boys hear me coming and look over their shoulders, they all take off like shots. "Go,

82

go, go!" one of them calls to his buddy, as though he's genuinely panicked at being passed by the new girl.

"You'd think you were chasing them with a bloody machete."

Over to my right, a boy with light brown hair is jogging back onto the road after stopping in the grass to retie his laces. His face is more freckles than regular skin, especially across his nose, and as he shakes his head at his teammates' backs, his eyebrows make a funny expression. I noticed him earlier, when we were leaving the gym after warm-up: While the other guys went ahead, he stayed back to hold the door open, which struck me as gentlemanly for the average high school boy. On the road, we fall into step beside each other. I'm not sure if I'm matching his pace or he's matching mine.

"Why did they take off as soon as I got close to them?" I ask.

"Because they're stupidly competitive about stuff that doesn't matter," he says. "And watch, they'll probably be walking again in a minute."

"I guess they won't be showing me where the turnoff is."

"You wanna run with me? I've done this route zillions of times. And I promise I won't bolt when I feel the pressing need to exert my masculinity."

"Are you sure? I wouldn't want to stand in the way of your caveman instincts."

"Positive, although I appreciate your concern."

Our banter carries on effortlessly. It's like when you find your perfect pace and feel like you could run forever. "Anyway," he says, "I'd rather stay at this speed than spend the whole time stopping and starting."

"Me too. You know, my middle school coach used to say that in distance running, you should try and keep a pace where you can talk comfortably without getting winded."

"Like what we're doing now."

"Exactly."

"We're naturals." I catch him smiling out of the corner of my eye. "It's really nice to meet you, Eva. And welcome to Hardwick, by the way." (Coach Rodriguez introduced me at the beginning of warm-up and mentioned that I was new. This guy must have actually been listening, unlike the other guys who were trying to pants each other, and the girls who were whispering, giggling, and critiquing the sturdiness of each other's running ponytails.) "I'm Erik. I'm also in the eleventh grade."

"It's really nice to meet you, too." The words don't feel as dorky as when I said them to Jenny. "So . . . if you've run this route a zillion times, does that mean you're a lifer?"

"Yup. Been here since the tender age of . . . uh, however old I was in the fifth grade."

"How do you like it?"

"School-wise, it's great." Erik pauses. "But, um, well . . . socially it's— Oh, here's the turnoff."

Branching off the road is a narrow dirt trail I definitely would have missed if I'd been running on my own. "Watch for tree roots," he says, leading me down the path as it snakes into the trees. A few boys who've already made it to the turnaround point pass us going in the opposite direction; I can't help but notice that while they joke around with each other, none of them pay much attention to Erik, though I suspect they've all been teammates for a while. That's odd. Erik seemed to be on the verge of telling me about his social struggles, but I don't want to make him feel obligated to go there.

"Tell me some fun facts about Hardwick," I suggest.

"Fun facts about Hardwick . . . ," he muses. "You know, the cheeseburger soup in the dining hall is actually really delicious, if you give it a chance."

"I don't know if my body can handle that."

"Okay, fine. Here's one. It's not a *fun* fact, per se, but it's definitely the weirdest story I know about the school."

"Tell me."

"Okay. So . . . a long time ago, my grandpa had a cousin who went to Hardwick." This time around, Erik's voice sounds a bit more serious. "This was in the early sixties, in the middle of the Cold War, when everyone was super freaked out that the Soviets were going to bomb the United States. Well, Hardwick apparently built this giant fallout shelter under the campus. I guess the idea was that you go inside and protect yourself from radiation? They built these things all across the country."

"Oh yeah—I've seen the signs in the city. The yellow-and-black pinwheels."

"Right. So, Hardwick builds one of these things," Erik goes on. "And they decide they want to train the students to survive down there, because, you know, Cold War. So, they lock some kids in the shelter for a weekend, and my grandpa's cousin *dies*."

"Erik. What?" I'm so baffled, I almost don't realize we've reached the edge of a babbling stream—Burk Creek, apparently—and it's time to turn back toward the way we came. "What happened?"

"It was a freak accident. Something falling from the ceiling, maybe? When I started here, my grandpa told me not to go down into any basements without a hard hat. I couldn't tell if he was joking or not."

"Jeez. I'm sorry for your family."

"It's okay. It was such a long time ago. But weird, eh?"

We pass by a few more runners. I wait until we're out of the trees and merging back onto the road to ask, "Have you ever wondered if the fallout shelter is still there?"

He mulls it over. "You do hear about people finding these shelters intact, all these years later. So yeah, I've definitely gotten curious. But . . . you know . . . I'm not sure I want to go poking around the underground tunnels of Hardwick Preparatory Academy on my own."

A few minutes ago, it started to drizzle, but suddenly, it's raining—hard. Erik and I start laughing hysterically as we sprint, soaked to the bone, back toward school. The whole time I'm thinking about how easy it was to talk to him, and whether the last thing he said about the fallout shelter might *possibly* have been a nervous attempt at an invitation to look for it with him.

☢

By late September, my days of feeling lonely at Hardwick are long behind me. I never know when I'm going to be doing my homework or brushing my teeth and magically get a text from Jenny inviting me to another Fives hangout. (I've now pieced together that Jenny is my "recruiter." In September, when it's time to fill the openings in the roster, each Five has the option to bring in a recruit of their choosing—except in the case of Niah, who was forced to recruit Simon Banbury because he's a legacy. Every year, there are five open ninth-grade spots, but they usually invite around seven recruits, just in case a few of them are duds. This year, there was also an eleventh-grade spot open because a former Five moved to California with his family.) Eventually, when I'm a full-fledged Five, I'll be able to hang out with Jenny again whenever I want. Maybe we'll find more ways to get out of math class and wander through the glen, or even just chill in the dorm and watch Netflix. Until then, I'm more than happy to be a law-abiding recruit.

One Friday night, all the Fives plus the six remaining recruits drive in a caravan deep into nowhere, parking on an empty road in the middle of a rolling field. We all climb up onto the roofs of the cars, lie down on our backs, and take in the stars. The night sky is startlingly clear—twinkling stars that you'd never dream of seeing in a light-polluted city— and I'm lying between Jenny and Niah, our bodies touching without any gaps in between. I take it all in: my almost new friend group, my sheer luck, the whole damn beautiful galaxy above me. Sometimes, thinking about the endlessness of the universe makes me feel like an insignificant pea, which is doubly depressing when you *already* feel like an insignificant pea on Earth. But tonight, I don't feel that way. Tonight, the universe looks to me like endless possibility.

The next Friday night, I get a text from Jenny as I read *The Great Gatsby* in the light of my bedside lamp.

> Sneak out. Meet in student parking lot 9:30.
> We're going for a drive.

I throw off the covers immediately, sending Nick Carraway and his stupid green light hurtling into the wall. I tuck my sneakers under my arm, slip out the door, and pad down the staircase in my socks, quiet as a shadow. I hold my breath as I creep past the door of our dorm supervisor, Mrs. Krakowski, who just finished making her rounds to ensure our lights were out. I hear the faint sounds of arguing coming from her room, which means she must be settled into her nightly *Real Housewives* binge.

When I get to the parking lot, I'm the first one there. I cross my arms and squint off into the distance, waiting for a glimpse of someone I recognize. I check the time. It's 9:30. Where are the other recruits? Simon's usually a little bit late to these things, but Drew, Henry, Jessica, and Clara tend to show up five to seven minutes early, like me.

For a split second, the ground lights up. I gasp and whip my head around, like a fugitive caught in a searchlight, only to find two cars full of junior and senior Fives girls waiting silently in the dark. Jenny and Heather are in the front seats of one; Niah and Raven are in the other. Their faces are smooth and expressionless. Jenny flickers her headlights again, which I now understand is my cue to get in the back seat.

It's pure silence when I open the door and slide in next to Nikki. As our two-car caravan rolls out of the parking lot and crunches onto the gravelly road, Heather twists around in the front seat, holds out a plastic water bottle that's only a little bit full, and says, "Drink."

Nikki stares.

I do as I'm told and uncap the bottle, trying not to wince as the nail-polish-remover smell slaps me across the face. I take a sip. It's warm. And terrible. It definitely came from the bottomest of bottom shelves, and it burns on the way down, leaving a raw streak down my esophagus.

Heather smirks. "Finish it by the time we get there." My face must give an involuntary twitch, because she adds, "You'll thank us." Then she turns back around.

My whole body rejects the liquid in my hands, but I'm not going to lose my Fives spot over a few shots of cheap vodka. I don't know how much time there is until we get wherever we're going, so like a warrior charging into battle, I steel myself for pain and knock it back in one giant gulp that makes my cheeks bulge out to the sides. I dig my nails into the fabric of my jeans as I will myself not to vomit all over the back of Heather's seat. *You're fine you're fine you're fine you're fine you're fine.* My whole head is on fire. Nikki wordlessly pats my thigh, which doesn't help the pain, but at least it makes me feel like I did the right thing.

The cars park at the edge of the woods. When their headlights go out, it's pitch-black. I hope I don't have to find my way through the forest again, because when I slide out of the back seat, the ground feels unsteady. It's like stepping onto a boat. Jenny slips her arm around the crook of my elbow, and Niah does the same on the other side. They both have flashlights, and they lead the group down a path through the trees, supporting my wobbling body between them.

We start to march uphill, large rocks towering on either side of us. The beam of Jenny's flashlight lands on a set of stairs carved into the stone, and that's where we go: up, up, up, until all of us are huddled on what seems to be a rocky plateau.

Jenny and Niah release my arms, and the girls form a circle around me.

"Strip," Heather commands. In the flashlight beam, her face is deadly serious.

My addled brain tries to put the pieces together. "As in . . . take off . . . my clothes?"

"Yes."

"Everything?"

"Everything."

I search the other faces, waiting for someone to tell me it's all been a prank, but nobody—not even Nikki, who patted my leg—shows any sign of letting up. And so once again, I do as I'm told, starting with my sneakers and moving on to my jeans, followed by my sweatshirt, and finally, humiliatingly, my bra and underwear. I feel cold air in way too many places. My arms, covered in goose bumps, dart across my body trying to cover everything at once. It's impossible. I'm so exposed. But maybe it's normal. Maybe they've all had to do this at some point. And maybe I'd make a fool of myself if I rejected the very ritual that binds us all together.

I take a deep breath and try my best to relax. As soon as I quit squirming, the circle parts, and Jenny, taking my hand, leads me across the stone surface until there isn't any stone to stand on anymore. It's a ledge. She backs away with her flashlight before I can see what lies at the bottom.

Then I hear Heather's voice behind me. "Jump."

"W-what?"

"Jump, Eva."

The first Fives test didn't scare me at all, but this one makes my breathing go shallow. I'm starting to get dizzy. "B-but I don't know where I'm landing."

"You don't trust us?"

In the tense silence that follows, I hear footsteps moving toward me. Then I feel a cool set of hands come to rest on my bare shoulders, and Heather's floral perfume creeps into my nostrils. "If you don't jump," she whispers into my ear, "I will push you. And if I have to push you, I will be very disappointed."

I've heard enough. With a deep breath, I launch myself off the edge.

Darkness whooshes around me.

The panic only lasts for a millisecond, until I crash through the surface of icy water: feet, waist, chest, head. I scream—both in relief and from the freezing temperature—but only bubbles come out. I kick as hard as I can to get back to the surface, and when I finally breach, I'm met by the greatest sound in the world: the girls all clapping and cheering my name from somewhere up above. "Eee-VA! Eee-VA! Eee-VA!"

"Over here!" Jenny waves her flashlight from a rocky beach a short distance away. She's holding a bundle that must be my clothes. I paddle toward her, laughing with relief. I slip as I'm getting out of the water, and my wrist collides with a sharp rock.

"Careful! Are you okay?"

"I'm fine," I reply, rinsing it off in the water in case there's any blood. And I really am; in fact, I'm *better* than fine. As the cries of my name rain down from above, I feel like I could soar to the moon.

With the exception of my test scores in Mr. Richterman's class, every facet of life at Hardwick keeps on getting better. I remember to wear my blazer on formal assembly days. I train myself to sleep through the incessant cawing of the crow that lives outside my window. I time my showers so I don't have to wait in a line that snakes down the hallway. I don't mean to brag, but I'm kind of crushing it at boarding-school life.

And running cross-country again . . . it's as good as I remember it from back in middle school. The routes around

Hardwick are stunning. We'll sprint to the top of bright-green hills that overlook miles of rolling countryside, then wind our way through wooded trails that look like something out of a fairy tale. Running on my own through the streets of Manhattan these past few years, I guess I didn't realize how much I missed the smell of dewy morning grass, the peaceful sounds of pounding feet and chirping birds just after sunrise. Not to mention the relief of not having to stop at traffic lights. Up here in the middle of nowhere, when I relax into my perfect pace, my legs carrying me on toward infinity, there's nothing in the world I'd rather be doing.

So far, we've had two meets. I finished first in my division at one of them, and second at the other—*far* ahead of any other girls from Hardwick, including Marissa, the team captain. After each of the medal ceremonies, where I went up on a podium in front of hundreds of runners from different schools, Coach Rodriguez clapped me on the back and exclaimed, "It's a damn good thing I let you on late!" He keeps telling me if I keep up the good work, we might have a decent shot at finishing the season ahead of St. Martin's, a nearby private school and Hardwick's bitter rival since the dawn of time.

I've even started to pick up bits and pieces of the girls' complicated cheer, which rears its head before every practice and meet. (The beginning goes, "H-P-A! H-P-A! HOP AND HIP AND HIP-HOORAY!" The dance moves, however, continue to evade me.)

During full team practices, where the guys and girls run

together, I always end up side by side with Erik. Our paces are perfect for each other, and we always have something to talk about. Turns out, we're both randomly into whiny emo music from the early 2000s, and we've both seen every single season of *Survivor*, including the ones from before we were born, when the host, Jeff Probst, basically looked like an infant.

"You know what's always bothered me?" Erik asks during practice one day. It's a deceptively warm morning, the kind where you set out with a windbreaker but end up tying it around your waist as soon as the sun hits.

"What?" I reply.

"How in every single *Survivor* episode, Probst says, 'Once again, Immunity is back up for grabs.' You don't need to say 'once again' *and* 'back.' You could just say, 'Once again, Immunity is up for grabs'—or, 'Immunity is back up for grabs.' The way he does it is totally redundant."

"And you are *totally* a nerd."

We bicker over Jeff Probst's diction all the way to Burk Creek, where I simply have no choice: I crouch down, scoop up some ice-cold water, and splash it at Erik. He gasps, shakes out his hair like a golden retriever, and then he does the same to me.

There's a pause as we both look at each other. A rivulet trickles down into my eyeball, and I blink furiously without breaking eye contact. And then we both lunge forward, scooping up water and launching into an all-out splashing war.

We both die of laughter.

Are we . . . flirting?

It's hard to say. Maybe we're just having fun. Erik hasn't mentioned us looking for the fallout shelter since that very first run to Burk Creek, so maybe I was wrong about him wanting to hang with me one-on-one.

The other guys on cross-country are honest-to-god idiots, but I've gotten friendly with some of the girls on the team—not enough to spend time in each other's dorm rooms or anything, but enough to sit together in the dining hall and laugh at a handful of inside jokes. Marissa does a hilarious impression of Coach Rodriguez talking about how much he hates St. Martin's, complete with incredibly accurate bouncing on the balls of her feet. I fully realize the opportunity is there to get closer to them—to actually *get* to that dorm-room-hangout level of friendship—but I don't know. I just don't feel the urgency to make it happen.

Probably because my Fives confirmation is on the horizon, and I spend almost every waking minute thinking about it.

All right, not probably—*definitely*.

As long as I don't screw anything up, my official confirmation will happen at the end of October, according to Simon's intel. But first, there's a very important dinner I have to go to at the dean of students' house during fall recess.

"It's basically the final step," Jenny says in the driver's seat of her black Jeep. It's just the two of us driving back from the grocery store in town, where she needed me to go in and buy a bunch of cases of beer with my fake ID and a wad of cash from the other Fives. No problem. (In her initial text message, Jenny said our two-person outing counted as a "group event," namely because the group had drunk through her free beer supply and desperately needed a restock. Once the cases were in the back seat of her car, she pressed her finger to her lips and said it would still count as a "group event" if we got hot apple cider and wandered around the quirky local antique store.)

"What do I have to do at the dean's?" I ask her, draining the last sweet dregs of my cider. "Do I have to pass some kind of test?"

"No, the the dinner is gonna be chill." She waves her hand in the air, showing off the vintage ring I helped her pick out. She got super excited when I pointed out how the chunky blue stone perfectly complemented her hair, and I felt like I'd won some kind of prize. "You just have to make it super clear that you love Hardwick, and you'd never, ever, *ever* say a bad thing about the school. That you'd basically die to defend its hallowed halls."

"That I'd *die* for it?"

"Okay, not that you'd die. But definitely let the dean know that you're loyal."

"That should be easy enough."

"Obviously." She takes her eyes off the road to cock an orange eyebrow at me. "I mean, aren't you?"

"Aren't I what?"

"Loyal."

Jenny's sudden seriousness surprises me. "Yes," I say quickly. "A hundred percent." She turns away again, but her intense stare hangs in the air like a ghost. That was kind of freaky. I've never seen that side of her before.

The dinner at the dean's house is scheduled for the first night of fall recess, when most non-Fives students have gone off campus—if not to their own homes, then to a friend's place for the four-day long weekend. We get a half day on the Thursday, and I spend the unseasonably warm afternoon reading the *Hardwick Herald* in the quad between the dorms and watching my classmates trickle out with their weekend bags slung over their shoulders. I snagged a copy of the school paper at lunch so I could brush up on Hardwick goings-on before tonight.

"Whatcha reading?"

It's Erik, standing at the edge of my blanket with his thumbs hooked into the straps of his backpack. He's wearing dark jeans and a delightfully autumnal maroon sweater, which looks very soft. I've never seen him *not* in some kind of Hardwick uniform before, and there's something strangely intimate in knowing these are the clothes he picked out for himself.

"Oh, you know." I pat an article about the drama department rehearsing for the fall production of *A Midsummer Night's Dream*. "Just trying to stay plugged in."

"Learning anything interesting?"

"Uh, let's see. The cast of *Midsummer* is apparently incorporating a fleet of hoverboards into the performance. . . ."

"Shakespeare would be proud."

"And the kid playing Bottom tripped on a hammer that was lying around and fell through one of the set pieces, which is now being repaired."

"And the paper put *Bottom* on blast?" Erik asks in exaggerated shock. "They should be printing the name of the kid who left the hammer lying around! This is an outrage."

"Hey, don't shoot the messenger."

"I demand justice for Bottom!"

"You should join the Young Activists Club. They meet on Tuesdays in the arts building, according to page seven."

Erik laughs. "I've found my calling."

I fold up the *Herald* for now. "So where are you off to?" I ask. "Have any big plans for break?"

"Oh, you know me. A real social butterfly." I've noticed Erik makes a lot of self-deprecating jokes about his social skills, but in all of our interactions so far, I've never found him to be awkward. The opposite, actually: I'm always surprised at how natural our conversation is. Like I don't even have to think about what to say next. "I'm just going home to New Jersey," he says. "Hanging out with the fam. My older brother's home from college this weekend, too, so I'll get to see him. It'll be nice."

"Well, have fun."

"You're staying here?"

"Yeah. My family kind of sucks, so . . . ." It occurs to me that even without the Fives, there's a good chance I'd have opted out of going home—which is comforting, because it means I'm not really lying to Erik.

"Ugh," he says, "I'm sorry."

"It's okay. I'm gonna get some good long runs in."

"Well, Eva, I look forward to running with you again upon my return." He furrows his brow. "Did that sound, like, bizarrely formal? I felt like a medieval knight when I was saying it."

"A little. But I liked it."

"Phew. Hey . . ." He scratches the back of his neck. "Would you by any chance want to go look for that fallout shelter sometime?"

An invitation to hang out, just the two of us? "Absolutely," I reply.

He grins. "I'll bring the hard hats."

"Size large for me, please. I have a lot of hair."

"Consider it done."

Erik adjusts his backpack and waves goodbye. I watch as his lanky runner's legs carry him toward the student parking lot, imaging what it would be like to climb into the passenger's seat and drive back to Jersey with him. Windows down, hair blowing in the wind, the old emo music we're both weirdly into blaring from the speakers. Would we stop at a rest station for snacks? And if so, what kind of trail mix would I buy? Maybe one with chocolate and one with fruit, just to cover my bases. And cheddar popcorn, for something savory, except then we'd get that dust on our hands.

My alarm bells should be going off right now, reminding me not to get ahead of myself. But the funny thing about Erik is that I'm not afraid of losing him, which is probably why I'm comfortable making so many stupid jokes in his presence. It's freeing . . . and also weird, because I'm not used to feeling so *chill* about someone I care about.

Or maybe that's it. The reason I'm so chill is that we're not on that level yet. I mean, we don't really know each other; we're only friends because we're both on cross-country. That would explain why I'm so relaxed around him.

I feel the opposite as I get ready for dinner with the Fives, my body crackling with nervous energy. Ainsley House is practically empty tonight, which means I can waltz right into the shower instead of waiting around in my towel while other girls walk past to use the toilets. I take advantage of the empty sink space to blow-dry and straighten my hair, and then I pull on what I hope is a dean-appropriate cable-knit sweater and skirt. I get a surge of adrenaline as I rush down the stairs, and it only gets stronger as I stride across the empty campus.

I'm the first one to get to the meeting spot just beyond the stone archway. Drew, Henry, and Jessica materialize a minute later. The two boys fist-bump me, and Jessica greets me with a warm hug. It's strange to be close with a bunch of ninth graders, but there's something about the shared experience of being recruited for a secret society that's bonded us over the past few weeks.

"Clara's probably still figuring out what to wear," Jessica says, squinting up the hill for any sign of the other ninth-grade girl. Clara's usually one of the early ones. "You look good."

I do a little curtsy. "As you can see, I went with college admissions interview chic."

Drew strikes a pose in his gray cardigan. "Same."

Just then, Simon strolls through the archway, wearing a preppy blue blazer and a belt with little whales stamped all over it. Simon—here before Clara?

"Greetings!" he calls out.

A tense silence settles over the group as we watch him amble down the hill, totally oblivious.

Simons frowns at us when he gets close. "What's the matter?"

"Did anyone talk to Clara today?" I ask the group.

Drew, Henry, and Simon shake their heads, but Jessica's eyebrows furrow with concern. "She texted me after they took her to the cliff last night. She knew we weren't supposed to be talking, but she was kind of freaking out. I feel bad about it, but I told her she had to stop messaging me, and I blocked her number. I didn't want to break the rules."

"Why was she freaking out?" Drew asks.

"She didn't jump. She refused to take her clothes off." Jessica groans and shoves her fingertips into her temples. "You guys don't think . . ."

Her voice trails off ominously, but I know exactly what she's asking: Was Clara kicked out of the recruiting process for failing one of the Fives' tests?

Drew looks around at the group. "Did the rest of us jump?"

Everyone nods.

"Banbury, you *jumped*?" Henry asks in disbelief.

Simon crosses his arms. "As a matter of fact, I did."

"Jackson didn't have to push you?"

Simon looks at the ground. "Only a little bit."

Meanwhile, an anxious-looking Jessica drags her fingers through her long brown hair. "Well, *shit*."

"Maybe she's just late," Drew offers halfheartedly.

But pretty soon the rest of the Fives start to trickle through the archway with no sign of Clara. When the group is done assembling, Heather makes a show of counting off the recruits on her fingers.

"One, two, three, four, five. Fab!" She smirks. "We're all here. Let's go."

So that's that. The Fives will only have four ninth graders this year, assuming the rest of them pass.

Poor Clara.

The dean of students lives in a big yellow colonial about halfway down the hill into town—Jenny pointed it out on our way back from the beer run. Heather, the Fives' leader, walks in front of the group; I bring up the rear next to Simon, who still looks kind of depressed after admitting Jackson pushed him off the cliff. He should have just jumped, like I did. Maybe I can lift his spirits.

"Simon, I need your wisdom." Sure enough, he perks up. "You seem to know a lot about the history of Hardwick."

"I do indeed," he replies.

"This is gonna sound superbly weird, but have you ever heard about a nuclear fallout shelter on campus?"

A second later, I collide with Raven's back. Someone at the

front must have stopped abruptly, causing the rest of the group to fold like an accordion.

"Oops, sorry about that!" Heather says sweetly, putting a hand on Jazmine's and Alyson's shoulders to steady them. "Did I just hear someone say something about a fallout shelter?"

Her blue eyes squint as she scans the group. As everyone else looks around curiously, I raise my hand. "It was me—I was asking Simon if he knew about it. Someone mentioned it to me, so I was just wondering . . ."

Heather cocks her head to the side. "Who mentioned it to you?" Her voice is bright and inquisitive, but her smile is as hollow as it was on the first night we met. I'm starting to feel like I did something against the rules, but what could it be? The Fives gradually part like the Red Sea, leaving Heather and me facing each other.

Instinct tells me not to give her Erik's name. "I think it was someone on the cross-country bus. I honestly can't even remember who."

Heather sighs and clasps her hands in front of her heart. "All right, well, that's just one of those things the school doesn't like people to talk about, okay?"

I plant my hands on my hips, thinking of Erik's family. "Okay, but can I ask *why*?" Oops, that came out a little more forcefully than I meant it to.

Heather seems taken aback. "I'm sorry, Eva, I didn't realize I had to get your approval on every school rule."

Her words cut like a dagger.

I let my arms fall to my sides.

The icy smile returns to her face as she looks around at the rest of the Fives. "By the way, if anyone else hears the topic come up, please feel free to let me know."

The groups nods. Heather turns back to me, a single eyebrow cocked expectantly. I nod too.

I feel people's eyes on me as we start to shuffle down the hill again, but when I swing my head around to catch them in the act, they pretend to be looking somewhere else. Fear starts seeping into my stomach—why the hell did I get so defiant back there? I just talked back to the person who ultimately decides whether or not I join the Fives.

What if I've ruined it?

What if I'm the next to go, like Clara?

Heather skips up the front steps of the dean's house and raps the brass knocker, shaped like a lion with a ring in its mouth. A few seconds later, the door swings open, and there's an old man standing on the threshold in a fitted blue suit that matches his piercing eyes. He has broad shoulders, a full head of white hair, and a handsome, lined face.

"My Fives," he says warmly, flashing us the hand signal. This must be the dean of students—I've seen him around campus.

"We're here!" Heather chirps.

Everyone shakes the dean's hand as they enter. He seems to know them all personally. He asks Raven how her Juilliard application is coming along, asks Xavier what he thought of some sports book he lent him, and proudly tells Niah what he's done recently to reduce his carbon footprint. Finally, it's my turn. I can do this. I take a deep breath, roll back my shoulders, and introduce myself.

"It's wonderful to meet you, Eva," the man says. "I'm the dean of students. Craig Allenby."

SIX

Connie

Darkness. Mr. Kraus just left us in total, pitch-black darkness. Not only that, but he gave us basically zero instructions for what to do besides use the radio.

This is terrible.

I want out.

"Found it," Craig says.

There's a click, followed by a humming noise, and an eerie yellow light comes on. When I'm done blinking, I see that we're standing in a large concrete room—roughly the size of three tennis courts—with no windows, a low ceiling, and an overall sewerish feel to it. Up until now, this must have been some kind of huge storage room, because no one in their right mind would ever *want* to spend time in here.

Organization puts me at ease, so I take stock of my surroundings like a store clerk checking her inventory. Directly in front of us, taking up the most space in the room, are six rows of metal cots, split down the middle by a wall of curtained dividers. It suddenly strikes me that even with the curtains, we'll be sleeping in the same room as boys. *Weird.* The cots stretch all the way to the back of the shelter, like beds in a hospital or an orphanage. They have thin green blankets that don't look very warm, and I wonder if I would have been happier in one of my long nightgowns after all.

Next to the door, there's a three-legged table with a handheld radio on it, like Mr. Kraus said. The radio is brick-shaped and black with silver edges. It has a silver antenna that sticks out the top.

To our left, a large part of the wall is hidden behind stacks of—I don't know what to call them—drums, maybe? They're these big beige cylinders stacked three high, each with the following words on the front:

CIVIL DEFENSE

SURVIVAL SUPPLIES

FURNISHED BY THE UNITED STATES GOVERNMENT

DRINKING WATER

Of course. There's no running water down here. Which makes me wonder: Where are we meant to use the bathroom? And brush our teeth? I pray the answer lies behind that door over there, and that I don't have to squat over a bucket in full view of Craig, Steve, and Bobby. I'd like to figure that out as soon as possible.

The wall to our right is equipped with shelves that go all the way up to the ceiling. These shelves are stocked with cardboard boxes, and the cardboard boxes—just like the water drums—have official-looking writing on them.

CIVIL DEFENSE
CARBOHYDRATE SUPPLEMENT
CONTENTS 72 POUNDS
DATE OF PACK: JANUARY 1962

I'm calm enough that I can think critically again. I wrinkle my nose at the typed black words. "Carbohydrate supplement" sounds like something we're supposed to eat. There are other boxes labeled Survival Biscuit, Survival Cracker, and Bulgur Wafer, none of which sound especially appetizing, if you ask me.

Bobby puts his hands on his hips and wolf whistles. "Hardwick isn't messing around. This place is the real deal!"

Helen crosses her arms over her chest. "This place is depressing."

Craig squeezes the back of her neck and plants a kiss on her cheek. "All right, all right, let's try to be positive." He claps his hands and walks to the front of the group, facing us with his feet slightly more than shoulder-width apart and his hips jutting forward. It's the same way he stands when he delivers announcements at assembly. Just the other day, he got up onstage to declare he was running for head boy; the entire auditorium erupted in cheers, including the teachers, who are technically supposed to be impartial. "I'm assuming this is new for all of us, and since this is where we'll be living for the next four days, I think we should try to get the lay of the land."

Even though Steve is a year older, and a good six inches taller, he listens to Craig with full attention.

"Steve, could you help the girls lift those boxes off the shelves?" Steve nods like a soldier taking an order from his commander. "And, Bobby, what do you say you and I go figure out how that radio works?"

"Aye-aye, Captain," Bobby replies.

Thunk. Thunk. Thunk. Thunk. Steve lifts four big boxes off the shelf and drops them on the ground. His movements are fast and powerful, and at one point, Betty yanks me out of the way of his flying elbow. When he's finished, he goes to join Craig and Bobby, leaving Betty and me to sort through the rations with Helen.

Although I've seen Helen just about every day since the fifth grade, I've never really interacted with her until now, largely due to our drastically different levels of popularity. This semester, I've come to learn about Helen through Craig's stories, and what I know is that she is quick to anger, is prone to complaining, and spends a great deal of time on her hair, which often makes her late to things. Today, her blond tresses are pushed back with a pink headband.

"Let's see what's in this one." In one swift motion, Helen tears open the box labeled Carbohydrate Supplement. From inside, she pulls out a large metal tin. "We're going to need a can opener."

"Over here!" Betty crouches down and pulls out a cardboard box from underneath the bottom shelf. "There's a bunch of them." She tosses one to Helen, who catches it in one hand.

"Nice move," I blurt out.

Helen smiles. "Thanks."

Using the can opener, she cuts around the top of the tin and pries open the lid. I'm surprised by what's inside. "Those are carbohydrate supplements?" I ask.

The tin is filled with hard, round red and yellow candies. Helen picks up a red one and places it on her tongue. Her eyes go wide. "Oh!" she exclaims. "It's sour."

Betty reaches for a yellow one. She pops it in her mouth and has the same surprised reaction.

"I guess it's kind of okay," Helen reasons. "Here, Connie, try one."

As far as I can remember, it's the first time Helen Honeyman has ever said my name. And when she holds out the tin, she smiles again.

Next, we open the bulgur wafers, which look distressingly similar to the cardboard box they came in. The taste isn't anything to write home about, and the texture is strange—very crunchy. I've never had anything like them before. The crackers and biscuits, which we open up next, are a bit more palatable.

"Andy, do you copy? Can you hear us? Over." Craig holds the radio up to his mouth while Steve and Bobby look on. I wonder if the instructions said to use the word "over," or if Craig knew to do that on his own. It sounds so professional.

There's a bit of static on the other end, and then Mr. Kraus's voice is in the room with us. "I hear you loud and clear, Mr. Allenby. Well done. Over."

Craig beams. Steve and Bobby clap him on his shoulders.

"Hey, girls." Steve stands with his arms crossed in front of his chest, his forearms and biceps bulging. "What's the deal with the food situation?"

"You can't *already* be hungry," Craig points out with a chuckle.

"I eat every hour, on the hour, except when I'm sleeping." Steve doesn't look amused.

"Every hour *on* the hour?" asks Bobby. "Isn't that a bit restrictive? Like, what if the clock strikes three, and you're sitting on the john?"

"Wait." Bobby's joke just reminded me of something very important. Everyone turns their eyes on me, which makes me want to shrink into a crack in the floor. Sometimes I don't know what's scarier: potentially saying the wrong thing, or saying the *right* thing too loudly. "W-where *is* the toilet, do you think?"

"Great question, Connie." I love how Craig not only is able to make me feel at ease, but also important. "That should be the next thing we figure out." When Steve begins to protest, Craig adds, "And *then* we'll eat."

In all my worrying about the bomb, I never gave much thought to the minutiae of living in a fallout shelter, such as how and where a person goes to the bathroom.

If I had, I never would have imagined it to be quite this bad.

I was right in assuming the door had something to do with it, but wrong in thinking we'd actually find a toilet. Instead, when we peer into the tiny room, all we see is an empty drum with a rubber seat lying on the floor beside it.

Helen gasps. "You don't think we're supposed to . . ."

"We are *absolutely* supposed to," Bobby confirms. "That's what a fallout shelter toilet looks like, baby. Once it's full, you pop on the lid and bring in another empty water tank. Then you just transfer the seat."

"That's completely disgusting."

"You would only have to use it for a couple of weeks."

"How do we wash our hands?"

Bobby points to a plastic bin on the floor with an orange bar of soap in it, and Helen wrinkles her nose.

Craig steps through the door and pulls the chain hanging from the light bulb. "Look," he says. "There's a first aid kit in here, too." He unclips the lid and holds it open so we can see what's inside: gauze, bandages, tongue depressors, and other basic stuff you'd find in the infirmary.

Bobby reaches in, pulls out a pamphlet, and flips through it. "Oh, this is helpful," he says sarcastically. "'How to treat sucking wounds in the chest.'"

"What's a sucking wound?" asks Betty.

"Not something you can treat with a dinky first aid kit."

"Well, let's hope we don't have any wounds to treat," she says. "Sucking or otherwise."

We wander back to the open area by the door. If I can

reduce my bathroom trips to two or three times a day, then I only have to go in there . . . ugh. Like ten more times. Maybe it'll be like the outhouse at Betty's lake house, which is always a shock at first, but eventually you get used to it.

"I think we should eat now," Steve grunts.

Since I don't have much of an appetite, and I've already tasted the full range of cardboard-adjacent survival delicacies, I wander over to the wall of drinking-water drums. There's one without any others stacked on top of it, and on the floor beside it, there's a pile of metal canteens. Following the directions on the front of the drum, I open the lid and find a sealed plastic bag full of water. I tip the drum on its side, open the spout on the bag, and reach for a canteen to catch the liquid that comes trickling out. I start to gulp it down, but then I remember the more I drink, the more I'll have to use that terrible toilet. I'm going to drink as little as humanly possible for the next four days.

"You're the best," Craig says as I hand him one of the six canteens I filled for the group. Our fingers brush, and my heart skips a beat. It's too bad he's sitting on the floor next to Helen, and his bent knee is casually resting on top of hers.

"I just realized a major problem with this place," Helen announces.

Craig grimaces. "Babe, I'm going to make a rule that you have to say something positive for every negative thing you point out."

She rolls her eyes and carries on. "Did anyone else count the number of beds?" Sitting in a circle around a packet of bulgur wafers, the rest of us shake our heads. "There are six going across and thirty going lengthwise. That's only a hundred and eighty. Hardwick alone has twice that many students—and this is meant to be a public shelter for people in the community, too."

"I'm sure the school has a plan in place. It wouldn't just be every man for himself."

"What would the plan possibly be?"

"Can we not argue about this?" He squeezes her knee. "I trust Hardwick. They wouldn't mess this up."

She sighs and drops the subject—but not before I realize that in addition to all the things Craig has told me about his girlfriend, Helen is also smart. She has a point about the beds. I picture a horde of people desperately banging on the door of the shelter, only to find out there's no more room. My chest tightens, and I pray there's another public fallout shelter somewhere nearby.

Helen's astute observation makes me curious if she has sides I don't know about. *What do people think of me?* I wonder. I'm currently nibbling on a wafer not because I'm hungry, but because everyone else is doing the same thing. They probably see a nervous wreck. I couldn't even walk to the shelter door without Craig leading the way. As the boys take turns trying the red and yellow candies, Betty leans in.

"You're doing great so far," she whispers.

Not much has changed since Betty and I met on the second day of fifth grade. I still remember the first time I saw her. Rather, I couldn't *not* see her, because she was standing right in front of me with a bow the size of Texas stuck to the side of her head. Hardwick has this horrible tradition where during the first assembly of the year, all the new fifth graders have to march into the auditorium while the rest of the school claps for them. It's called the Welcome Parade, and it's mortifying—especially when you're the one forced to do the parading.

We were lined up in the hall outside the theater, waiting to go in. I could hear the rumble of voices—could already feel the hundreds of eyes staring at me—and gradually, I started hyperventilating.

Betty spun around when she heard my labored breathing. "Whoa. Are you okay?"

"I don't. Think so." It was a struggle to talk.

"What's wrong?"

"Everyone. Looking. At me."

She squeezed her eyes shut and opened them again: my very first glimpse of Betty's famous idea face. "Okay," she said, with the confidence of someone much older than eleven, "I'll take care of it."

"What?"

"I'll make sure they look at me instead."

I still didn't know exactly what she meant until the doors opened and Dean Denton summoned Hardwick's newest students into the room. When we entered, I'm certain not a single person paid me a lick of attention; they were busy laughing at Betty, who skipped into the room pumping her fists in the air. At one point, I think she even whooped. She looked ridiculous, and she didn't care one bit. Like I say: she's fearless.

There's a *ping!* as a half-sucked yellow candy flies from Steve's hand into the metal leg of a cot. "I'm gonna get real sick of eating this stuff," he grumbles. He pulls out a pocketknife and twirls it between his fingers, occasionally flipping out the blade and stabbing at the concrete floor.

"Steve." Betty cocks her head at him. "Why are you even *down* here?"

It's a question I'm sure we've all been pondering. Steve O'Leary isn't particularly friendly with any of us eleventh graders, and besides the football team, he's not the type to get involved in extracurricular *anything*.

"Gotta get my grades up if I wanna keep my football scholarship for college," he mutters. "And my grades blow, so the dean said I could do this for extra credit if I signed up in time." His next floor-stab is extra powerful. I wince. "Sucks," he says, "because I was gonna go to my girlfriend's place this weekend. Her parents are outta town."

"Well, *I* think we should try to be happy," Craig says. "It's a big friggin' deal that we're down here doing this. We're making Hardwick history."

"And, you know, practicing how not to die," Bobby adds. "Always useful."

Betty's idea face makes another appearance. "You guys. We should document it." Her eyes home in on Steve. "Can I borrow your pocketknife?"

"Why?"

"I'm going to carve our names into the wall."

"Let me do it."

"You sure you know how to spell?" Bobby asks. He immediately puts his hands up when Steve gives him a death stare. "I'm kidding! It was just a football-player joke."

We form a semicircle around Steve and watch as he carves our names into the concrete wall next to the main door. The letters are jagged and thin as the blade's edge, but still legible. He *does* end up spelling my last name wrong, writing "Abbott" with only one B. I don't say anything as he starts on the O, but Betty lunges forward and forces him to turn it into another B.

As we stand around marveling at our creation, static erupts from the radio. And then we hear Mr. Kraus's voice.

"Everything okay in there, survivors? Over."

Craig runs to the table and picks up the device. "All's well. We got the lay of the land and ate dinner. Over."

"Glad to hear it," he says. "Now, I want you six to get some rest. I'll be paying you a visit first thing in the morning, and that's when our training is really going to kick into high gear. Are you ready? Over."

We all look at each other. Craig, Betty, and Bobby grin wide with excitement; Steve nods and pounds his fist into his palm; Helen chews her bottom lip. I'm not sure exactly how to respond, but when Craig and I lock eyes, I decide the best thing to do is mirror his smile.

He holds the radio up to his mouth. "We're ready as we'll ever be, Andy. Over and out."

SEVEN

Eva

Dean Allenby's house is . . . scholarly. Lots of wood paneling. Books without their jackets stacked on the windowsills and end tables. In the dining room, there's a huge fireplace at one end of the room, and hanging over the mantel is an oil painting of the entrance to the school. It's a bit aggressive, really. Like, we get it: you love Hardwick. But maybe Allenby didn't pick the painting. Maybe they give you this house when you're the dean of students.

These are the meaningless details I try to distract myself with as I take my seat at the massive dining room table, long enough for ten people to sit comfortably on each side. I'm on the very end, next to Simon and across from the other recruits. I'm trying to be present—trying to join them in complimenting the pinecones and rosemary sprigs that serve as centerpieces— but I can't stop replaying my confrontation with Heather on the walk down here and wondering if my head is on the chopping block.

Allenby taps his knife against his wineglass, and the room quiets down. In the chair at the head of the table, the only one with armrests, he rolls back his shoulders and puffs out his chest.

"My Fives," he says again, the same as when he opened the door. "It's such a pleasure to have you here this evening. I look forward to all of our dinners, but there's something about the first gathering of the year that really makes me excited. It's probably that I get to meet our new recruits. To the five of you at the far end of the table, welcome. I'm delighted to meet you and to welcome you into this historic society."

The dean smiles at each of us in turn. Even from a distance, I feel his piercing blue eyes looking straight into mine, like we're the only people in the room. The closest I've come to interacting with Allenby before this was passing him on the way to lunch, but now that I'm sitting at a table with him, I can see that there's definitely something intriguing about him.

He opens his palms to the rest of the group, like a pastor. "You are the most promising students on campus," he continues. "All of you are going places. We have Ms. Ossington here"—he gestures at Heather—"who recently finished up a prestigious summer internship with a friend of mine in investment banking in Manhattan. And we have Ms. Fontana"—he nods to Raven—"applying to Juilliard's violin program, where I'm told by a former Five in the admissions department that she has a wonderful shot at getting in. No surprises there."

I mean, *I'm* surprised—that's a huge deal. Raven's amazing at the violin, but Juilliard is next-level impossible to get into.

There was this piano prodigy at my old school—this kid who performed for the Obamas when he was like ten and then got invited on *Ellen*—and *he* got rejected by Juilliard twice.

"And of course, we have Ms. Storm, who I hear is a stellar addition to the Hardwick cross-country team," the dean continues. "A job well done! A month in, and she's already rising to the top."

Thanks, but probably not anymore! The whole table looks at me, including Heather. I don't want to know what she's thinking right now, so I glance down at my place setting, where a man in a catering uniform has just set down a bowl of creamy-looking soup. It smells like truffle.

Allenby carries on congratulating the Fives on their accomplishments. I desperately want to enjoy myself, but I just can't shake the thoughts about our altercation on the walk down here. My fear of being axed from the society is now layered over with frustration: Why did Heather have to make such a scene in the first place? Instead of singling me out, she could have just waited and texted the group later. Then I never would have talked back to her. If she's mad at me, then it's partly her fault, too. *Take that, Heather.*

Also, why *is* it such a big deal if people mention the shelter? Don't get me wrong, what happened down there was obviously tragic. But Erik made it sound like his family had gotten over it, for the most part—I mean, it happened back in 1962. If they've managed to move on, why is *Hardwick* still being so delicate about it?

"To our new recruits." Allenby picks up his soup spoon. "As your fellow Fives will know, in lieu of saying grace, I like for us to recite our group's motto. This will be an excellent opportunity for you to practice."

I didn't know we had a motto, but Simon nods. Drew, Henry, and Jessica watch the Fives expectantly.

Then the entire table chants in unison, like a church congregation: "Order, unity, power. Order, unity, power." The chanting gets louder and louder, and some of the Fives, to my alarm, start banging their hands on the table. Silverware clinks against porcelain. Looking around, I realize everyone except for the recruits is wearing a gold class ring with the letter V stamped in the middle. "Order, unity, power. Order, unity, power. ORDER! UNITY! POWER!"

The hairs on my arms are *fully* on end.

And then, as if nothing out of the ordinary just happened, everybody tucks in. I drag the bottom of my spoon in circles along the surface of my soup, feeling not entirely connected to my body. Something's off. Was the chanting a little . . . weird? Or is it just that I'm still riled up and searching for things to be angry about? It's probably the latter. I need to chill.

I try to ground myself by tasting the soup. I was right, it's a truffle-cream-potato kind of thing. Then the plates are cleared, and the caterers bring out steak. *Steak!* At a school dinner. I've gotten used to eating turkey sandwiches and medium-temperature spaghetti in the Hardwick dining hall.

As the waiters clear the dinner plates, I excuse myself to use the bathroom. As I'm crossing the foyer, I hear footsteps following me on the hardwood.

"Hey."

I turn around. It's Jenny. "Hey, what's up?"

She puckers her fire-engine-red lips. "Need to touch up my lipstick." Then she nods me into the corridor where the bathroom is, and where the people at the dining table won't be able to see us.

In the shadowy hallway, she touches my forearm. "You looked kinda . . . off in there. Are you okay?"

"Off?" My voice comes out an octave higher than normal. "No, no. I'm totally fine."

She puts her hands on her hips. "Look, I know things were tense on the way down, but just let it go, okay? Everyone still loves you."

"There is *no way* Heather loves me."

"Dude, stop. I'm telling you the truth. Just, like, try not to escalate things next time. She takes being the leader super seriously, and she wants to make sure she enforces all the dean's random rules. You gotta go along with it."

"All right. I can do that." My shoulders start to relax. I didn't even realize I was holding them up by my ears. "Thanks for stalking me over here."

"You got it." Jenny smiles.

I nod at the bathroom door. "You want to go in first?"

"Nah, I didn't actually need a touch-up." She taps her

bottom lip and examines the pad of her finger. "This new stuff they sent me is super long-lasting."

"Post coming soon?"

"You know it." She smiles again, flips her hair over her shoulder, and walks into the foyer.

I use the toilet and wash my hands as quickly as possible. Now that I'm certain Heather doesn't want to punch me in the face with her golden Fives ring, or send a steak knife spinning through the air in my direction, I'm actually kind of antsy to get back to the dining room. Just going by the first two courses, dessert's probably going to be unreal.

Someone raps on the door as I'm drying my hands.

"Just a second!" I call out.

"Okeydokey." It's Jackson.

When I pull open the door, he's right there in front of me. He's leaning with his elbow on the frame, his hand running lazily through his dark, shaggy hair. His eyes rove my body like they did on the first night we met. "What's up, little lady?"

"Um, I just peed?"

"Charming!"

I usually get a spark from Jackson's not-so-subtle flirting, but now, when it's just the two of us in a very small space, it feels . . . a bit overwhelming. "Er, Jackson . . . do you mind if I squeeze by?"

He shifts his weight ever so slightly, giving me *just* enough room to slip past him. There's no way to avoid the sides of our bodies rubbing up against each other. Once I make it into the hall, he spins around and leans against the doorframe with his other elbow.

"So, Eva. How'd your jump go?" He waggles his eyebrows.

I feel safer on this side of the door. "I did okay. I went with a reverse dive, and I actually managed three back somersaults, but my pike could have been cleaner."

He blinks a few times, furrows his eyebrows, and shakes his head. "Wait, *what?*"

"Sorry. It was a joke."

Jackson's face relaxes. "*Oh.* See, I just do music. I'm not an 'intellectual.'" He makes finger quotes. I roll my eyes at him for the second time, which makes him laugh. "Well, all *I* know, Eva, is that I bet you looked real good doing it."

He winks, and before I have time to fire something back, he closes the door. I wrinkle my nose.

The good news is, I'm not about to get kicked out of the Fives. I hurry back to the dining room and take my seat next to Simon.

"So," Allenby says, patting his stomach and smiling faintly as the waiters set down enormous platters of dessert, "this semester is off to a good start, isn't it?" He reaches for a chocolate chip cookie, breaks it in half, plucks out a single chip, and places it between his teeth. "Although I have to be honest, I was dismayed to see our groundskeepers cleaning up graffiti from the back of the equipment shed."

"That was Jesse Karp," says Jackson, sliding into his chair upon returning from the bathroom.

"Jesse?" the dean asks. "Are you sure?"

"I walked by his window and happened to look inside, and I saw him packing the cans into a backpack."

"Well, it's a good thing I assigned him to a ground-floor room," Allenby says with a laugh. At least half the table joins in; the rest are busy eating their dessert.

"I heard Alex McGrath and Trevor Winter were part of it, too," Xavier adds. "Winter was the one who bought the spray paint."

My chest tightens. There's a mountain of pastries in front of me—cookies, tarts, brownies, macarons in every color of the rainbow—but I've lost my interest in any of them. What's going on right now? Is the point of this dinner to rat people out? Trevor Winter is in our gym class—I've seen Xavier joking around with him.

"I also saw something kind of worrying," Jenny chimes in.

Allenby raises his eyebrows. "Oh?"

"Well, actually, I didn't see it, but in the library, I overheard people talking about"—she giggles—"some kind of performance art involving stealing all the single-use plastic products from the dining hall."

"Well, that is something, Ms. Price! I should probably have a word with the drama department. And might I ask which students you overheard?"

"I'm not sure. They were a few stacks over."

"Did they say when they were going to do their, ah, *piece*?"

"No, not that I heard."

"All right. We'll keep an eye out."

"For what it's worth," Niah says, "single-use plastic products *are* pretty bad for the environment."

"That's true," the dean replies. "And I'm all for self-expression. But unfortunately, not in exchange for our ability to feed our students." He smiles apologetically.

As Niah and Allenby discuss eco-friendly alternatives to the cutlery that's currently in the dining hall, Heather clears her throat to get the dean's attention.

"I'm so sorry to jump in." She sets her half-eaten white macaron on the rim of her plate. "There was just one more thing I wanted to add, if it's okay."

"Of course, Ms. Ossington. What is it?" Allenby asks.

Her eyes flit in my direction ever so quickly, and just like that, I know exactly what's coming. "It's come to my attention that someone on campus is talking about one of the off-limits areas of the school: the *shelter*." She drops her voice on *shelter* the way some people do when they're talking about *cancer*. "I don't know who first brought it up, but *someone* did, because it recently worked its way back to me."

The dean's mouth wilts at the corners, and he steeples his fingers in front of his chest. "I see. We'll have to be on somewhat high alert for that." He looks around at the rest of the group. "I'm going to need your help. If you hear any of that talk, I need you to tell me immediately, and I'll deal with whoever it came from—for safety's sake. We've had accidents in the past with students getting into areas that are off-limits, and we really must make sure we avoid that sort of thing going forward. I don't want people getting hurt. Understood?"

"Understood," the table replies in unison—myself included. Thank god I never mentioned Erik, because it sounds like he could've ended up in trouble.

If Heather knew I was withholding his name, would she accuse me of disloyalty? I dunno—I still feel okay about doing it. At my old school, my friends and I had an unspoken agreement that we'd never snitch on each other, even if the principal tried to pressure us into doing it. It was considered poor form.

Down at the other end of the table, Allenby lets out a long sigh. "A quick reminder," he says, opening his palms again. "As you go about your day . . . as you look at and listen to everything around you . . . I want you all to remember how lucky you are to be a part of this elite community going back generations. Any opportunity your heart desires is right at your fingertips."

He makes a gesture like he's catching a fly in midair, and he leaves his hand in a raised fist as he keeps on talking.

"I'm going to tell you a quick personal story. As some of you may know, when I was a young man, my father left my family with nothing. It made me feel like *I* was nothing. But then I came to Hardwick, thanks to the profound generosity of my mother's parents, and I met some truly inspiring people.

I ended up starting a society for high achievers known as the Fives. I think you're all familiar with it now."

Polite laughter.

"Surrounded by the greatness of my fellow Fives, I realized I could do something great with my life, too. The Fives gave me purpose like you wouldn't believe." He unclenches his fist, smooths out his tie, and takes a long look around the table. "The point is, you're all in a very enviable position, having so many advantages available to you. All I ask is that you show your appreciation through cooperation."

I nod along with everyone else, mulling over the dean's last request. Cooperation? What did that mean? I'm not about to rat anyone out for spray-painting or planning performance art or talking about the fallout shelter, I can tell you that much.

As we file out the door at the end of the night, Allenby has a word with each person individually.

"It was a pleasure meeting you," he says to me with a twinkle in his bright-blue eye. "I look forward to seeing you back here soon. You'll have to be ready to recite the Fives motto. Do you remember it?"

I try to think back to earlier in the dinner. How many words were there again? Three. Yes. And they said them five times in a row.

"Um . . . Order?" Allenby nods, so I keep going. "Unity . . ." He grins. "And finally, there's . . ." Shoot. What was the last part?

"Power," Allenby says. "Order, unity, and power. Those are the keys to success."

"Right. I'll remember that for next time."

"Remember it for *life*. It'll serve you well."

Instead of feeling inspired, I walk back up the hill with a weird taste in my mouth, and not because of the three-course meal. (That part was great—I'm going to miss it when I'm fighting with the toaster in the dining hall tomorrow morning.) It's the "cooperation" stuff—the implied expectation that I'm going to hand over people's names to the dean. The whole situation makes me uncomfortable—it even makes me kinda mad. But if I refuse to do it, does that make me a bad future Five?

My thoughts are running in circles. All I know is that as soon as I see Erik, I need to warn him not to talk about the fallout shelter with anyone else but me.

"Anything interesting happen over the break?"

Erik and I are wandering across campus in the golden late-afternoon light. Coach Rodriguez split up the boys and girls at practice today, so we didn't get to talk until I came out of the locker room and found him leaning against the water fountain, long after the other guys had left the athletics building. At first, I didn't get why he was standing there, but when he perked up at my arrival, I realized he'd been waiting for me—and that now would be a perfect time to tell him everything.

"Um . . . yes," I reply. "You could definitely call it interesting."

I steer him into the glen, where we're much less likely to be overheard. Since the dinner at the dean's house, I've been mulling over what to do, and I've finally made my decision.

Granted, I feel awful about it. The Fives still mean a lot to me, and I hate turning my back on them, even a little bit. This morning in gym, Xavier went out of his way to partner with me for soccer drills, turning down some other guys who asked him first. On my way to lunch, Jazmine smiled at me from all the way across the quad. This afternoon, Jenny and I spent math class passing notes and making faces at each other in the window, and I kept thinking how great it'll be when we can finally hang like normal friends again. All of these little moments—not to mention the middle-of-the-night stargazing, the middle-of-the-woods bonfires—make me want to keep following the Fives' rules to a tee.

But the other part of me wants to make sure Erik doesn't get himself in trouble—for both of our sakes. I still remember the dean's exact words: "If you hear any of that talk, I need you to tell me immediately, and I'll deal with whoever it came from." I don't want Erik to be *dealt with*! On top of that, I've imagined myself sitting at Allenby's dining room table, my stomach plummeting as someone tosses out Erik's name as easily as Jackson tossed out Jesse Karp's for spray-painting. There's no question I would immediately jump to Erik's defense, but then what would happen? Would I be kicked out of the group? I'd rather not have to find out, which is why I've decided to stop this train in its tracks *now*.

"Erik, there's something I need to tell you. But I'm really nervous."

He raises an eyebrow. "What is it?"

"I don't even know where to begin," I say. "It's kinda hard to put the whole thing into words."

"Oh?" He looks surprised. And then his cheeks go beet red. He rubs the back of his neck. "Um, you don't have to say anything if you don't feel ready . . . There's, um, there's no rush . . . We have plenty of time, if that's what you . . ."

Oh my god.

Does he think I'm about to tell him that I like him?

Do I like him?

There *was* that time our knees touched on the cross-country bus and I felt like my chest was imploding.

And the time—

No. Focus, Eva. Even if you like him that way, there's no way he feels it back.

"No—no, no, no. Erik, it's about the nuclear fallout shelter."

I watch his reaction. His mouth twitches in a funny way I can't explain. Then he rearranges his face into a look of polite curiosity.

"Did you go looking for it?" he asks. "Did you *find* it?"

"No, but . . ."

This is it: the moment when I go against the rules I swore to follow. *You will not breathe a word about the group to any nonmembers.* But I'm in an impossible situation: either protect Erik or keep my mouth shut and put us both at risk. If he casually mentioned the shelter to me, then who's to say he wouldn't casually mention it to one of them—not knowing they were going to go straight to the dean? Besides, it's not like I'm posting about the Fives on social media; I'm telling *one* person, and I know I can trust him. I take a deep breath.

"This is going to sound ridiculous, but there's a secret society at Hardwick. And they recruited me at the start of the school year . . ."

As we walk through the mottled light, just him and me and the blanket of orange leaves, I tell him everything about the Fives, including their rules about fallout shelter talk. By the time I'm done explaining things, Erik's eyebrows are two perfect semicircles; his mouth is opening and closing like he's trying to form questions but doesn't know exactly what to ask. Finally, he blinks and asks, "What in the actual heck?"

"Yeah. Sorry for dropping this bomb on you."

"Fallout shelter pun intended?" he asks.

"Of *course* that's your response." I poke him in the arm.

"*Ow.* Sorry. I'm still just trying to process everything." Erik laughs in disbelief. "I can't believe we have a secret society— let's get that out of the way first. Like, WTF."

"Wild, right?"

"But on top of that, how bizarre is it that they don't want people talking about the shelter?"

"I don't know. Is it?" I ask. "At first, I was confused, but then when the dean said it was a safety issue, it seemed kind of legit. Didn't your grandpa's cousin die from some kind of structural collapse?"

"Well, yeah, but . . ." He scratches the top of his head for a few seconds. "That was in the sixties."

"What do you mean?"

He slides his hand down the back of his neck, his eyebrows knit in concentration. "I know my grandpa talks about hard hats and everything, but I feel like they would have fixed whatever the structural problem was. The school still needed a functioning fallout shelter in case of an attack, right?"

I hadn't even thought about that, but Erik has a point.

"Also," he goes on, "Cold War or not, if you're a fancy private school like Hardwick, and something on your campus *kills someone*, you'd probably take care of it immediately. You wouldn't just leave it and hope nobody else goes down there."

"That's also a good point . . . but why would Allenby lie?"

"I dunno," Erik says, rubbing his freckled chin. "Maybe there's some other reason he doesn't want people to know about the shelter."

"What if it has to do with your grandpa's cousin?" I don't know why I just whispered that. Maybe because we're verging into conspiracy theory territory. "What if something shady happened in the shelter, and he's trying to make sure it doesn't get out?"

Erik's eyes go wide. "Do you think so?"

"I mean, no. Not actually. Detectives would have investigated it at the time, right?"

"Yeah, fair. And my grandpa has never seemed suspicious about how his cousin died. It doesn't come up that much, and when it does, it's always very 'case closed.' Nothing mysterious about it."

"Figured," I reply. "You're right, though. It *is* a weird rule."

"Listen," he says, "I totally understand if you're not comfortable anymore, but if you're willing to risk it, we could still go looking for the fallout shelter."

It would be fun to have a project with Erik, something for the two of us to do together outside cross-country. I'd be subverting the Fives for a second time . . . but this feels like an adventure, and if there's anyone made to stealthily skirt the rules, it's me. "Let's do it," I reply. "But, Erik, you really can't tell anybody *anything* I just told you. If it gets out, and it gets traced back to you, they could report you and—"

"I'm not going to tell anyone."

"It has to stay between us. Our secret."

"It will. I promise you, I don't have anyone to tell."

I look at Erik, who's looking at the ground. His hands are in the pockets of his navy-blue track pants, and his shoulders are hunched forward. Suddenly, it feels like we're talking about something else.

"Erik . . ." I'm not exactly sure how to phrase this. "Why do you always joke about your social life?"

He shrugs. "Because my social life is kind of a joke?"

"Do you wanna talk about it?" I ask gently. "I've been talking for like half an hour straight, so . . ."

Erik sighs. For a minute or so, we walk in silence. Maybe he doesn't want to go there; he'd rather be self-deprecating and leave it at that. But at the fork in the path that leads toward the dorms, he turns the other way, toward a path that goes deeper into the trees. "You have a few more minutes?"

"Yeah. Plenty of time."

By now, the light in the glen is pure magic. As we pass through a golden beam that made it through the branches, Erik says, "You ever notice how I don't really hang out with the other guys on cross-country? Like, I don't even really talk to them?"

"Well, yeah," I reply, thinking back to the first day I met him, when the other guys went bolting off ahead of me on the run to Burk Creek. "But Dylan and Avery and all those guys are always trying to pull each other's pants down, so I just figured you *correctly* didn't want anything to do with them."

"You're basically right," he mumbles, "but it's more complicated than that."

"How so?"

"Those guys used to be my best friends."

Come again? I can't imagine Erik being buddies with Dylan, who's constantly calling the other guys "pussies" for not running as fast as he does—or Avery, who pretends to have sex with inanimate objects, including plastic Gatorade bottles. Erik's the kind of guy who uses semicolons in text messages, for god's sake.

"What happened?" I ask him in disbelief. "No offense, but I can't really picture you hanging out with them."

"None taken." He shrugs. "I didn't really like doing it. But I always did cross-country in the fall, basketball in the winter, and track in the spring, so I was automatically part of their group: the 'jocks,' or whatever you wanna call them."

"You must have watched Avery hump so many Gatorade bottles."

"I'd like to burn it from my memory. They were pretty unbearable, but at the same time, we'd all been in this friend group for so long that I didn't even know what the alternative looked like."

He fiddles with the zipper on his jacket.

"But it got to the point where if I had to hear Dylan or Avery make one more sexist or homophobic joke, I was literally going to punch them in the face and get myself expelled," he continues. "And I'm bi, by the way—which they *knew*—so that made their idiot jokes even more infuriating."

"*I'm Bi, By the Way* would be a great title for a memoir," I point out, and Erik laughs. "But I digress. What did you end up doing?"

"Oh, you know. Called them out on it at the end of last year, on the bus ride back from our final track meet. They said it was stupid locker-room stuff and they didn't really mean it; I said that still didn't make it okay. It got a lot more heated than I expected. Rodriguez hadn't been paying attention to what the fight was even about, and he banned us all from the athletic banquet for 'unsportsmanlike behavior,' *et voilà*, Erik Ellis no longer has any friends at Hardwick."

"Well, I'm still happy you spoke up."

"I am too. I mean, it sucks to make yourself an outcast, especially at a place like this. But I can deal with it. Hey, you wanna climb up there?"

He's pointing off the trail to a giant mossy boulder, nearly as big as the ones people picnic on in Central Park. I don't see why not, so we scramble up on all fours, finding a flat spot on the edge big enough to sit next to each other with our feet dangling off.

It's hard to focus on anything except the one-inch gap separating the outsides of our pinky fingers.

"Okay, Storm, it's your turn."

"What do you mean?"

"I just told you my sob story. Now you gotta tell me yours." His pinky finger dances to the left and taps mine. It feels like two wires coming together, completing a circuit. But I'm definitely reading way too much into this. "What's up with your family? Why do you say they suck?"

I sigh wistfully and stare off into the trees. My mom would probably say I'm being dramatic. "It's a long story," I mumble. "The abridged version is that they basically don't want me around. I'm, like, a stain on their perfect little unit."

"You know you don't have to give me the abridged version."

It's funny. The first time I locked eyes with Jenny in the reflection of the window, I felt like she really saw me. But Erik takes it to a whole other level; Erik makes me feel like he's seeing inside me.

"All right, fine. You asked for it." I bounce the heels of my sneakers off the rock. "From what I understand, my mom accidentally got pregnant with me from a random hookup. She definitely didn't want a kid at the time, and I think my grandparents made her feel really shitty for not being more careful, because they're hella Catholic. So she resented me from day one. Like, I literally didn't stand a chance.

"Then, when I was two, she met her husband, Caleb."

"You sound like you're not a fan."

"In preschool, we made these arts-and-crafts cards for Father's Day. My mom and Caleb had just told me they were getting married, and I was pumped to do a card for him. I remember trying to sound out his name so I could write it in finger paint. I spelled it with a K, not a C. That night, I get home, give him the card, and he laughs. He says something like, 'You spelled my name wrong. And I'm not your father. Maggie, she knows I'm not her dad, right?'"

"Shit."

"Yeah. Anyway, they get married, and then they have my half sister, Ella. And she's literally a flawless child. Straight As, super well-behaved, always doing the right thing. My mom got the perfect family she always wanted . . . except I was still there. And I think it makes both of them angry—but of course, they could never come out and say that. Instead, they just compare me to her *constantly*. All I hear about is how I'll never be as smart or successful as Ella. Even when I ran cross-country in middle school and I was the best one on the team, they didn't care.

"And the really frustrating thing is that Ella and I actually get along, but we can't get close because I think she feels trapped between me and our mom and Caleb."

Wow. It feels good to talk about this stuff. Alicia, Nina, Celeste . . . my apathetic allies . . . they weren't into these kinds of conversations. They were more into complaining about all the ways my old school sucked. Erik still seems to be listening, so I take a deep breath and go on.

"Anyway, honestly, I was never a bad kid. I was a perfectly average B-plus student who had trouble paying attention in class, because my mind likes to wander. But when your parents keep reminding you what a disappointment you are—like, every freaking day—you get tired of trying to prove them wrong, because it's pointless. You won't win. And so, you give in and lash out like the shitty kid they say you are.

"You start high school and you quit cross-country even though you loved it and you were really freakin' good at it, because you just don't want to *try* anymore. You stop doing your homework, and you stop going to class all the time, and then you get caught hanging out on the roof of the school with the other delinquents, most of whom are stoned out of their minds.

"Just like that, your mom and her husband have a ready-made excuse to ship you off to boarding school and have the life they always dreamed of. They don't ask you if you want to go. They just secretly enroll you and announce it over dinner a week before the semester starts. And then, *boom*: You're here. With no friends. Knowing your family is happier without you."

I feel spent. Maybe I've already said too much and Erik's freaked out. He's the first person to hear the full story of how I got to Hardwick. Why did I have to go and burden him with all that?

But then he says, "Eva, I'm so sorry. I'm trying to imagine how that feels, and I can't. It's horrible."

"Thanks," I reply. "It just sucks to know you're not wanted."

"Well, for what it's worth," he says, "*I* want you." When he hears his own words, he blushes and grabs fistfuls of his light-brown hair. "Oh my god, I'm sorry. I'm so awkward. I, um, I mean, I want to be your friend. We should keep on being friends, because it sounds like we both could use one."

Well, I guess that's what we are: friends. He's into me, but not *into me*. Glad he cleared that one up before I potentially embarrassed myself. "You're telling me," I reply. "I'm here for you whenever you want to rant about stupid Dylan and Avery."

"And I'm here if you ever want to rant about stupid Mom and Caleb."

"Thanks."

"Any time. Seriously."

When the golden light starts to fade and the orange leaves on the ground turn bluish, we climb down from the boulder and pick up our walk again.

I'm exhausted from purging my emotions, so I steer the conversation back to the fallout shelter. Erik tosses out a slew of ridiculous theories about why Dean Allenby doesn't want people to know about it, including the hypothesis that he's secretly been using it as a sex dungeon all these years.

"Oh my god, *stop*," I plead through a fit of laughter.

"For real though, I want to know more about this shelter," Erik says.

"I forgot to tell you: since we'd talked about going to look for it before you left for fall recess, I actually watched this Netflix documentary on the Cold War so I could get a bit of historical context."

"And you say *I'm* a nerd."

"Fine, we're both nerds—I'll admit it. Anyway, here's the deal: In 1961, JFK was like, 'Oh crap. The Soviets are gonna bomb us.' So, he put all this government funding toward public fallout shelters, which were basically just converted basements. You'd die instantly if a bomb landed anywhere near you, but they could maybe protect you from radiation if you were far enough away."

"Imagine if we found the shelter, and it was totally intact."

"I mean, it's possible! Like you said before, there are tons of stories of people finding perfectly intact fallout shelters." When I finished the documentary, I stayed up late reading all about this shelter found under a school in Washington, D.C. It was still stocked with nasty old crackers.

Erik rubs his palms together. "We should do some research, too. I'll ask my grandpa if there's anything else he remembers, just in case there *is* more to the story. Although, warning: he's slightly senile."

We drop the conversation as soon as we're out in the open again. At the door to Ainsley House, Erik hugs me goodbye. He smells like the boy deodorant he must have slathered on after cross-country practice; something with a name like *Arctic Crush* or *Musk Tsunami*. It makes my skin prickle in a good way.

But apparently, we're just friends.

This is a friend hug.

As I reach for the handle, I turn back to ask him one more question. There's no one around to hear us talking.

"Erik, I meant to ask you, what was your grandpa's cousin's name?"

"Let me think about what her last name would have been." He traces what appears to be a family tree in midair, murmuring names under his breath. Then he nods.

"I'm pretty sure her name would have been Honeyman," he says. "Helen Honeyman."

EIGHT

Connie

The first night in the shelter is, in a word, miserable.

It starts with my first time using the "toilet" in our make-shift bathroom, where I forget that the rubber seat isn't actually attached to the drum beneath it. A mortifying sequence of events follows: The seat skids to the side when I put my weight on it, which in turn makes the whole drum teeter dangerously, like a car rounding a sharp turn at full speed, except this car is full of pee. I crouch down to steady it again, and somehow, in the process, the seat *touches my face*. I stand up in an attempt to start over, except this time, I forget that my pants are around my ankles. I stumble—thankfully not into the drum, but I do crash into the wall, which hurts. I shuffle back to the drum for take three, at which point Steve bangs on the door and asks what's taking me so long. Now all of my classmates think I'm having gastrointestinal troubles in the tiny bathroom we all have to share for the next four days.

When we get into bed, it's unfathomably dark with the

lights off—and cold. The green blankets are basically paper, and they make crunching noises every time one of us moves. Steve snores, and Bobby mumbles in his sleep. The curtained dividers do nothing to muffle the sounds. Eventually I drift off from sheer exhaustion, only to be jolted awake by Mr. Kraus slamming the door behind him and flicking on the light.

"Rise and shine, survivors," he calls out. "In five minutes, I want you standing at attention next to your beds."

This is *weird*. Teachers are not supposed to see where you sleep. Also, why is he barking directions like some kind of military commander? And why is he wearing a red whistle around his neck? While Mr. Kraus rolls the curtains out of the way, we take turns using the bathroom and changing into our clothes—I'm a lot more coordinated with the toilet this time—and make our way back to our cots. I'd very much like to cancel whatever today's training is, but Betty is practically bouncing on the balls of her feet; she keeps tightening her pigtails for no reason. Craig, who has a very cute case of bed head, looks remarkably alert and enthusiastic—unlike Helen, whom I catch disguising a yawn behind the back of her hand, which in turn forces me to do the same.

Mr. Kraus is carrying a briefcase, which he sets down at his feet. He straightens up again and surveys us through somber-looking eyes. He announces, "I have devastating news to report."

Here we go.

"While you were down here, the Soviets in fact carried

out twin bombings yesterday, not just one. In addition to New York City, Washington, D.C., has been flattened to the ground, with total casualties numbering in the hundreds of thousands. I am afraid to inform you that all top government officials are dead, including President Kennedy."

"Wow," Bobby interrupts, "thank god the damage wasn't extensive."

"No talking, please," Mr. Kraus snaps. "Let this be a warning not to interrupt me."

The teacher begins prowling up and down the rows of beds, making eye contact with each of us individually. After Bobby's reprimanding, nobody says a word, although Betty visibly lengthens her posture as he walks by. When his gaze lands on me, I get the unnerving sensation he can see into my brain. *Remember*, I tell myself, *none of this is real.*

"Welcome to day one of a whole new world," Mr. Kraus says from the front of the room again. "The American way of life, as we know it, is over. Democracy couldn't save us from destruction. We're going to need a new kind of society if we survivors hope to have any kind of future. A society based on discipline and allegiance. Where one leader makes decisions and everyone else follows. Where big things actually get done. For now, I will be your leader, and I will train you for success."

Mr. Kraus bends down and opens the briefcase with two metallic *snaps*. Of all things, he pulls out a hammer, followed by a piece of paper with red lettering on one side. Then he marches over to the wooden shelves, fishes a nail out of his shirt pocket, and methodically hammers the sign into a vertical strip of wood.

"Our first training principle." He steps back so we can read it.

ORDER

"What's that supposed to mean?" asks Bobby.

"It means, among other things, that you *do not interrupt me.* I have now made a note of your poor discipline."

Bobby smirks. No one in our grade is more impervious to reprimanding. I think he likes the attention—and on some level, I even think the teachers like giving it to him. But not Mr. Kraus. Not today. His face is still serious as can be.

"Order," Mr. Kraus muses. "What does that signify? It means you will only prevail in this new landscape if you're capable of following rules—of acting with precision and efficiency. We are building ourselves back from *absolute ruin*, and there's no room for error."

He fingers the whistle around his neck. "Which brings us to our first exercise," he says. "Obedience drills. All of you, please go line up along the far back wall from shortest to tallest. Shortest on my left. Go."

The shrill scream of the whistle fills the room.

We all chose cots that are closer to the door, so it's a bit of a trek to the back wall, especially first thing in the morning, when we're all still a little groggy and uncoordinated. Betty and I opt for a straight path up the side, but some of the others weave through the beds in the middle. Steve stubs his toe on a metal leg and curses loudly, which seems to be the only way Steve knows how to curse.

Then, at the wall, it's a struggle to figure out who's shorter and taller than whom. Betty is clearly the shortest and Steve's clearly the tallest, but Bobby and I have to stand back-to-back while Craig places his hand on the tops of our heads to determine I am, in fact, a tiny bit taller. Next, I have to measure myself against Helen, who beats me by an inch or so. In the end, from left to right, it goes Betty, Bobby, me, Helen, Craig, Steve.

Mr. Kraus looks up from his watch. He does not look pleased. "Two minutes and forty-seven seconds," he says. "An embarrassment. You can do much better than that."

"I stubbed my toe," Steve argues.

"No talking out of turn, Mr. O'Leary! That's a warning for you. Now, everyone, back to your starting points. We're going to do this again."

The second time Mr. Kraus blows the whistle, everyone races for the back wall. It's an even bigger mess than the first time, because we're all bumping into each other as we go for the same routes through the rows of beds. Betty bursts out laughing as she and Bobby nearly trip over each other at the wall, which earns her a warning from Mr. Kraus, too. Nobody so much as giggles after that.

"Again!" Mr. Kraus demands.

How long are we going to go on like this? My stomach

rumbles, and I wonder if we'll be stopping at any point to eat breakfast. Not that I'm exactly craving any of those survival crackers, but I'm going to need some sustenance if he expects us to keep running these drills.

"You've only gotten it down to forty-five seconds," Mr. Kraus declares. "This really shouldn't take you any longer than thirty."

Eventually, we start to make some progress. If Betty and I stick to our side path, and Craig and Helen go up the other side, and Steve and Bobby each choose a middle route, we can make it to the back wall without anyone tripping over each other.

The fifth or sixth time we do the exercise, I steal a glance over at Craig and find a familiar look on his face. I've seen it during his soccer games, and when he debated James Moseley ahead of elections for class president, and all the times he's fretted over how to win back Helen. His jaw is clenched, and his eyes are ever so slightly squinted. It's his competitive face—and it's inspiring. It makes me want to be competitive, too. I have to admit, it's satisfying to see our time get quicker with each new round.

When at last we get it down to thirty seconds, Mr. Kraus springs a brand-new drill on us. This time, we have to start at the back wall and end up seated in a circle at the front of the shelter.

"The sooner you get this one right, the sooner you eat breakfast," he commands.

We manage a strong first run, like soldiers marching across

the concrete floor. It's kind of . . . I don't know . . . *impressive*, how we've learned to move with such precision. Like I said, organization has always been calming to me, even if I don't appreciate Mr. Kraus or this fake apocalyptic scenario.

"That was well done," he says when we're seated on the floor. "Would you like to have your meal now?"

Steve, no doubt the hungriest of the group, locks eyes with Craig. Then he looks up at Mr. Kraus.

"Can we try it one more time?" he asks. "I just want to see if we can get it under thirty."

And we do.

Craig is so thrilled that he picks up Helen and swings her around in a circle. At first, she yelps in surprise, clutching at her skirt, but by the time he sets her down after three full spins, they're both windswept and laughing.

When we're all arranged in a circle again, Mr. Kraus steps into the middle. He plops a box of survival crackers at his feet. "Well done, survivors. As your leader, I'm very pleased with your progress."

Betty turns up her face like a flower tilting its petals toward the sun.

"I'm going to leave you for the day now, but I'd like you to keep practicing those drills. Mr. O'Leary?" Steve raises his eyebrows. "I'm going to put you in charge of supervising that. Now, there's one last thing: before you begin eating, please wait for my message on the radio."

Everyone nods.

Although I'm not sure I like the idea of Steve directing the obedience drills.

When the door slams shut behind him, nobody says a word; we all just sit and blink at each other. Then Helen shakes her head like she's snapping herself out of a daydream. "We can talk, you guys. He isn't here anymore."

"Oh yeah," I reply. I'd genuinely gotten used to principle number one.

There's a crackle on the radio, followed by Mr. Kraus's voice. "Thank you for waiting, survivors. Mr. Tackett, I have something to tell you." Bobby perks up. "I had to warn you twice about your poor behavior, which led me to make a note of it. Disorder is *not* the key to success in our new world. Therefore, you will be punished." Bobby's face falls. "Please leave the circle and go sit on your bed. You will not be partaking in this meal. And to the rest of the group: you are not to bring him food. Over."

Bobby laughs, but he sounds nervous. "Good thing Andy can't actually see us," he says, reaching for a cracker.

"What are you doing?" Steve asks.

"I'm taking a cracker."

"But Andy says you're not supposed to."

It seems incredibly unfair that Bobby wouldn't get to eat with us, but at the same time, Steve is pretty intimidating—and he seems to be empowered by his newly assigned supervisor role. I'm too scared to get involved. Betty and I exchange a look. She isn't saying anything, either.

"Come on, Steve," Helen says. "Don't be stupid."

"Babe." Craig puts his hand on her knee. "We're supposed to be following Andy's rules. We promised him."

"Yeah," Steve grunts. "We promised."

Craig clears his throat. "Bobby, I think you should just do what Andy says and sit this one meal out. And the next time we do training, we'll know what the rules are. That seems fair, right?"

Craig Allenby. Ever the voice of reason.

Bobby's eyes make one more sweep of the circle, but no one comes to his defense. "All right." He sighs, climbing to his feet. "Um, I guess I'll just be, um, over there." He pads across the floor and sits down on his bed, watching us with a vacant expression as we plunge our hands into the depths of the cardboard box.

After we eat, Helen announces she's going to take a nap in one of the far back corners, away from the noise. Bobby, who eventually lay down instead of staring at us, now seems to be doing the same. Steve mumbles something about an important meeting and heads over to the bathroom, and Betty wants to go comb her hair, leaving me and Craig alone on the floor together.

It's like we're back in chemistry class as he scoots toward me. "What do you think so far?"

I glance at the radio as though Mr. Kraus could be listening in, but of course, that's not how radios work. "It's a lot different than I expected," I admit. "I didn't think we'd be learning, um, these kinds of survival skills." I gesture to the Order sign tacked to the shelving unit.

"I didn't either. But it's interesting, isn't it?"

I think about all the progress we made on those obedience drills. "Yeah, I guess so."

"I just feel really inspired by Andy, the way he's taken charge of the whole operation. I hope he could tell how hard we were working this morning." Craig nods over my shoulder, toward the faraway corner where Helen is resting. He lowers his voice. "Helen's being so negative," he says. "I know she's just doing it to get under my skin, but I'm worried it's bringing down the group—and pretty soon, Andy's gonna notice. What should I do? Should I go talk to her?"

I rub my chin and consider the possible answers. "Maybe if she gets worse?" I suggest. "It's still pretty early on, so for now, I think you should just keep on being positive. And even if it doesn't help Helen, it's definitely helping everyone else. Including me."

Craig nods repeatedly. "You always give the best advice. Thanks, Connie."

Just then, Betty plops down beside me. I don't think either of us saw her coming, because Craig looks surprised and clamps his mouth shut. A second later, Steve emerges from the bathroom and beckons for Craig to come help him set up a new course for our drills this afternoon. Craig leaps to his feet, salutes us, and hurries off.

As soon as he's gone, Betty whips her gaze in my direction,

her pigtails swinging with the movement of her head. She looks confused. "Did Craig just say you 'always give the best advice'? Is there something I'm missing here?"

Now that she's overheard us, there's no point in lying to her. I make Betty promise she'll keep it a secret, and then I explain how Craig has been coming to me for dating advice all semester.

"But why didn't you tell me sooner?" Betty asks at the end of my story. "You've been in love with him since the first day of ninth grade—"

"Shh."

She rolls her eyes and repeats herself in a whisper this time. "You've been in love with him since the first day of ninth grade. Now you guys are secret pals. You didn't think this was worth mentioning to your best friend in the whole world?"

"Don't flip out, Bets. He made me promise not to tell anyone because he didn't want it getting back to Helen."

But Betty continues glaring at me. She knows I'm not being totally honest, because she and I tell each other everything, including stuff we're not supposed to repeat—like how her mother got a nose job last summer. I have to tell her the whole truth. "I was worried if I told you, you'd make it a big thing," I whisper. "Like, maybe you'd make me confess my feelings to him. Because you're a hundred thousand times braver than I am."

"Connie." She takes one of my hands between both of hers. "I would *never* make you do something you didn't want to."

I consider reminding her of the time she made us both try out for the volleyball team, even though we both couldn't play, and how about two seconds into the tryout, I bumped her a ball that shattered her glasses. (We didn't make it.) Or when she made us dress up as clowns for the Halloween dance, with full face paint, even though I told her no one else would put *that* much effort into their costumes. (I was right.) Or how she would have made me sign up for this fallout shelter test, even if I hadn't come around to it on my own. She must be able to see the reel spinning through my mind of a dozen other such examples.

"Okay, fine. Sometimes I push you to do stuff, but, Connie." She squeezes my hand. "You can always say no if you really don't want to do something."

Logically, I know she's right. I *could* just say no—but deep down, I never really want to. Bets is so confident; she's who I might be if I weren't so worried all the time. That's why on some level, I've always trusted that my friend knows what's best for me—even more than I do. I always defer to her, and except for the time it left her with broken glasses, it usually works out okay. When she convinced me to sign up for stage crew last fall because *she* got a part in the play, I ended up discovering I really liked sewing costumes. The costume designer, an eccentric older woman named Graziella with flyaway gray hair, invited me back to work on the spring show, because she said she liked my work ethic; apparently, I'm very good at following directions, even if she tends to shout them in her native Italian.

I look Betty in the eye. "I know I can say no, Bets. It's just that you're usually right about stuff in the end."

She winks and tosses a pigtail over her shoulder. "Oh, darling. I know."

When Bobby rises from his cot an hour later, it's with a new sense of resolve. "Well?" He plants his hands on his hips and looks from me and Betty to Craig and Steve to Helen, still curled up in the corner. "When are we going to get started again? I'm ready for Andy to not think I'm a total dick."

Betty and I get to our feet and walk over to the boys. Craig looks pointedly at the green lump that's his girlfriend. "We're ready whenever everyone else is."

With his chest puffed out in a show of authority, Steve stomps over to Helen's cot and does a back-kick into one of its legs, shifting it over by a foot. Helen gasps and bolts upright. "Jesus Christ. What the hell are you doing?"

"Don't kick her bed, Steve," Craig says in a raised voice.

Steve crosses his arms impatiently and looks down at Helen. "Wake up. It's practice time."

"You know, this isn't what I thought we'd be practicing when I volunteered to come down here," Helen replies.

"Take it up with Andy, then."

"Maybe I will," she fires back.

Craig's right: she *is* being kind of a downer. Although she did just get jolted awake.

"Come on, babe," Craig calls to her, and she eventually

gets out of bed, glaring at Steve as she smooths down her hair and straightens her clothes. Craig puts his arm around Helen when she finally walks over, and as he hugs her into his side, he smiles at the rest of the group. "Let's do this."

"Let's show those damn Soviets who's boss!" Bobby cheers, and I'm relieved to see he's not too upset about his punishment earlier.

In fact, as Steve starts to bark the instructions for our next routine, I realize that for the first time since we got down here, I'm starting to feel comfortable—like I can actually do this for the next three days and not have a nervous breakdown. It's exciting to be spending this much time with Craig, and I even feel closer to Betty after the talk we just had. I've gotten the gist of what Mr. Kraus is going to be putting us through, and so far, it's been manageable. I even sort of *enjoyed* the obedience drills, once we got the hang of them.

"Three, two, one, *GO!*"

At Steve's command, the six of us set off on a complex path through the beds. When, after a few more run-throughs, we get it down to twenty-seven seconds, I get this familiar warmth in my chest. I felt the same way when I watched from backstage as the curtains parted on opening night of the fall show: this glowing sense of pride that I'd been part of a team, and that our team had gone on to achieve something beautiful. I'd mended the hems of the girls' dresses and sewn buttons onto the boys' coats; I'd sorted through a giant box of garish jewelry to find the glittering brooch Betty was wearing on her chest. I was an integral part of something. It was a feeling of belonging that I wasn't used to at Hardwick.

"Is it weird that I feel really proud of us?" Betty asks.

Craig grins. "I feel the same way."

"Me too!" Bobby cries.

"Again!" Steve roars.

Helen rolls her eyes and crosses her arms. What's the matter with her, anyway? Oh well, I don't have time to analyze Craig's girlfriend right now. The fire inside me is burning bright, and as soon as Steve says the word, I race back to the starting line.

NINE

Eva

On the bench next to someone else's sweaty gym uniform, my phone buzzes with a text from Erik.

The coast is clear.

Deodorant under one armpit will have to do. I jam on the cap, shove it in my bag, and slip out the door of the locker room while the other girls are still talking and blow-drying their hair over by the sinks. I purposely didn't join the group conversation about Kelly, another junior on the team, having a crush on Avery of Gatorade-humping fame: a) because it's *Avery*—ew; and b) so that no one would notice if I had to bolt.

We figured it would look kind of suspicious if we lingered around until the building emptied out, so instead, we're sneaking into the basement of the athletics complex while everyone else is too busy getting ready for dinner to spot us.

I meet Erik at the water fountain, and we zip down the hall

to the door labeled Stair B without anyone seeing us. According to Erik, there's a rule that student athletes aren't allowed to go down to the storage area due to "safety concerns," which reminded me of Allenby's speech at dinner. That's why we decided to start here.

We poke our heads through the door. Coast still clear. No footsteps coming from anywhere else above or below us.

I nod at Erik. "Let's go."

After tightening the straps on my backpack so it doesn't bounce, I lead the way on tiptoe down two long flights of stairs and gently—gently, gently, gently—push the metal bar on the door. It opens into pitch blackness.

"Imagine if we found it on our first try," Erik whispers.

As soon as we step through the door, there's a soft *click*, and then I'm blinded. Harsh fluorescent lights assault my eyeballs. "Jesus, it's bright!"

"It's okay, Storm." Erik puts his hand on my shoulder. "I got you."

I blink a few times. "All right, I think I'm good." Erik lets a few seconds go by before removing his hand and awkwardly returning it to his side.

We're standing in a giant space that seems to be part equipment room, part garage for all the lawn tractors they use to maintain the athletic fields. There are basketball hoops, rolled-up nets, lacrosse and field-hockey sticks, giant containers of basketballs, volleyballs, footballs . . . everything you'd ever need for gym class. On the far wall, behind the tractors, there's a freight elevator with polished stainless-steel doors. I take in the bright-white cinder-block walls and scuff-free poured concrete floor.

I plant my hands on my hips. "Well, this obviously isn't it." It's just a storage area that genuinely *would* be dangerous for kids to be in by themselves.

Erik goes over to inspect a bronze plaque by the door. *"The Felix Lopez Athletic Storage Facility,"* he reads. *"Donated in 2009."* He runs a hand through his still-kind-of-wet hair and sighs. "I knew parts of this building were newish, but I thought it might still have a crusty old basement. Ugh, I bet they've renovated a ton of buildings on campus since 1962. What if they just cleared out the fallout shelter and turned it into another high-tech garage?"

"It's possible, but I don't want to give up yet. We should look in the older buildings."

"And do research," he adds. "There's an archives room in the library where they keep all these old yearbooks and newspapers. I stumbled in there this one time when I was looking for the bathroom. Weird place, but I wonder if we could find a clue in there."

My phone buzzes.

It's a text message from Jenny.

Girls' night in Heather's room. Come
ASAP. Collins House, room 210.

I read the message again, soaking in the words. *Heather's room*. The mystical place that was off-limits the first time I met Jenny.

"Hey, you wanna go grab dinner?" Erik asks.

"I would, but I have this Fives thing." I hold up my phone and try to look super bummed about it, so I don't hurt his feelings. I'd gladly have dinner with him on any other night.

"No worries," he says. Then his eyes light up. "Maybe you'll get some more shelter info. Maybe you'll find out about Allenby's *sex dungeon*."

I laugh again at the theory. "I'll keep an ear out for clues, but I'm not bringing it up."

"Why must you crush my dreams?"

I cross my arms. "Because I don't wanna get kicked out."

Erik smiles. "I *suppose* I can forgive you. As long as you don't abandon our secret quest."

"I would never. I promise."

"Good. Because we still have a lot of basements to search."

We slip out of the athletics building and part ways at the dining hall with a promise to text each other tomorrow. When we friend-hug goodbye, I swear he gives my body an extra squeeze before he lets go—just for a millisecond, but it feels like a coded message.

I walk back to the dorms with butterflies in my stomach, wondering what it meant.

Until now, I've never had a reason to set foot inside Collins

House, which is where all the senior girls live at Hardwick. Directly across the quad from Ainsley House, the stone building is almost identical from the outside, but the rooms are allegedly bigger—a reward for making it through seven years of dorm life.

"I for sure got the biggest room in the building," Heather says as she nibbles off the top half of a grape.

Her corner bedroom has windows on two walls, and plenty of room for the twelve of us—me, Jessica, and the ten confirmed Fives girls—to sit comfortably on her immaculate white area rug. (Our shoes are stowed safely on the floor of her walk-in closet.) In the center of our circle, set on a lacy white tablecloth, is a giant platter of cheese, crackers, nuts, and grapes. Over on the desk, there are six bottles of white wine and a tray of actual wineglasses—like, glasses made of *glass*, instead of our usual Solo cups.

"How did you get it?" I ask, taking in the huge expanse of wall space next to Heather's bed. It's decorated with framed black-and-white photos of skyscrapers, hung in a perfectly geometric grid.

She laughs and bites the remaining grape half into quarters. "I mean, *obviously* Dean Allenby was going to give it to me. And I'm sure he'll give it to whichever of you he picks for leader next year." She looks pointedly at Niah and Jenny, who each straighten up. "Unless it's Xavier," she adds. I guess I'm not even in consideration, seeing as I haven't been confirmed yet.

"When did you find out?" asks Niah.

"Toward the end of the year," Heather replies coolly.

Jenny bites her lip and exchanges a glance with Niah. "Guess we'll have to wait and see," she mumbles. This is getting kind of awkward.

"Whoever it is, you'll have to approve the new recruits, schedule the trials, and plan the group events all year," Heather chirps, plucking another grape off the vine. "You have to be really organized, and also *respected*, you know? I'm sure the dean will pick the best person for the job."

"So, uh, are we gonna open that wine?" Alyson nods toward the desk. I wonder how she, Nikki, Raven, and Jackson felt when Allenby chose Heather to be the leader over them.

"Oh, right," Heather replies. "Jessica, you're closest."

"Got it!" Jessica squeaks. She leaps to her feet and races to the desk—apparently before realizing she's never used a corkscrew before. While the other girls slide into side conversations, I watch as Jessica picks up the metal appliance nervously, like it's a torture device, and pokes the pointy end with the pad of her finger. Then she jabs it into the cork without taking the wrapping off and jerks it around like she's using a crowbar.

I want to go help her, but there's no way to do it subtly. I'd have to step over the cheese plate and part the crowd on the other side.

"What is *taking* her so long?" Heather mutters to Raven. She pauses their conversation and peers across the room, to where Jessica is still engaged in a battle to the death with the first bottle. Heather shrieks with laughter. "Oh my god, Jessica! What the hell are you doing?"

The other girls laugh, too, and it makes me feel sick. Poor Jessica's trying her best! Normally, she's super smart—she speaks, like, five languages fluently: English, French, Spanish, Italian, and German. She might even be able to converse in Latin, come to think of it. She's just new to wine opening.

Then again, I knew how to open wine in ninth grade. But I was also drinking it in Central Park when I should have been in class, so I'm not sure how much of an accomplishment that really is.

"I'll help," I say quickly, scrambling to my feet. No need to be subtle anymore, now that everyone's eyes are on Jessica. When I reach the desk, she looks at me like I've just saved her life and hands over the bottle and corkscrew.

I pop it out no problem.

"*Thank you*, Eva!" Heather calls out.

I open a second bottle and fill the twelve glasses, and then Jessica and I hand them out to the group. This feels so sophisticated—especially the way no one seems concerned about getting caught drinking in a school dorm room.

When everyone has a drink in hand, we raise our glasses in the middle of the circle.

"Order, unity, power," Heather commands.

"Order, unity, power," we repeat.

At Heather's suggestion, we end up playing truth or dare. After a few rounds (and two glasses of wine), I accept a challenge to take two shots of vodka from a plastic bottle she fishes out from the back of her underwear drawer. It's the same terrible, warm liquor I chugged on the night of my cliff jump, but there's nothing I can do about it—Eva Storm does *not* default on dares. The first shot goes down quickly, but the second one puts up a fight.

"You can't spit it out," Heather hisses.

A bunch of the other girls laugh at me, including Jessica. Seriously? That's the last time I rush to save her from a corkscrew fiasco. I ball my hands into fists and swallow, wincing from the mixture of pain and humiliation.

Soon, I'm at the point in a night of drinking where I'm pivoting my head like an oscillating fan to see if the room moves at the same speed, a trick I learned at a party to determine whether you're tipsy or not. Heather's desk lamp takes a while to catch up.

Meanwhile, the group is busy ganging up on Nikki. The senior originally picked truth, but when Heather demanded to know if she'd gone all the way with her girlfriend, Nikki got shy and asked for a dare instead.

"That means she's still a virgin," Heather mutters, loud enough for everyone to hear. (It's an open secret that Heather and Jackson slept together at some point last year, when she snuck him into her dorm in the middle of the night.) Again, the others laugh.

This is such bullshit.

"Hey, Nik, join the club!" I exclaim, launching myself

across the circle to high-five her. Nikki's whole face brightens. She keeps on smiling, even when I miss her palm and accidentally smack her in the shoulder.

Shortly before curfew, I stumble through my door and flop into bed. I wake up in the morning to a dull headache and the realization that I slept with my shoes on and streaked mud all over my sheets.

My phone buzzes with a text from Erik. Seeing his name makes my stomach feel . . . fluttery. I stop worrying about the sheets.

How was the party?

Hmm. How *was* the party? I stare at his message for a while, contemplating how to respond.

Eventually I go with:

Meh. More shelter hunting soon?

Yesterday, I'd been so excited to go hang out in Heather's room. But looking back on the evening, part of me wishes I'd gone to dinner with Erik instead.

In the days that follow, Erik and I stay true to our mission by searching for basements—especially in the old buildings that look like they haven't been renovated since the early 1900s. Our goal is to go as deep as we can, to find some hallway nobody's visited for decades—somewhere that's been vacant for so long, no one on campus even remembers it's there.

One morning after cross-country, instead of going to breakfast, we slip into the math and social studies building, which is still empty before first period. After listening in the entryway for teachers roaming around and hearing only silence, we hurry down the wooden staircase as far as it'll go, down into a cold, dark room that smells like wet clay. Beams of light shine through small rectangular windows near the ceiling, illuminating all the dust swirling through the air. There's nothing in here; it's just a dank unused basement.

"From what I've read, a fallout shelter probably wouldn't have had so many windows," I point out.

"And there would have been a door separating it from the rest of the building," Erik adds.

A few days later, I go exploring on my own. Class time is when the halls are most likely to be empty, and also, they lock some of these buildings outside of class hours. At the bottom of three flights of stairs, I find myself in a dreary hallway that stretches in both directions. I pick the one that looks darker and dustier, and then I turn a corner into an even *more* dismal-looking corridor with no windows and a door at the end of it.

My pulse quickens.

I start to make my way forward.

Halfway down the hall, the door bursts open, and Ms. Pell comes marching out with a stack of papers under her arm.

When she sees me, she jumps, but quickly her surprise turns to anger.

"What are you doing down here?" she snaps. "Aren't you supposed to be in class?"

Time to think fast. "I'm, um, looking for a bathroom. There's someone taking forever in the stall upstairs, and it's kind of an emergency." She needles me with her sharp eyes, so I cross my legs and wrap my arms around my lower abdomen for added effect. "Please."

She breathes out a long jet of air. Finally, she says, "You have to go *left* at the bottom of the staircase. This is the staff copy room."

"Thanks!" I reply, before sprinting away.

Another strikeout.

But at least she bought my act.

That night, as I fight a losing battle with my homework from Mr. Richterman (Euclidean proofs should honestly be illegal), my gaze wanders over to the window. It's dark outside—nothing to distract me, unfortunately—so instead, I stare at the window itself. It's rounded on top, in an old-fashioned way, with—*wait.* Ainsley House is old as hell.

It's 8:47. I still have thirteen minutes before Mrs. Krakowski makes the rounds. The basement of Ainsley House is a big laundry room—same with all the Hardwick dorms—but I think there are doors leading off the main space. I've never thought twice about them before, and I don't think I've ever seen them open. A dorm would be a convenient place for a fallout shelter. If something happened in the middle of the night, the students who lived in Ainsley House could go right downstairs; the others could run over from the neighboring buildings.

I put on the closest pair of sweatpants, jam my feet into slippers, and hurry down the hall. I don't run into anyone as I take the wooden staircase to the musty old laundry room with its row of white washers and dryers on one side. This place is a thousand years old. It has cobwebs in the corners. There's a prehistoric couch shoved against the wall with moldy orange foam bursting from the seams.

And behind the couch, there's a metal door.

It's 8:52. I can totally do this.

I grab hold of one of the arms and shove with all my might, like a strongman moving a monster truck with his bare hands. The couch has bulky wooden finishes that make it unbelievably heavy, but with enough straining, I manage to move it enough to expose the door. Here goes nothing.

With a deep breath, I yank it open.

A broom falls into my chest before clattering onto the floor.

It's a dusty old supply closet.

Foiled again.

Disappointed, I put away the broom, close the door, and slide the eight-thousand-pound couch back into place. It's 8:57. I'd better bolt.

Taking the stairs up to the foyer two at a time, I'm moving too fast to see the person coming in through the front doors.

We collide at the top of the steps, hard enough that I almost fall backward, except she reaches out and steadies me by my upper arms. I let out an *oof!* sound. I'm pretty sure my nose just collided with a collarbone, and it hurts like a bitch.

At first, I assume it's Mrs. Krakowski.

"Eva?" Oh no. It's Jazmine. Now's not the time to run into another Five. "Are you okay?"

Keeping my mouth clamped shut, I gingerly touch the spot under my nostrils to make sure I'm not bleeding. It's dry. Phew.

Jazmine leans in and lowers her voice. "Look, I know you're not allowed to talk to me, but can you please just let me know your nose isn't broken?"

I give her a double thumbs-up, smiling to let her know I mean "yes, I'm fine," and not "yes, my nose is shattered."

She takes a step back and cocks her head to the side. "What were you doing in the basement? Laundry?"

Shit. I nod.

"It's getting pretty close to curfew. You don't mind that your clothes are gonna sit in the machine all night?"

I shrug and shake my head. Please stop asking me questions about what I was doing in the freaking basement.

Jazmine taps her phone and checks the time. "Ugh, we only have two more minutes. We should go." She looks over both shoulders before flashing me the V sign and striding off down the first-floor hallway.

That was my second close call in a day. Maybe Erik's right,

and it's time we hit up the library before I get myself reported to the dean.

Now that it's the end of October, there's a constant cool breeze that smells like overripe leaves. A few determined students still walk around in their short-sleeved dress shirts, but for the most part, people are bundling up in fleeces and scarves whenever they go outside. Halloween decorations go up in the dining hall, including rows of giant pumpkins flanking the front steps, fake cobwebs stretched over the doorways, festive gourds in the center of every table, and plastic tarantulas nestled (a little jarringly) in among the salad bar offerings. There's fall magic in the air, made even more potent by the fact that my Fives confirmation is happening any day now.

After nearly two months of rule-following, I'm excited to leave recruit life behind me. I'll be able to see Jenny and the others whenever I want to, and talk to them outside our predetermined time slots. Reminding myself *not* to say hi to my friends in public is getting pretty old.

Sometimes when I think about the Fives, I get a pinch in my heart. Not always—just sometimes. It's when I remember the bad stuff: the way they ratted out our classmates to Dean Allenby, eliminated Clara for refusing to take off her clothes, and laughed at Jessica and Nikki that night in Heather's room. The fact that they *keep making me drink that awful vodka*.

But maybe they just act meaner in the first few months of the school year to intimidate the new recruits. I still want to be a part of their group, so I push the bad stuff away. My mind is a football field with the negative thoughts relegated to the opposite end zone.

The big night is cold and windy—the kind of evening that chills you to the bone, and that I'd much rather spend in the comfort of Ainsley House, burrowed into my blankets. Instead of lying in bed watching Netflix, I'm yanking on a pair of jeans, zipping up my fleece jacket, and making the bleak trek toward the glen.

The wind howls and whips at my cheeks and sends dried leaves skittering across the walkways. I hunch my shoulders as I walk straight into it, but even still, it makes tears stream from my eyes.

It's better once I'm finally under the cover of the trees. There, I meet up with the ninth-grade recruits, and as instructed in the text message we all received, we follow the twisting path to the clearing where we attended our first Fives party in September.

As miserable as I was on my solo walk to the woods, as soon as I'm surrounded by my fellow recruits, I can't help but get excited; I barely feel the surprise gust of wind that permeates the branches and shoots debris into my eyes—or at least, I'm not bothered by it. That's what happens when you're in a group on a mission. Especially a group so exclusive that no one else at Hardwick knows about it.

I lead the way around the final bend. That first night, I could start to hear music by now, but tonight it's total silence. Did I lead us down the wrong path? No . . . I'm sure this is the one. Finally, we emerge into the clearing.

Whoa.

This is . . . freaky.

The general setup is the same as it was on that first night:
There's a roaring bonfire that looks *extra* enticing, given how
cold it is, surrounded by a ring of quilts, and then a ring of
lanterns. But this time, the ring of lanterns is surrounded by
a ring of Fives, all of them standing silently at attention, the
reflection of the flames flickering in their eyes. There's a gap
in their circle, with just enough room for the five of us recruits
to join them.

Heather steps forward onto the blankets and strides around
the bonfire. "Come join us," she beckons, gesturing to the
empty space between Jenny and Jackson.

Simon, Drew, Henry, Jessica, and I join the ring of Fives. I
purposely take the spot next to Jenny, who stealthily squeezes
my hand for a split second when Heather's back is turned. I
smile with the right side of my mouth and hope she sees it.

"Close your eyes," Heather commands.

I do as I'm told.

The warmth from the bonfire licks my skin.

I feel like I'm about to be forced to my knees and branded
with a white-hot poker.

Would I let them do that to me?

No.

Maybe.

I don't know. I'll decide if and when it becomes relevant.

Which, thankfully, it doesn't. Heather, while pacing in front of us, judging by the sound of her voice, makes a speech about the wonders of Hardwick Preparatory Academy and our newfound responsibility to guard its spotless legacy. It sounds like she's reading off a piece of paper.

"Remember," she concludes, "Hardwick protects those who protect Hardwick."

There's that pinch in my heart. I squeeze my eyes shut even tighter and banish the bad thoughts to the other end of the football field in my head. I think I'm standing too close to the bonfire; the flames are hot on my cheeks and forehead. I feel kind of woozy.

"Hold out your hand and keep your eyes closed until I tell you to open them," Heather orders.

I extend my arm.

I hear Heather speaking softly a few paces away. "Simon Banbury, open your eyes and repeat after me: order, unity, power."

"Order, unity, power," Simon says.

The process repeats with Jessica, Drew, and Henry. Then it's my turn.

"Eva Storm, open your eyes and repeat after me: order, unity, power."

When I open my eyes, the first thing I see is a gold ring in the middle of Heather's left palm. It's stamped with the letter V. With her right hand, she picks it up and holds it between her thumb and forefinger. It's like we're about to get engaged.

"Order, unity, power," I recite. *Those are the keys to success.*

Heather nods her approval. The ring is heavy and cool on my skin.

And just like that, I'm officially a Five.

"Did they make you drink blood out of a skull? Or sacrifice any small animals? Any *large* animals?"

I swat Erik on the arm as we walk across the damp grass to the library after cross-country practice and dinner. "I'm gonna sacrifice *you* if you don't stop talking about it. We have to be careful. They might overhear us."

"Come on, Storm, we're not in the dining hall anymore. Give me *something*."

To be fair, there's no one on the quad but us. Whispering, I relay everything I remember from the evening. At certain parts—like Heather's line about Hardwick protecting those who protect Hardwick—Erik grabs my arm and then releases it almost immediately. I wonder what's going through his mind every time he touches me, and whether each of those touches is a friend touch or a more-than-friend touch.

Because I like Erik. I'm sure of it now. I see it in the fluttery feeling I get whenever his name appears on my phone screen and whenever he touches me—like when he grabbed my arm a second ago, even though he took it away quickly. I felt it. When Coach Rodriguez splits up the boys and girls for cross-country practice, I want to scream; when he keeps us all together, I want to sing.

I know Erik said we were just friends that day we talked in the glen, but sometimes I wonder if his feelings have changed. The other day, I showed up to practice with my hair in French braids, and he said I looked pretty—not just that my hair looked pretty, but that *I* looked pretty. And he blushed. Then again, he's also gotten into the habit of addressing me by my last name, which is exactly how guys talk to their buddies. Not to people they're *into*. And that night with Jeffrey on Alicia's roof, there wasn't any confusion: he wanted one thing and one thing only. Erik leaves me with so many questions, it makes me think he can't possibly like me back.

He opens the door of the library for me. Inside, small groups of students hunch over circular tables, their heads jerking back and forth between their textbooks and laptops. Nobody speaks; a laminated sign on the wall says DRY SNACKS ONLY.

"Second floor," Erik whispers.

Our footsteps hardly make a sound as I follow him up the carpeted staircase. Every noise—every sign of life in this place—seems to get sucked into the spongy gray floor. We journey deeper and deeper into the stacks, past "autobiographies" and "art history," until we're face-to-face with a windowless wooden door that I've definitely never noticed in the handful of times I've wandered up here.

Erik starts to push it open. "Watch out for cobwebs."

Then, from inside, comes a bloodcurdling cry: "I SHOOT MY CROSSBOW AT THE GOBLIN'S HEART!"

More voices follow: "Roll for damage! Roll for damage!"

"Your arrow pierces the goblin's armor. He dies instantly."

"We're in the fortress now!"

On the other side of the apparently soundproof door, four students sit on the floor, screaming and pumping their fists. Scattered on the carpet between them are dozens of dice in different shapes and colors, and several impressively detailed hand-drawn maps. They're the only people in the room, which is small, windowless, and otherwise filled with shelf upon shelf of identical brown storage boxes.

They seem too engrossed to notice us. Erik clears his throat. Only then does the girl nearest to the door look over. She smiles at us and pushes her rectangular wire-framed glasses up the bridge of her nose. I know her from math class; she sits at the front of the room and has a way better handle on those godforsaken proofs than anyone else does. I know her name— Luisa Luna—because of how often Mr. Richterman calls on her to explain the answer.

"Sorry to interrupt." Erik does a small awkward wave. "Do you mind if we . . ." He points to the shelves.

"Of course not," Luisa says. "Are we being too loud? We've never actually had anyone come in here before."

"Oh no—you're good!"

She flashes us a double thumbs-up. "Cool. Well, if we start to get annoying, just holler."

While the four of them go back to slaughtering goblins with reckless abandon, Erik and I quietly study the labels on the boxes until we find the ones marked 1960–1961 and 1961–1962.

Inside both are stacks of the *Hardwick Herald*, presumably a copy of every issue that came out in each school year. I'm not sure exactly what we're looking for, but I figure the school paper must have written *something* on the shelter, or Helen, or both.

"Where should we start?" he asks.

"Nineteen sixty-one is when JFK started telling people to build shelters," I whisper. "Did your grandpa remember exactly when his cousin died? That would give us a general time frame."

"When I asked him over fall recess, he said it happened a few weekends ago," Erik whispers back. "He's really struggling with his memory. Let's just start with the earlier one and see what we can find."

It takes us fifteen minutes apiece to scan an issue from front to back for any mention of the fallout shelter, but no luck. Two more issues down, and my eyes are blurring. "Honestly, how did people find stuff before Control+F became a thing?"

"It would be way easier if any of this were google-able," he says. "Kids of the future are gonna have a way easier time finding details on *our* mysterious deaths."

We continue searching, our necks and backs bent over the yellowing paper. Meanwhile, the kids at the front of the room are having the time of their lives. I hear snatches of whatever game they're playing: Someone uses a spell to hypnotize a bunch of evil elves; another person has a sword fight with a drunk wizard. Erik and I have started following along and silently cheering whenever they seem to have some kind of victory. Even though we're sitting on the floor of the most depressing room at Hardwick, on a research mission that may or may not yield any actual answers, I'm finding this whole thing very enjoyable.

And then an article from October 1960 catches my eye. There's a grainy photo of a boy posing with a soccer ball under his arm. The headline: "Sophomore Soccer Star Scores Winning Goal in Big Game." And underneath: "Craig Allenby breaks tie to bring home 3–2 victory for Hardwick over St. Martin's."

"Erik, look!" I slide the paper across the carpet.

He raises his eyebrows. "You don't think that's the same Craig Allenby, do you?"

We have to talk so quietly that our heads are almost touching. I wonder what it would feel like to have him tuck one of my curls behind my ear.

"Yes. It definitely is. He mentioned he used to be a student here, but I didn't put it together that he was actually here when they built the shelter. That means there's a chance he would have known your grandpa's cousin. That's pretty interesting."

"Uh, Storm, look! What the heck?" He jabs his finger into the paper and reads out loud from the article about the soccer game: *"Sophomore Helen Honeyman cheered Allenby on from the bleachers with a homemade 'GO CRAIG GO' sign. 'My boyfriend works harder than anyone else I've ever met,' she told the* Herald. *'He's a real inspiration.'"*

My jaw drops. "Boyfriend?"

Erik nods. "Boyfriend."

"Helen and Dean Allenby . . ."

"Dated, apparently."

179

This takes the mystery to another level of weird. But as I mull it over, I land on a new possibility. "What if the dean just doesn't want people talking about the fallout shelter because it's too upsetting for him?"

Erik considers it for a moment. "That would be really sad . . . but I'm not sure it adds up to him asking the Fives to report people."

"True. It seems a little extreme."

"But it was a really smart idea," he adds quickly. He turns away, but I think I catch him blushing again. "Maybe I should start in on this one while you keep going over there. Just to see if anything changed dramatically from school year to school year." He peers inside the 1961–1962 box.

"Hey, Storm." He frowns at the contents. "Does this pile look . . . smaller to you?"

He's right. The papers in my box came up to the brim, but in his, there's a bit of space at the top. "It's almost like . . ."

"Some are missing."

We look at each other skeptically before pulling out each paper and checking the date in the top right-hand corner. Sure enough, there are gaps in the archive. There's an issue missing from January, and a bunch gone from April and May.

Erik scratches his head. "Well, that's weird."

"These papers came out a long time ago," I point out. "Maybe they just sucked at maintaining the archives back then." To compare, I peek under the lids of a dozen more boxes from the sixties and seventies—but they're all filled to the brim, just like the first one we looked at.

"It feels like someone took them out on purpose," Erik says. "Like someone wanted to hide something."

The cogs in my brain start to turn. "If Helen died the way everyone says she did, what would there be to hide?"

Now I'm feeling less wary about venturing into conspiracy theory territory: the "safety concerns" about the shelter seem dubious, and it looks like someone removed certain records of what happened here during the 1961–1962 school year. What if the dean is trying to cover something up, and he's using the Fives to help him do it—by asking them to report back to him?

I whisper the same questions to Erik, and we stare at the *Hardwick Herald*s fanned out on the floor, as though the answers might appear out of nowhere.

By now, the four others have safely rescued a sorceress from a barricaded tower and are calling it quits for the night. As they gather their things, reliving the highlights of the night's conquest, it occurs to me that Erik and I are about to be in here alone. They start to leave the room, and my hands get all clammy. I wipe them on my kilt. *Nothing is going to happen. What am I even thinking?*

"You know, I'm really happy we're doing this together," he whispers.

"Me too."

"Eva." Erik is looking directly into my eyes. I look back. If we stayed this way long enough, I could count every freckle on this bridge of his nose. "There's, um . . . there's something I wanted to tell you."

Then he sort of . . . reaches for my head. The sudden movement surprises me, so I pull back, and he freezes. Too late, I realize he was about to do exactly what I'd wanted: he was *actually going to tuck a curl behind my ear.* Now his hand is hovering in midair with nowhere to go. "Ha," he says. He picks up the end of one of my curls. He pulls it straight and lets it spring back again.

"Erik, what—"

"Sorry." He jams his hand under his leg. "I, um . . ."

"Hey, you guys!"

We both jump about twelve feet in the air. Luisa is standing at the end of the row, grinning at us, her thumbs tucked into the straps of her backpack like a Girl Scout. Erik shimmies away from me as though we just got caught making out. *Come back!*

Luisa hurtles on obliviously. "I totally should have invited you when you first came in, but if you guys ever wanna come to D and D Club, we meet here every Tuesday night at six thirty."

"What's D and D?" I ask.

"Dungeons and Dragons," Luisa and Erik answer in unison. I raise my eyebrows at him.

"Listen," he says quickly, still blushing from our awkward interaction, "I've always been a nerd, even when I was a jock."

"Do I have to know how to play?"

"Not at all!" Luisa says brightly. "Hassan was new this year, and he learned super quickly."

It did sound like they were having fun. I could definitely be into goblins and sorceresses; I used to spend hours in my room reading fantasy books—mostly because I liked the idea of traveling to another world that wasn't Mom and Caleb's apartment. Yeah, it's kinda dorky, but whatever. I'm willing to own it. "I'll definitely think about it," I tell Luisa, whose grin gets even bigger.

After she bounces out the door, Erik fixes his gaze at a spot on the carpet. I need to rectify this.

"Erik, what did you want to tell me . . . before?"

"Um . . ." He bites his bottom lip. "It's, um . . . it's funny, actually!" He rearranges his face into a smile. "I was going to suggest we come back and play Dungeons and Dragons sometime. And then Luisa came over and said the same thing. Weird, eh? It's like a sign from the universe."

He breaks eye contact and directs his energy toward sorting the newspapers back into a single stack.

"Yeah," I reply as nonchalantly as possible. "I guess it was meant to be."

TEN

Connie

"Rise and shine, survivors. It's time to show me what you practiced yesterday. Five minutes, and I want you lined up at the back."

Mr. Kraus blows his red whistle, and I leap out of bed like the mattress caught fire. Across the shelter, the others jump to their feet too. Bobby salutes Mr. Kraus. After helping Craig roll the curtains out of the way, he's the first to the bathroom and the first to line up on the back wall. It's bizarre to see Bobby Tackett acting so . . . obedient. It's so different from his usual antics. He must be trying to make a better impression than yesterday. Maybe this whole experiment will be good for him.

I slept better last night, probably because I was exhausted from not sleeping at all the night before. Steve's freight train snores still woke me up a couple of times, but all in all, I feel rested. As fast as I can, I unzip my toiletry bag, spray deodorant under my arms, and drag a comb through my tangled hair. I use my finger to rub toothpaste over my teeth and wash it all down with a swig of water. A shower would be nice, especially after yesterday's physical activity. Only two more nights to go.

At the scream of the whistle, we speed in formation through the beds and into our seated circle at the front. It's easy as pie, after what Steve made us do yesterday: course after course, each one more complicated than the last. By the end, we were splitting into pairs and seeing how fast we could carry the metal cots from one side of the shelter to the other.

"Well, well, well. Twenty-one seconds. I am *very* impressed." Mr. Kraus paces around the edge of our circle with his hands clasped behind his back. "I think you're ready to move on to our next training principle. Ms. Walker, please bring me my briefcase."

Betty scrambles to her feet, grabs Mr. Kraus's briefcase, and meets him at the shelving unit. After she hands it over, she races back to the circle to fill her empty space. Meanwhile, Mr. Kraus takes out his hammer and a new piece of paper. We watch quietly as he nails it in below the first one, so now the signs read:

ORDER

UNITY

This time, we know better than to pipe up with questions. If my stomach is rumbling after a day and a half with only flavorless crackers to eat, I can't imagine how the boys are feeling; nobody's going to risk losing their next meal.

"Unity," Mr. Kraus says as he wanders back over to the group, "is our next key to success in this turbulent time. I ask you: When you're up against the forces of evil, what difference could any *one* of you make on your own? Individually, we fall; together, we rise. We must commit ourselves wholeheartedly to our cause. We must—"

Mr. Kraus abruptly stops speaking.

Helen's hand is in the air.

"Ms. Honeyman," he resumes, "this is your warning. It isn't orderly to throw up your hand at random. If your leader wants to hear you speak, he will ask you to do so."

"Well, I just wanted to know exactly what this 'cause' even *is*. Because this isn't what I was expecting when I agreed to do this. I thought we'd be learning actual survival skills."

She has a point: Mr. Kraus hasn't really explained what all of this training is adding up to. I'll admit I enjoy the obedience drills, but it would be nice to know *why* we have to master them. At the same time . . . doesn't she want to eat? Craig looks exasperated, and Betty seems stunned by Helen's comment.

But Mr. Kraus's face is as calm as a shark. "I *am teaching* you 'actual survival skills,' Ms. Honeyman. I have made a note of your poor discipline."

Helen frowns, but she keeps her mouth shut.

Mr. Kraus glares at her. "You should think twice before you interrupt your leader. About our cause: I was just about to get there before you cut me off."

I try not to let it show on my face, but my spine tingles

whenever he says "your leader" to refer to himself. It makes me think of him not as a human, but something bigger and more intimidating.

He clears his throat. "Do you remember I told you we need a new kind of society, something that will make us stronger than democracy ever could?"

I find myself nodding along with the rest of the group.

Mr. Kraus points at the new sign. "In order for this new society to have *unity*, it needs a name, for starters. So." He opens his palms to us. "Our movement is called the New Americans. This is our hand signal."

He forms a triangle by making a steeple with his fingers and touching his thumbs beneath them. What the . . . Oh. I see it now. If you add in his forearms, it looks like an A—for *Americans*, I guess. I don't really understand the purpose of a hand signal—it even gives me secondhand embarrassment, like when I'd listen from backstage as Betty and her acting friends got way too into their vocal warm-ups—but the others seem to be excited about it. When Betty turns to show off her sign, I can see a big smile through the gap between her palms. Tentatively, I flash the sign in return. I'm sure I'll get used to it—or even kind of enjoy it, like with the obedience drills. Across the circle, Craig nudges Helen with his elbow until she rolls her eyes and shows him her A.

Mr. Kraus smiles at us. "Good work, survivors—or should I say, New Americans. This hand signal is how we'll greet each other from now on, and how you'll demonstrate your loyalty to the movement. Show me if that sounds good to you."

Six As go up in the air.

"Excellent." Mr. Kraus is beaming. "Now, I want all of you to say it with me: New Americans. New Americans. New Americans."

It sounds like a chant.

"Come *on*," he urges. "New Americans. New Americans."

I join in at low volume. Now I feel even more embarrassed, but the others seem to really be getting into it. Craig chants the loudest; Bobby pumps his fist in the air; Betty's shoulders bounce up and down.

I start to lose track of how long we've been going, and it's right around this point that I realize I'm not as embarrassed as I was before. I've gotten used to the weirdness, and besides, everybody else is doing it. And then, it actually becomes *fun*; Betty and I mimic Bobby's fist-pumping, while Craig and Steve slap out a beat on the floor. The same rhythm courses through all of us, like a shared bloodstream. As we look around the circle and lock eyes with one another, my heart races with excitement. Then I get a lump in my throat. Right now, in this very moment, I'm not afraid of what the future might hold. We can handle it. *We're the New Americans! New Americans! New Americans!*

"Aaaaaand, stop!"

Mr. Kraus waves his hands in the air like an orchestra conductor, and the group falls silent, panting. What just happened? Is everyone as energized as I am? Judging by the fire burning behind everyone's eyes, I think we can all feel the shift in the room.

Everyone except for Helen, that is. As usual, she looks like she has a permanent bad smell under her nose.

Mr. Kraus picks up his briefcase. "You all did very well," he says. "I'm going to leave you now for breakfast. As usual, please stay tuned to the radio for further important messages."

After our teacher locks the door behind him, Helen gets to her feet. She doesn't even wait for Mr. Kraus to announce her punishment; she crosses her arms and stalks off to a bed in the back corner of the room.

I expected Craig to chase after her, but he stays on the floor and watches her walk away, his mouth slowly melting into a frown. Betty and Bobby shake their heads disapprovingly. Steve, not even paying attention anymore, crams a fistful of wafers into his mouth. The crumbs collect in the folds of his shirt, which he then shakes out to release them.

I nibble at the edge of a wafer, trying to sort out my thoughts on what just happened. Yes, Helen behaved out of line when she demanded information from Mr. Kraus—I never would have done that in a million years.

But I can't deny the truth: in that moment, while I watched her in disbelief, I also wanted to know the answer to her question.

I look around at the four remaining faces in our circle, and my stomach drops. How come they didn't seem to feel the same way?

When we're done with breakfast, the boys decide they want to do some redecorating. Specifically, they want to build a New American clubhouse in the center of the shelter, using whatever supplies we have available.

When he's finished washing down an entire sleeve of survival biscuits, Steve wanders over to survey the stacks of water drums.

"Are you guys sure about this?" I ask. "Those things are really heavy."

Craig winks at me. "*Unity*, Connie."

I know he meant it playfully, but the words sting. I can't believe I messed up already. I get to my feet and follow him over to the wall of water, with Betty and Bobby hopping along in our wake.

Craig assigns Betty and me to "bed duty," which entails sliding the cots closer to the walls to make room for the new structure. Steve and Bobby's job is to lift the drums down individually, so we can roll them across the floor.

Eventually, Craig does end up retreating to the back of the room, where he crouches down beside Helen's bed and speaks to her in a voice too quiet to hear. I assume he's trying to counsel her about her attitude, and again, I feel conflicted. She asked a fair question.

"He should really call it quits with her for good," Betty whispers in my ear. "She is such a downer. He could do so much better." She nudges me in the ribs.

"As if, Bets."

Craig stands up and runs a hand through his hair. He seems frustrated. Just then, there's a yelp from Bobby, who looks like he's about to collapse under the weight of the water drum he's lifting to the ground. Craig bolts to his assistance, while Helen lazily gets out of bed and wanders over to me and Betty.

"I guess I'll help you guys," she mumbles. "I'm not gonna get any rest with all this noise, anyway."

Betty looks at Helen suspiciously, like she's worried she might sabotage our efforts somehow. But what's she going to do, sit on every single bed to prevent us from moving them? I smile to let her know she's welcome to join us.

Helen smiles back.

When we're done with the cots, we help roll the drums into the empty space we just cleared, and then do the same with a bunch of cardboard ration boxes. Craig, Steve, and Bobby—but mostly Craig and Steve, the two athletes—stack the drums and boxes in pillars of four each, using another drum as a make-shift step stool to reach the highest spots. Then they line up the pillars to form four walls, leaving a gap to use as a door. Craig mops the sweat off his forehead as he and Steve slide the final tower of drums into place. Steve snatches Bobby's canteen from his hands and downs it in one gulp before returning it.

We take a step back to admire our handiwork. I really can't believe we built this with our bare hands. Craig wolf whistles and slings his arm around Helen's shoulders. "That's one far out New American clubhouse." She shrugs him off and crosses her arms over her chest. Craig looks wounded.

"I'm sorry I doubted your idea at first," I confess to the boys. "It looks great."

"Hell yeah it does," Steve says.

Betty claps. "I'm jazzed for Andy to see it!"

"Hear, hear," Bobby agrees.

"Come on." Craig puts on a grin and waves us forward. "Let's go in."

"I'll wait out here," Helen says. Good lord, she is *really* trying to give him a hard time.

There's just enough room for the five of us to crowd inside the walls, but it sure is tight. I can smell the boys' sweat from all the heavy lifting they just did. Maybe this clubhouse was more fun to build than it is to actually use. Just when I'm thinking of slipping out the door, Bobby starts to whisper, *"New Americans. New Americans. New Americans."*

The same thrill from earlier takes over. Craig, Betty, Steve, and I join in. The five of us are chanting as one, our voices getting louder and louder: *"New Americans. New Americans. New Americans.* New Americans. New Americans. New Americans. NEW AMERICANS. NEW AMERICANS. NEW AMERI—"

"Aaaaaahhhhh!"

Betty's scream is followed by a deafening crash as a pillar of cardboard boxes goes tumbling to the ground. One of the boxes springs open and spits out a metal tin, which in turn springs open and spits out hundreds of red and yellow candies.

The carbohydrate supplements skitter every which way across the ground, disappearing under beds or coming to a rest at the spot where floor meets wall. A spasm of fear courses through my chest; it's a good thing the boxes fell out, not in. Betty could have been seriously hurt.

She must be thinking the same thing, because her face is white as a ghost. "I'm so sorry! It was an accident. I started jumping, and I landed all funny and—"

"It's okay, Betty." Craig flashes her the A sign. "Remember? Unity. New Americans don't blame each other for accidents. We're happy you're okay."

"Whew." She puts her palm on her chest. "Thanks, you guys."

There's a crackle from the radio. "Everything okay in there, New Americans? I heard a crash. Over."

Craig rushes over to the table. "Everything's fine. Some boxes fell over, but no one was hurt. We just have to clean up some candies. They went everywhere. Over."

"Remember, New Americans: *order*. Over."

"It won't happen again. Over."

"Good. Well, when you're done cleaning up, I want the six of you to form a circle around the table for your next training session. Let me know when you're in position. Over."

"Betty, you're bleeding." Bobby points to my friend's forearm, where a thin trickle of blood is making its slow progression from her elbow toward her wrist.

"Oh no!" she yelps, and holds out her arm. "What do I do?"

"I'll get the first aid kit." Bobby rushes over to the bath-room. "My dad's a doctor," he adds over his shoulder, as though that qualifies him to handle the situation. Although better him than me: blood gives me the creeps. He returns with the kit already open, pulls out a roll of gauze, and tears off a square with his teeth. He sets the metal container on the floor, and then uses the gauze to wipe up Betty's blood. I watch her eyes flicker back and forth between the focused expression on Bob-by's face and the spot where his free hand holds her wrist steady. She almost looks disappointed when he finishes putting on the bandage.

"You're all set," he says.

"Thanks," she replies, her voice wavering.

When Bobby is done tending to Betty's wound, every-one gets on their hands and knees to collect the carbohydrate supplements. I'm sort of surprised to see the boys helping out, since usually men expect women to do the cleaning up. At home, at the end of dinner, my father sits at the table while my mother and I clear the dishes. She washes, I dry; he pours a glass of whiskey to watch the Huntley-Brinkley report on NBC. Next to me, Bobby flattens himself against the floor and thrusts his arm under a cot. When he withdraws it again, his hand full of candies, he smiles at me triumphantly.

This unity thing, it's pretty good.

And sure enough, as I'm crouching to retrieve another candy from underneath a bed, Betty crawls over to me and whispers, "Is it just me, or is Bobby kind of hunky? In a way?"

I giggle and poke her in the shoulder. "I *knew* that's what you were thinking back there."

"I mean, I always thought he was funny, but I didn't know he had that *caring* side, you know? Could you see us together?"

"Yeah, totally."

"Eee! Okay, let's see what happens."

When we're done collecting the candies—at least, all the ones we can find—the six of us take our spots for the next round of training.

"We're all standing around the table," Craig speaks into the radio. "Over."

My chest tightens at the crackling on Mr. Kraus's end. What are we going to do next? "Good to hear from you, New Americans," he replies. "This morning we talked about unity. Individually, we fall; together, we rise. I trust that you've been employing this principle over the course of the day. Over."

"Yes, sir." Craig nods enthusiastically, even though he's talking to a machine. "We built a New American clubhouse using the boxes and water drums. Over."

"Oh, did you? Fantastic! Absolutely fantastic. You continue to impress me. And I have every reason to believe you'll also excel at this next step. Now, my New Americans, I want each of you to reach one hand under the table. Over."

Every face in the circle looks confused, but we do as Mr. Kraus says. I hold my hand under the table and nothing happens. I run my fingers along the underside of the wood, until I come across what feels like a playing card held in place with tape.

"Does everyone feel a card?" Craig asks.

I nod.

So do the others.

He presses the button on the radio again. "We found the cards. What should we do next? Over."

"Congratulations," Mr. Kraus says. "These are your New American membership cards. You may peel them off, but please do not look at them until you're each off on your own. There are six cards in total, and two of them are marked with a black dot in the center. If your card has a black dot, it means you have a special role in our new society."

I chew my bottom lip. Things have been going better than I expected so far, but I'm not so sure I want a special role any time soon. What if it means I have to make decisions for the group? Or tell people what to do? I'm much more comfortable in the background.

"As we discussed today," Mr. Kraus continues, "our movement can only be successful if we are united. Your job, if you find a dot on your card, is to quietly keep an eye out for any weak points in our group—any fault lines that threaten our stability. If you discover such weakness, I encourage you to report it to me, either via the radio or the next time I'm present in the shelter with you, so I can deal with it accordingly. Over."

Weakness? What did that mean, exactly? Was it technically "weakness" when I questioned the boys' clubhouse-building strategy? How about when Betty accidentally knocked over the boxes? With the rules so open-ended, it seems like *anything* could get someone in trouble. The thought makes me panicky. The others don't seem scared; they've always trusted Mr. Kraus.

But I've certainly never felt that way. Mr. Kraus is all about being spontaneous. He does things without thinking them through—like that dangerous exercise with the blindfolds, or his stupid road trip to Alaska. He and his ex-girlfriend got lost and ran out of gas somewhere in the Canadian prairies, and they had to wait *two whole days* with minimal food and water before a stranger drove by and offered to help them out. I don't even know if they made it to Alaska in the end! In any case, I'm a little wary of this new plan he's announcing.

In the time it takes me to pick off the edge of my tape, Craig, Steve, Betty, and Bobby tear off their cards and race to separate corners to examine them. When Betty looks at her card, her eyebrows go up and her lips form a small O. I can read her face like a book, and I *know* she must have one of the cards with a black dot on it.

At least I won't have to worry about her reporting me.

Still, I hate the way everyone scurried off to look at their cards in private. Mr. Kraus said the secret black dots are to help make us more united, but suddenly, I feel like I can't trust anybody but myself. And just when I was getting kind of comfortable down here.

I turn away from watching Betty, worried that someone else might see me and think I'm trying to peek at her card. Across the table, I find Helen still standing there, a thin vertical line formed between her eyebrows.

We lock eyes.

She looks as uneasy as I feel.

Then she peels off her card and, breaking the rules, flips it over and examines it right in front of me. It's blank—no black dot.

Emboldened by her action, I reach under the table and peel off mine, too. Even if there's a dot, I'm not going to report Helen. I'm not going to report *anyone*.

My card's blank, too.

"This feels wrong, doesn't it?" Helen whispers.

In a panic, I glance over my shoulder. Now I don't know who might be listening, and I sure as heck don't want to be reported to Mr. Kraus. When I look back at Helen, I make a noncommittal grunt.

The line between her eyebrows deepens. "Connie, this is basically McCarthyism."

That name alone makes my stomach turn over. I can't help but wonder if Helen is being a little dramatic. This exercise isn't sitting quite right with me either, but it's not anywhere close to as bad as Senator McCarthy accusing people left and right of being Communist spies seven years ago—almost all of them innocent.

"Babe!" Craig calls to Helen from across the room. "Grab some crackers and come sit with me. You must be starving."

We hold each other's gaze for one more second before she leaves to join her boyfriend. As she slumps away, a troubling thought occurs to me.

All this time, I figured Helen's bad attitude was a way of aggravating Craig. But just now, when she was whispering about McCarthy, I was the only one who could hear her. Craig wasn't anywhere close to us; there was no way her comments could have any effect on him whatsoever. There are some things you do to get a reaction out of people, and other things you do because you really mean them, from your core.

Helen wasn't trying to make a scene just now. She was almost trying to tell me something.

She was almost saying *help*.

ELEVEN

Eva

The invitation's there one crisp November morning, lying in a spot on the floor that was definitely empty when I went to bed last night. I sit up and rub my eyes with the heels of my palms, just in case I'm imagining the navy-blue card stock printed with the words "You're Invited" in silver cursive. I blink hard. It's definitely still there.

Someone must have slid it under my door while I was sleeping, which is simultaneously unsettling and kind of thrilling. I crouch down on the carpet and turn over the invitation, and sure enough, there's a V at the top. Underneath, it says:

Fivesgiving

COME CELEBRATE THE SEASON

THE DEAN OF STUDENTS' RESIDENCE

SUNDAY @ SIX O'CLOCK

I place the invite on my bedside table, laying it down as delicately as if it were made of glass. Then I transfer it to the windowsill, where it's less cluttered, but I don't want anyone to see it from outside, so I move it back to the bedside table. Maybe I could put it—

Oh god, I'm being so stupid. It's morally wrong for me to be excited about this.

You don't know for sure they're trying to hide something. Maybe there really is a safety issue. Or maybe the dean is still traumatized from losing his girlfriend.

Enough that he'd make the Fives report any overheard mention of the shelter? Enough that he might have destroyed all record of it in the school archives?

Okay, but you can still go and hang out with the Fives.

But the Fives might be complicit in whatever the dean is doing—I've seen the way they hand over people's names. I used to feel a pinch in my heart when I thought about the Fives, but after the archives room, it's more like a twisting sensation—and it's getting a lot harder to keep the bad feelings at bay.

I run my finger along the edge of the card stock. I picture the real Thanksgiving I'll be forced to attend the following week, a.k.a. a painfully awkward dinner featuring me, Mom, Caleb, Ella, and Caleb's parents, whom I've literally met dozens of times, yet they still pronounce my name *Ay-va* instead of *Ee-va*.

I can't help it. Bad feelings aside, I'm still kind of flattered that someone took the time to sneak a secret invitation under my dorm room door.

Especially when I don't even know what to make of my relationship with Erik anymore.

On Saturday, the day before Fivesgiving, Erik and I board the bus together for Hardwick's final cross-country meet of the year. Coach Rodriguez high-fives each person as they get to the top of the steps. The team has been having a much better season than usual, and today's our chance to cement our victory over our rivals—which explains why Rodriguez looks like a kid on Christmas morning.

Erik and I sit together and talk the whole way to St. Martin's, but with each bump in the road, I can tell he's taking steps to prevent our legs from touching; he grips his bare knee and uses his hand as a sort of buffer, so that every once in a while, his knuckle slams into the side of my knee, a literally painful reminder that things are still weird between us. Since the awkwardness in the archives room, we've both been going overboard acting platonic around each other. And it's totally my fault: I got startled and made it seem like I wasn't interested, when in reality, I simply wasn't expecting his hand to come flying out of nowhere.

At least being in Platonic City means we're still hanging out; at first, I worried he'd never want to see me again. But in the past week, we've still snooped around the basements of several buildings (all busts, plus one alarming mouse sighting), texted each other for homework help, and eaten meals together after practice. No one has brought up the hand debacle, so it hovers between us like an elephant-shaped balloon. Sometimes I lightly poke it to see if he'll notice.

"So . . . we're not going to see each other as much once the season's over."

Erik shifts in his seat. "No . . . I guess not. Unless you're planning on finagling your way onto the boys' basketball team, which would be extremely impressive."

"Yeah . . . no. But I was thinking . . . I was thinking maybe we should check out Dungeons and Dragons on Tuesday. If you're down. I know you used to be into it. And it sounded kind of fun."

For some reason, my sentences are coming out in short bursts. When I work up the courage to look at him, he's smiling wide. "Yeah. That would be great."

"Okay, cool. Cool, cool, cool." Oh my god, stop saying *cool*. "I'll tell Luisa."

The bus grinds to a halt on the gravel road leading into St. Martin's. On the way up the aisle, we pass by Dylan and Avery, who seem to be waiting for the last possible minute to step out into the chilly air. Dylan looks up at Erik and snickers. Avery cups his hand over his mouth and gives a pretend cough where he clearly says the word "loser" underneath.

I stop in my tracks, deciding which one of them I want to punch first, when Erik grabs my sleeve and tugs me along. "Just ignore them."

"Doesn't it bug you?" I ask as we join the throng of students on the ground.

Erik shrugs. Somehow, it looks as though he's genuinely fine. "Once I learned it's better to be alone than hanging out with people who make you feel bad about yourself, I gotta say, those idiots really lost their power over me."

At the meet, Erik goes on to beat Dylan and Avery by three whole minutes, which is almost as satisfying as punching them would have been. And I end up placing first in my division, which helps Hardwick eke out a second-place finish overall—the best we've done in years, and two spots ahead of St. Martin's, which earns me a bone-shattering double high-five from Coach Rodriguez. As the team walks across the dewy grass, our shiny new medals bumping against our chests, he thumps me on the back with his dinner-plate-sized hand.

"I better see you at track tryouts in the spring, Storm!"

"I'll be there," I promise.

He lowers his voice by a few notches and slows his pace, so we fall behind the rest of the group. "I gotta tell you, when Allenby mentioned your name to me, I was skeptical. I don't like to make exceptions for people who miss tryouts. But damn, Storm. Your times this season? You earned every bit of your spot on this team. I want you to know that."

"Really?"

"You better believe it."

Right now, my legs may feel like jelly, but I could skip the whole way back to the bus. I could skip the whole way back to Hardwick.

I can't say the same on Sunday, when the walk downhill to the dean's house has my quads screaming in pain with every step, leaving me waddling side to side like a penguin in boots, tights, and a black velvet dress. My muscles are always sorest the day or two after a big workout, but on a cosmic, sign-from-the-universe level, I wonder if my body is telling me I should be wary of everyone at this party.

Well, if it is, I ignore the warning. The next thing I know, I'm sipping a flute of sparkling apple cider on an Oriental rug in Allenby's formal living room. The whole house smells like warm bread and pine-scented candles, and light jazz plays from a vintage turntable. Servers bring around trays of Thanksgiving food in bite-sized portions: turkey sliders with cranberry relish and gravy, cornbread fritters, cubes of roasted sweet potato with a single marshmallow on top. As I pop one of the cornbread fritters into my mouth, I notice Allenby start to turn in my direction, but before he can get there, Simon intercepts and asks him about the origins of an oil painting on the wall.

A hand closes around my wrist.

"Hey. Over here."

Jenny tugs at my arm, and once again, I'm following her blindly—out of the room and down a narrow hallway branching off the foyer. I hear whispers up ahead, and for a heart-stopping second, I think I'm about to be let in on some kind of big Fives secret. Or that my confirmation was fake, and I still have to do some other initiation.

Instead, it's just Jackson and Xavier perched on a window-sill, pouring clear liquid from a flask into their flutes of cider. Jesus Christ, I can't drink this crap *again*.

Jenny thrusts me forward. "Eva needs some, too."

Jackson flicks his hair out of his eyes and holds out the flask. "C'mere."

"No thanks." I take a step back from the boys. There's no way I'm subjecting myself to another round of liquid torture, and besides, I probably shouldn't dabble in hard alcohol on a Sunday night before school. "I have a math test in the morning."

"So?" asks Xavier.

"*Sooo*, I'm already terrible at proofs, and a hangover isn't gonna make me any better."

Jackson shakes his head and makes a *tsk-tsk* noise. "Don't you remember our motto? *Unity*, Eva." As Jenny and Xavier try to muffle their laughs, Jackson swipes my glass—sloshing some onto my dress—and tops it up with liquor. When he hands it back to me, I force a smile, lift it to my lips, and pretend to take a sip. The smell alone sends a wave of nausea rolling through me.

"Atta girl," he says. "Cheers."

"Cheers," I mumble.

Jackson takes a hefty swig straight from the flask, while Jenny nudges Xavier to make room on the windowsill and squeezes in next to him. They hooked up at a party in the glen the other week, and they're kind of a thing now. "You know, your grades don't matter much anyway," Jenny says to me.

Xavier rests his elbow on Jenny's shoulder and nods. "Yeah. You're gonna get in wherever you wanna go."

"Perks," Jackson drawls, before taking another swig.

I'd still like to not fail my math test tomorrow, and the chances of that seem to get slimmer the longer I stay in this hallway. Eventually, they'll be able to tell I'm not really drinking, because my glass won't be getting any emptier.

"I'm gonna go to the bathroom." I flash them a V and hold up my flute with the other hand. "Thanks for this."

Jenny returns the signal. "Enjoy."

I go around the corner to the powder room, where I proceed to dump the contents of my glass directly into the toilet. When I flush it away, I feel lighter, like I released something big that was dragging me down. I wash my hands, dry them on the Hardwick-crested hand towels, and slip back into the hall, thinking I'll grab another cider and linger in the corner of the living room until it's time to go back up the hill.

Instead, I open the door and find myself eye-to-chest with Jackson. *Again.* Why is he always lurking outside the bathroom when I'm in here? I step to the side to let him go in behind me, but the next thing I know, his arm is around my shoulders and his nose is pressed up against the side of my head. "This way, little lady."

Oh god, I am *so* not in the mood for his drunken antics right now. At the same party where Jenny and Xavier hooked up for the first time, Jackson thought it would be fun to throw a can of body spray into the bonfire, and the explosion was terrifying. I almost got hit by a piece of flaming metal as it whizzed past my elbow.

"Jackson, where are we going?"

"I just wanna talk," he slurs. "We *never* get to talk."

Up ahead, Jenny and Xavier have progressed to making out on the windowsill: a bold choice for a party at a teacher's house, but then again, the Fives follow their own rules. Neither of them comes up for air as Jackson guides me into the empty kitchen, around a table—where I stash my empty glass so he can't refill it—and finally, to a sliding-glass door that leads out to the backyard. Jackson pulls it open with his free arm.

"Oh my god, it's freezing out there." I try to pull away, but he yanks me closer. "Jackson, no."

"C'mon, it's not that bad. Once the vodka kicks in, you'll be totally fine."

And then he tugs me into the frigid night air.

Now I *wish* I'd had some of that nail polish remover to keep me warm. I cross my arms, shivering. Somewhere in the darkness, a cricket is chirping. A lamp on the back of the house casts a dim orange glow onto a barbecue and an outdoor seating area. Jackson steers me across the grass to the patio, where he releases me and flops onto a recliner.

"Come." He shuffles against an armrest to make room for me. We'd basically be lying on top of each other, so I sit on the edge instead. "Well, *that's* no fun," he says.

His charm isn't working on me tonight. He's being annoying, and I'm cold.

"What did you want to talk to me about, Jackson?"

"If you wanna know, you have to come closer."

"I can hear you fine from here."

"No, seriously, Eva." He touches my arm. All of a sudden, his goofy grin is gone, and his eyes are focused on mine. "It's a secret."

"Wait, really?"

"Yeah."

Secrets are good, I need secrets; they're going to help Erik and me solve the mystery of the fallout shelter. I scoot a foot back, so my butt is touching his hip, and lean even closer with my ear. "What's the secret?"

"You can't tell anyone."

"I won't."

The cricket chirps. My arms prickle with goose bumps. I can feel his warm breath. "The secret is . . ." He's so close that the *S* sound sends chills down my spine. "You know how I'm a senior?"

"Yeah."

He sighs into my neck. "I really wanna do it with you before I graduate."

I scream and jump to my feet and clap my hand over the side of my head—not because of the vulgar thing he just said, but because of the horrible slippery wetness that filled my ear for a split second. "Jackson, was that your *tongue*?!"

Cackling like an idiot, he falls back against the recliner. If I still had a drink in my hand, I would dump it on his head and then smack him with the glass.

"You are *so* disgusting." Rolling my eyes, I make for the house.

"Wait!"

I throw my whole body weight into pulling open the door and sliding it shut behind me. I don't even want to *think* about what I might have felt pressured to do out there if I'd still been a new recruit, desperate for the Fives' approval. Panting, I stomp past Jenny and Xavier, who are still going at it.

Striding down the hall, I think about what Erik said: how sometimes, it's better to be alone than around people who don't make you feel good. Well, the Fives don't always make me feel good—so why have I always stuck around? These people made me jump naked into ice-cold water. What if I'd hit a rock on the way down? What if I'd split my skull open? I didn't even think about those things in the moment. All I wanted was for the Fives to want me back.

I find my way back to the living room. My mind is on filling my arms with fancy hors d'oeuvres and hiding in the corner until it's time to go home.

I literally have one foot through the archway when I hear a silky-smooth voice say my name. "Ms. Storm. There you are. I was looking for you earlier."

No, no, no. It's like I'm trapped in a labyrinth with forty-seven minotaurs. Dean Allenby plucks a drink off a tray and hands it to me.

He clinks his glass against mine, and I put on a polite smile like a mask. I can feel the slimy ghost of Jackson's tongue in my ear. "You and I still haven't had much of a chance to get to know each other. Tell me, how's your first semester going so far?"

The dean has no idea what Erik and I have been up to, and I can't give him any reason to suspect me of anything, so I decide to keep my answers short. "It's going well, thanks."

"How are your classes?"

"Good."

"And you're making friends? Besides everyone here?"

"Yep."

"Good, good, good." He takes a sip of his drink, his eyes never leaving my face. *Fabulous.* I fully expected him to drift away in search of a better conversationalist after my last one-word answer, but Allenby's still standing there with that placid, close-lipped smile. Well, I guess it's my turn to ask *him* something—something boring that makes him want to wrap this up.

"So . . . how's the semester going for you?"

The ends of Allenby's smile stretch wider, crinkling the skin around his eyes. "Oh, the school is doing fine. Hardwick basically runs itself after all these years, you know what I mean?"

"Yeah."

He swirls his drink and takes another sip. "However, there is one minor issue that's causing some concern. The safety issue I believe we all discussed previously."

I squeeze my glass so tight, it's a wonder it doesn't shatter in my fist. "Oh, you mean the . . . parts of the school that are off-limits?"

"Precisely." He raises his glass. "Cheers to you for paying attention to the ramblings of an old man."

He laughs. To an unsuspecting person, I can see how Allenby would come across as charming.

"Anyway," he continues, "I'm grateful to have such a perceptive and loyal group of students helping me get to the root of this potentially dangerous matter. So, thank you, Ms. Storm."

"Um, you're welcome." I steal a glance toward the foyer, calculating how I might execute an escape.

"A quick question, while I have you."

He must have caught me looking antsy. I re-up my polite smile. "Mm-hmm?"

"In the dining hall, I've noticed you spending time with your cross-country teammate, Erik Ellis."

As soon as Allenby says Erik's name, a weight settles at the bottom of my stomach. Why would he be bringing up Erik right now, if not for his connection to Helen? *Short answers.*

"We hang out sometimes. Being on the same team and all."

"I'm sure you're quite close. I remember the bond I had with my soccer teammates back in the day. We were like brothers." He crosses his middle and index fingers, holds them up, and smiles wistfully.

"Yeah, I mean, we're pretty good friends."

Allenby nods. "He's a good kid, isn't he?"

"Yeah, he is."

Now his smiles fades, replaced by a look of concern. Uh-oh. "I'm aware he's had some trouble with the other boys

212

on the team. That must be really tough, to go through the season without those strong bonds." He takes another sip of his drink and watches me closely.

I shrug, picturing Dylan's and Avery's annoying faces. "I think he's confident he can survive without them."

Allenby chuckles. "Mr. Ellis confides in you, then."

It feels like we're playing four-dimensional chess. I cross my arms, careful not to spill my cider. "What do you mean?"

"My apologies, Ms. Storm! That must have seemed like a strange thing for me to say." He shakes his head ruefully. "The thing is, ever since the end of last year, I've been worried about Mr. Ellis's well-being. I guess that's what happens when you're the dean of students, right?" Another chuckle. "Anyway, it sounds like Mr. Ellis is doing just fine."

"He is."

"Wonderful! Well, I just wanted to say—as someone, again, who cares about his well-being—if Mr. Ellis ever confides in you anything out of the ordinary, anything you think I should know about, please don't hesitate to tell me." He leans in and adds in a low voice, "He'll never have to know it came from you."

Oh my god. I see what he's doing. He's probing me for intel and disguising it as concern for Erik's "well-being."

"Nothin' to tell you," I reply.

Allenby sighs. "I see. Well, you know my door is always open. Anyway, enough about that!" He puts his empty glass on a passing tray and picks up a fresh drink. "Ms. Storm, why don't you tell me more about yourself? What do you want to do in life? I love to hear students' plans for the future."

Finally, a change of topic. "Um . . . honestly, I'm not completely sure yet," I admit. "Probably not math, though."

He laughs. "I was never one for math, either. I wanted to be a leader—not sit around and stare at numbers all day. But don't repeat that to Mr. Richterman." He winks. "What would you say you most look forward to at Hardwick?"

That one's easy. "Running."

"Ah! Of course! I should have guessed that."

"The other day, I was thinking I might like to keep doing it in college," I tell him. "And then, I don't know. Maybe I'd want to be a coach someday, or, like, a physical therapist for athletes. I'm still figuring it out, I guess."

Allenby snaps his fingers. "Well, we can definitely work with that. I know coaches at dozens of colleges. Actually, I recently introduced Robert"—he points to a tenth-grade boy who's built like a brick house—"to the wrestling coach at Duke. That's one of the benefits of being in this group, Ms. Storm. I'm always happy to facilitate a connection for a loyal Five."

And that's when I realize: Allenby never changed the subject after all. He's bargaining; he wants me to become one of his informants in exchange for a coveted introduction.

There's that awful wringing in my chest. What if this is what Jackson meant when he talked about "perks"? What if this is how Raven got a boost on her Juilliard application—how Heather got a fancy Wall Street internship while she was still in high school—and why the other Fives were so eager to snitch at that first dinner? Hand over a name to Dean Allenby and get help from one of his many connections.

I feel viscerally angry, not just because the Fives are willing to sacrifice other people for their own success, but also because the option even exists for them to do so. The whole system is so messed up.

Well, not only would I never rat out Erik, but I also crushed it at yesterday's meet without anybody's help, thank you very much. No fancy introduction necessary.

I thank the dean for his offer, before excusing myself so I can go to the bathroom and text Erik everything I just learned—and then maybe hide there for the rest of the night, away from the rest of the Fives.

I've never been happier to leave a party than I am to leave Fivesgiving. When I finally get back to Ainsley House, I Face-Time Erik so we can *really* talk. I do a dramatic reenactment of my intense conversation with Dean Allenby, and I explain everything I know about the Fives' system of snitching on their classmates in exchange for "perks."

"How is that even allowed?" Erik asks in disgust. He's dressed for bed in a faded Power Rangers T-shirt, which I'd find totally charming if I weren't still so angry. "That's, like . . . corruption!"

"*Right?!*" I pound my fist into my bedspread. "They're basically getting special privileges for being spies!"

"The dean is out of control."

"So are the Fives! They're apparently okay with this whole arrangement."

Until now, Erik's been leaning against the cinder-block wall of his dorm room. Now, he lies down on his side. I can't help but notice it's the view I'd be getting if we were sharing his pillow. He yawns—then I do, too. It's been an exhausting evening. "This feels like one big, rotten mess, doesn't it?"

"Tell me about it." I let out a long sigh. "I just wish I knew what to do next."

On Tuesday night, wrapped in our winter jackets, Erik and I fight our way through a blustering wind from the dining hall to the library. We just had our first *planned* dinner together, instead of happening to wander over to a table together after cross-country, which made it feel kind of like a date—to me, at least. Probably not to him. And it wasn't exactly romantic: he was eating his favorite, cheeseburger soup, and together, we were developing our Dungeons and Dragons characters in preparation for their big debut at tonight's gathering. Mine is a swordfighter I named Xena, after the Warrior Princess; his is a magical elf he named Gordon.

Luisa introduces the rest of the group as we take our seats on the floor of the archives room. "This is Hassan, Candace, and Max," she says. We all exchange hellos. I know Candace from a few classes we have together—in English class, she's the one who's always being asked to read her writing out loud. It's *really* good. Hassan and Max are both seniors, and I vaguely recognize them from around campus; Hassan occasionally makes announcements at assembly for Model UN Club, and Max is just so tall—we're talking, like, six-foot-eight—that he's impossible to miss, especially with his bright-red hair.

"Hassan and Candace are both elves," Luisa explains. "Max is a human with killer crossbow skills. And I'm dungeon master, which means I lead the game. So, here's the deal: the last we left off, the group followed the sorceress to the mouth of a cave and heard ominous growls coming from inside . . ."

The group is patient with me as I learn how to play. Luisa keeps hurling ridiculous plot points at us—an encounter with a dragon, an avalanche of poisonous snow—and together, we decide how we want to respond. Then we roll our dice to see how successful we are. The first time I try to swing my sword at the dragon, I end up rolling a one. "Your blade flies out of your hand and goes flying at Gordon's head, nicking the top of his ear off," Luisa announces somberly. Erik gasps in mock horror.

I have no idea how much time has passed until Candace looks at her phone. It's almost 8:30; we've been at it for two hours. "I hate to cut things off before we get to the mystical shrine, but I have this feature for the *Herald* due in the morning, and Allenby's gonna kill me if I don't get it to him on time."

"Allenby?" I ask. "As in, Dean Allenby?"

"That's the one. Everybody's favorite."

Erik and I subtly exchange a glance as Candace scoops her dice back into their velvet drawstring pouch.

"Does Dean Allenby edit the *Herald*?"

Candace laughs darkly as she gets to her feet. "Not officially, 'cause it's supposed to be a student-run paper, but we all joke that he does."

"Why?"

She jams her beanie over her buzz cut and jerks the zipper of her jacket with a lot more force than she needs. "Because he makes us show him *every single story* before it goes to print, which seriously holds up closing. But he wants to make sure we're not gonna make Hardwick look bad."

Max looks appalled. "What is this? State-run media?"

"Yeah, basically." Candace sighs. "Apparently he's been doing it ever since that guy Kelvin Liu was expelled."

Erik and I lock eyes again. His are even wider than before.

"Oh yeah, I remember hearing about that when we were younger," Erik says slowly. "What exactly happened, again?"

"Plagiarism," Candace replies. "I heard he turned in an essay that was really similar to some college student's thesis that was posted online."

Erik looks skeptical. "Why would that suddenly make Allenby paranoid about the *Herald*?"

"Well, Kelvin was on staff, so I guess he wanted to make sure his plagiarizing ways hadn't spread to the rest of the paper? I dunno."

"Seems kind of weird."

"Yeah, but from what I've heard, Allenby already had his

issues with Kelvin and the *Herald*. That same semester, Kelvin was trying to publish some story on the school's history, and he reached out to Allenby for comment, because, you know, he actually used to *go* here—back in the fifties or sixties, or whenever it would have been. I think the issue was that Allenby agreed to an interview, but only if he could approve the story before it was published. *Big* no-no in journalism—you never let your sources do that, even though they always demand it. So Kelvin refused, and I guess he started trying to research the story without Allenby's help, which was kind of an epic F-you to the dean. Anyway, that's why some people at the *Herald* think Allenby had been waiting to crack down on the paper, and then when Kelvin went and plagiarized, he finally had his opportunity."

"How convenient," Erik says.

I was just thinking the same thing.

"It's *so* annoying." Candace shakes her head and shrugs. "But anyway, I definitely don't want to incur his wrath, so I'll see you guys later. Peace."

When she flashes the V with her fingers, I forget where I am for a second. It feels like I'm back in Allenby's living room, carrying around a hundred-pound weight in my stomach. Then, of *course*, I remember Candace isn't a Five, and all she's doing is saying goodbye. The weight evaporates, and I feel so much better.

"See you guys next week?" Luisa asks as we pack up our things.

"Yes," Erik and I answer at the same time.

"And Eva," she adds. "If you ever wanna join, some friends and I always stop by the dining hall for a snack after Mr. Richterman's class. You're welcome whenever."

Happiness spreads through my body like a sip of hot chocolate. "I'd love that."

"Awesome! Well, I'll see ya tomorrow." She puts her backpack on both shoulders, waves, and leaves the room, followed by Hassan and Max.

As soon as they're gone, Erik marches over and closes the door behind them. His friendly goodbye face has been replaced with the wide-eyed look he was wearing a few minutes before. "Storm. Are you thinking what I'm thinking?"

The truth is, I'm standing here thinking how nice it'll be to have a few new friends to spend time with. People who aren't Fives. Which snaps me back to reality: Allenby; the *Hardwick Herald*; the story about Kelvin Liu.

"Yes. Kelvin. He's our next lead."

Erik whips out his phone. With just twenty minutes until curfew, and our dorms on the other end of campus, his thumbs move in a blur as he opens up Instagram and clicks around.

"My brother would have been closer in age to him," he murmurs. "I'm gonna go to Ryan's page and search the people he follows . . . Aha! Bingo. This must be him: Kelvin Liu. I remember his face."

"Should we message him? Would that be . . . intrusive?"

"Let's do it. It's not like he got expelled yesterday—look, he seems happy." Erik shows me a recent photo of Kelvin Liu on vacation with his parents.

"Ah yes, vacationing with parents. Always a recipe for happiness."

"Ha-ha."

"Okay, fine. What do we say?"

He taps the message button, and together we stare at the empty text field. He types: "Hey, Kelvin." Then he pauses. "What next?"

"Um . . ." I start to dictate: "I'm Erik, a student at Hardwick. I know this is totally out of the blue, but I have a relative, Helen Honeyman, who died at Hardwick back in the sixties, and I'm trying to figure out what happened to her. I hear you might know stuff about Hardwick's past. Let me know if you'd be open to talking sometime. Thanks!"

Erik hits send.

We stare at the screen for a few seconds, but there's no immediate indication that Kelvin's typing anything back.

The time is 8:44. "Shoot, we need to head out. I'll have to keep you posted." Erik slips his phone into his pocket, and we bundle up to go back out into the cold.

Later that night, after two demoralizing hours of English homework, I flop into bed feeling totally exhausted and turn off the light. Did F. Scott Fitzgerald even *mean* to stuff all that symbolism into *The Great Gatsby*, or did English teachers just invent it to mess with us? As my head hits the pillow, a buzzing from my phone stops me from closing my eyes. I pull it off the charger, praying it's not a late-night Fives thing; I really don't feel like going outside again—or seeing them at all right now, for that matter.

But the message is from Erik. He doesn't usually text me this late.

Which can only mean . . .

Wide awake, I slide the notification so I can see his message. It's a screenshot of his Instagram DMs with @kelvin_liu222:

> Hey, Kelvin. I'm Erik, a student at Hardwick. I know this is totally out of the blue, but I have a relative, Helen Honeyman, who died at Hardwick back in the sixties, and I'm trying to figure out what happened to her. I hear you might know stuff about Hardwick's past? Let me know if you'd be open to talking sometime. Thanks!

shit man
listen
i have a story for u

TWELVE

Connie

I wake up to a hand covering my mouth.

What

Is

Going

On?

I snap my eyes open, but of course, it's pitch-black. Panicked, I jerk my head to the side, breathing quickly through my nose, but the hand doesn't move, so I thrash the other way.

"*Shh*. Connie. It's me."

Helen.

Her voice is so quiet, I can hardly hear her. I stop moving, but my heart's still hammering at ninety miles a minute. She takes her hand away, and as my eyes adjust to the dark, I see her crouched beside my bed. She puts her finger to her lips and beckons for me to follow her.

As quietly as I can, I slide out from under my blanket and follow her over to the clubhouse, still groggy and completely confused about what the heck is going on right now. Inside the structure, she sits down cross-legged and motions for me to do the same.

She leans in, her voice barely above a whisper. "Sorry I scared you. I wanted to talk to you for real this time."

I draw my knees to my chest and wrap my arms around them, first shifting the fabric of the nightgown to make sure Helen can't see up my skirt even though it's dark. I probably shouldn't have gotten out of bed; if anyone realizes we're in here, we'll be singled out as weak points immediately, and I really, *really* don't want to get reported to Mr. Kraus. But on the flip side, I'm also grateful for a chance to talk to Helen, the only other person besides me who seems disturbed by the new dynamic down here.

"We have to be careful," I whisper.

"I know." Her tone is urgent. "It's like they're brainwashed. We're the only ones who aren't."

I think back to the obedience drills, the chanting, the feeling of building this very clubhouse. I remember the strange sensation of sharing a single heartbeat with everyone else in the group. "Helen, I kind of *was*, for a little bit," I admit. "But I'm not anymore—I don't like these cards."

"Me neither," she replies. "And I don't like Mr. Kraus one bit."

I want to squeeze my eyes shut and shake my head to see if I'll wake up. I know I'm not dreaming, but it's just impossible to believe I'm talking one-on-one with Helen Honeyman, and that we have more in common than I would have guessed. "You don't call him Andy, either," I whisper.

"No. I never have. I'm not obsessed with him the way everyone else is."

"I thought it was just me."

Helen sighs. "Craig *loves* him. He made me come down here, you know. I never should have listened." She runs a hand through her hair and looks at the ground. "I don't know why I always let him boss me around."

My brain doesn't know how to process this new information. He's always been so friendly to me. And everyone loves him. He's class president and soon-to-be head boy. He rescued an owl.

"I feel bad, because in every other way, he's perfect, you know?"

I nod.

"He's smart, and talented, and everybody loves him. My mom's *dying* for us to get married. But . . . at the same time, he's become fixated on this idea of success. He wants everything in his life to be perfect, including his grades, and his reputation, and me—his girlfriend."

I picture all the times Craig has asked me for advice, and all the times he's reminded me not to tell anyone. Did he only come to me in the first place because he knew I didn't have that many people to tell?

"Sometimes I get so tired of him bossing me around, and I call it quits." In my mind, I see an Erlenmeyer flask rattling on the chemistry table. "But then he'll say he's sorry, and he'll do something really nice for me, and I'm head over heels all over again."

A memory comes back to me, of a lunch period toward the end of February when Betty and I were sitting at the outsider table, as usual. There was a commotion across the room, and when we looked over, Craig was climbing onto the table where Helen and her friends were eating. It was the kind of thing that would get Bobby Tackett in trouble instantly, but when Craig was the one towering above the rest of the room, the teachers on duty smiled and let it slide. They trusted him. Standing in the center of the table, Craig announced to the whole dining hall: "I don't want to take up too much of your time, but I just wanna say, in front of everyone in this room, that I'm friggin' wild about this girl right here. Helen, baby, I love you."

In chemistry the day before, Craig had told me that Helen picked a fight again. Now here he was, putting himself out there in an attempt to win her back. Craning my neck, I watched in frustration as Helen put her face in her hands with embarrassment. I wanted to throttle her. She had the best guy in the whole school—couldn't she be a little more appreciative? And couldn't she stop bickering with him in the first place?

Now I'm beginning to wonder how often Helen *actually* picks fights for no reason.

Another memory: this one from last spring, the morning

of Craig's debate with James Moseley for class president. It was seven a.m., and I realized I'd left my blazer in the costume room after play rehearsal the night before. I needed to pick it up before class, otherwise I wouldn't be let in to formal assembly.

When I slipped through the backstage door, I heard two voices arguing onstage, which was strange, given how early it was. Peering out from the shadowy wings, I saw the voices belonged to Craig and Helen.

"Let's do it again," he said. "I want to get it right."

"Craig, I'm just holding your hand and walking you out to the podium," she replied with a groan. "How could I possibly get it wrong? Also, I'm hungry, and we're running out of time before class starts."

"One more time, babe. I'm still worried our steps are a little out of sync."

"I don't know what to tell you, Craig. This is how I walk."

"Just one more time. Then we can go get breakfast, I promise."

"But we've already done it thirty times!"

I'd assumed Helen was exaggerating and selfishly refusing to help him on his big day. But what if he actually *did* make her practice walking onstage thirty times?

Across from me in the small space between the walls of water drums and cardboard boxes, Helen sighs. All this time, it never made sense to me why Helen treated Craig as badly as she did.

Maybe it's because she *didn't*.

"Anyway, I don't know why I'm telling you all this," she adds, scratching her opposite elbow. Then she looks up and rolls back her shoulders. "My point is, I just want to know that we'll look out for each other, okay? I'm dreading whatever the next two days are going to bring."

"Yeah. Of course."

"And I'm kind of thinking . . ." She leans her head in even closer. "That maybe we should even . . . I don't know . . . *resist* them. To remind them that none of this is real. It's just some stupid scenario Mr. Kraus invented."

"Resist them *how*?"

"I don't know. I'm going to think about it. I haven't been able to sleep all night, but you should go back to bed. I don't want us getting caught."

I get to my feet, being extra careful not to disturb any of the surrounding boxes or water drums. It's strange saying goodbye to Helen. Even though we only talked for a few minutes, it feels like we've been through a lot together.

"'Night, Helen."

"'Night, Connie."

I tiptoe back to bed and pull the crunchy cover on top of me. It's cold, so I curl up on my side. Betty is only a few cots away, but right now, as she sleeps with her New Americans membership card under her pillow, there might as well be a million miles between us.

By eight o'clock in the morning, there's been no word from Mr. Kraus, so Craig makes the executive decision to get out of bed, roll the curtains out of the way, and flick on the light.

"Rise and shine, New Americans!"

From a few beds away, Helen and I lock eyes for the briefest flicker of a second. Then she nods her head toward the shelving unit; it's so subtle, I wouldn't think twice about the gesture if we hadn't had our secret conference in the middle of the night. At the same time, Craig goes, "Huh. That's weird."

I look over at the shelves. The others do, too. The Order sign is still nailed in place, but Unity is lying on the floor with a rip at the top.

"Could it have fallen down?" asks Betty.

"How could it have fallen down?" Steve fires back, stomping over to inspect it. While I don't typically think of Steve as being the sharpest tool in the shed, in this case, I know he's right. First of all, a piece of paper weighs nothing, so it wouldn't just slide off a nail. But I also have a very good feeling that someone tore that sign off the post—and a very good feeling about who exactly it was.

I don't say anything.

"Who was it?" Steve barks, his hands planted on his hips. "Connie? Betty? Tackett? Helen?" As his head swivels back and forth, I'm pretty sure I sense a look of fear in his eyes, as though he's scared that people might think it was him. I wonder if Steve got a blank membership card, too.

Nobody says a word. Craig walks over to Steve and strikes the same pose. In a softer voice, he says, "Come on, you guys. Who was it?"

"Not me," Betty and Bobby say at once. They both dutifully make their New American hand signals.

"Not me, either," Helen says with a shrug.

Five sets of eyes turn on me, just because I'm the last one to speak up. I feel like a gazelle in the center of a pack of lions. I want to cry. Or throw up. Especially because it really *wasn't* me. "I d-didn't do it," I stammer.

"You don't sound so sure of that, Connie," says Steve. He takes a threatening step toward me. I think about the knife in his pocket, and a wave of panic crashes against my rib cage.

Helen leaps to her feet. "Leave her alone, Steve."

"Oh?" This time he rounds on her. "*Was* it you?"

She crosses her arms. "How do we know it wasn't *you*?"

Steve scoffs at her. "It obviously wasn't me. I was the one who realized someone did it."

Then Betty marches over to Steve and holds out her palm. "Can I borrow your pocketknife, please?"

He looks at her like she's a gnat buzzing around his head. "What for?"

"To do something on behalf of the people who *didn't* tear down that sign. For all of us who actually believe in what those signs stand for."

His expression softens, and he hands her the knife. *"Thank you,"* she says pointedly, before heading for the spot on the wall where Steve carved our names the other day. Everyone trails after her except for Helen, who hangs back by her bed with her arms still crossed.

Underneath our names, in markedly neater lettering, Betty chisels the words "Order" and "Unity," one on top of the other. When she's finished, she returns the knife to Steve with a satisfied smile. Craig gives her an approving pat on the shoulder.

"Thanks, Betty. That looks really good." Then he turns to the rest of us. "As for everyone else . . . Listen, if no one is going to admit to tearing that sign down, we're gonna have to start interrogating people."

My eyes dart to Helen, who looks seriously ticked off. With her hands balled into fists, she marches over to us and glares at her boyfriend. "Did you just say 'interrogate people'? What are you, blitzed?"

Craig puts his hands on her shoulders. "Calm down, babe, will you?" She tries to wriggle free, but he holds her in place. "Helen, calm down. You heard Andy yesterday: We have to be united if we're going to survive. And to do that, we have to find the weak points. We have to know who tore down that sign."

"'If we're going to survive'? Craig, there hasn't even been an attack! And even if there had been, how would our twenty-four-year-old sociology teacher know the best way to restructure American society?"

"Because he's really friggin' smart, Helen! And he knows how to lead people!" Craig's usual levelheadedness has gone out the window, and I'm seeing a side to him I don't recognize. This isn't soccer star Craig Allenby, or soon-to-be-head-boy Craig Allenby. This is the Craig Helen described, who desperately wants to win at everything. "And I'm sorry," he says, "but

231

I just have to point this out: this whole experiment would be going *fine* if not for your terrible attitude."

Helen groans in frustration. "I don't have a bad attitude, Craig. It's just that I'm not brainwashed by a person who has no idea what he's actually talking about, and who's probably having fun messing with all of our heads."

"And why would he do that?"

"Because he likes the power of it all! I don't know!" She looks like she wants to tear her hair out. "But I can promise you: this is never gonna be applicable in the real world, and you're all taking it way too seriously."

Seething, Craig jams his hand into his pocket. When he pulls it out again, he's holding his card. As we all watch in silence, our mouths at varying degrees of openness, he takes a few deep breaths. When he speaks again, his voice is almost too quiet to hear. Then I realize his hands are trembling, and I think Craig Allenby is trying not to cry. "Ever since we came down here, I've tried to help you be your best. Just like I always try to do. But there's only so much you can help someone who doesn't want to help herself. I'm doing this because I care about you, and because I care about everyone else, which you apparently don't." He flips over his card and holds it up like a policeman's badge. In the middle, there's a black dot. "I'm going to have to report you, Helen."

Her face doesn't even flinch. "And I'm going to have to break up with you, Craig."

He looks like he's been slapped.

"For good, this time," she adds.

It's all happening too fast for me to keep up, but I can feel my allegiances breaking and shifting like ice on a river in springtime. I'm so used to trusting Craig's judgment, but I also believe in what Helen is saying. Meanwhile, Betty is staring daggers at Helen; she probably wants to pop her head off like a Barbie Doll's for insulting Mr. Kraus.

Craig opens his mouth to reply.

And then the door bursts open.

Mr. Kraus strides into the room, and everyone freezes. We must look awfully theatrical: Craig and Helen glaring at each other, the rest of us in a semicircle around them, and the New American clubhouse towering in the background. When Mr. Kraus sees the structure, he smirks to himself and nods. "Well I'll be," he mumbles. He sets down his briefcase and flashes the hand signal. "Good morning, New Americans."

In the awkward silence that follows, everyone but Helen does the signal back at him. My heart isn't in it anymore, and I feel like a fraud doing it, but the idea of going against the group—especially at a time like this, when tensions are already high—is unthinkable. Resistance has never come naturally to me; I'd always rather blend in and deal with my apprehensions privately.

"Ms. Honeyman?" Mr. Kraus asks expectantly, eyeing Helen's hands.

"Yes?" she replies.

"Do I have to give you a warning for not displaying unity?"

"Please feel free."

Mr. Kraus's smirk disappears. Then Craig steps forward and opens his mouth.

"And by the way," Helen adds before Craig can say anything, "I tore down the Unity sign. In case anyone was about to report me, I'll just own up to it myself."

She's going so much farther than I would ever have the guts to go. Our teacher eyes the ripped sign on the floor. When he looks up again, his jaw is hardened like cement. "Ms. Honeyman, go sit in the corner, please. Now."

Helen stalks off. Craig sniffs and straightens the bottom of his sweatshirt.

"The rest of you, please take a seat on the floor."

We do as we're told, and sit in a tighter version of the semicircle we were standing in before. Mr. Kraus bends down, unclasps his briefcase, and straightens up again with another piece of paper in his hand. He walks over to the post, picks up the Unity sign, and nails it back in place. Then he hammers in the new sign, so that all together, they read:

ORDER

UNITY

POWER

Power? What's this one going to entail? At this point, the only thing I care about is going through the motions as peacefully as possible and beating it out of here before we all end up killing each other.

"This will make sense to you shortly," Mr. Kraus says as he wanders back over with his hands behind his back and his gaze on the ground. Then, surprisingly, he sits down on the floor with us. He crosses his legs, straightens his back, and places his palms on his knees. His expression is still grave as can be. "New Americans, there's something very important I need to tell you this morning."

I steal a glance toward the very back corner of the shelter, where Helen sits with her head against the wall. She's too far away to hear what Mr. Kraus is saying, which means I can't look to her for any sort of encouragement.

"I haven't been totally honest with you," he continues, and I can hear the shallow breathing coming from everyone else in the semicircle. "On day one, I told you this was a test to prepare you for a hypothetical nuclear attack by the Soviets. And since then, we've practiced skills that might serve you well, should such an attack ever happen. But the truth is . . ." He takes a deep breath. "The truth is, everything you've learned is much more real than I've let on. Until now."

I look at Betty. Her eyes are as wide as 45s, and her lips are slightly parted. My heart is beating faster and faster, like mallets striking a giant drum.

"I didn't just invent the New Americans for the purpose of this test," Mr. Kraus says. "They are a very real, very *secret* new political party gaining traction across the country. I became involved with them about a year ago, and they've asked me and several other educators to begin recruiting younger members, like yourselves, and teaching them what it takes to be a member. Their principles are the same ones we've been practicing down here: order, unity, and next, power. Because . . ."

The drumbeat in my chest is getting faster and faster. The pressure is so intense, it feels like it's squeezing my lungs, and I'm finding it harder and harder to get air in.

"Because the New Americans' leadership has recently received intelligence that an attack *will* happen, and soon. And when it does, our party will be waiting in the wings to rise up and shape a better, stronger future for America." He points at the three signs. "*This* is what I mean by power. I mean we are literally going to step forth from the ashes and show the world what we can do."

"There's going to be an attack?" asks Bobby.

"Yes."

"Are we all going to die?" asks Betty.

"No. You're already on the winning side. All of you. You now belong to a very special group that will change the course of history."

"New Americans," Craig chants, a strange gleam in his eye. "New Americans. New Americans. NEW AMERICANS."

The others join in. "NEW AMERICANS! NEW AMERICANS! NEW AMERICANS!"

Any minute now, my heart is going to thump through my chest and splatter onto the floor. I'm starting to feel dizzy. It's because I still can't get any air in. It's like trying to breathe through a straw, and the straw keeps getting thinner and thinner.

I know what's happening: I'm having a heart attack. I'm having a heart attack and I can't breathe and I'm going to die right here on the shelter floor and no one will notice because they're too busy chanting. I need to get out of here. I need help. I try to clamber to my feet, but I don't have any oxygen and the room is going dark at the edges. Someone says my name, but it's too late—I'm falling down—I'm sprawled across the concrete floor.

Dark powers of destruction.

The deadly atom.

It's all about to happen for real.

For sixteen years, I've lived with this weight pressing down on me. Now it's going to crush me for good.

My lungs are empty.

I think I hear voices calling my name.

But the

Room

Goes

Black.

THIRTEEN

Eva

A delivery guy on a motorbike nearly plows me over as I step onto the curb. I'm rescued by a Cookie Monster with one eye hanging at a disturbing angle, who holds his hand (or paw?) out for money as soon as he's finished yanking me to safety. Ask any New Yorker, even one who's been sequestered at boarding school for the last four months, and they'll tell you the Port Authority Bus Terminal is, without a doubt, the ninth circle of hell.

So I'm surprised when I walk through the doors—into even *more* chaos—and the hellishness melts away at the sight of Erik Ellis in a woolly gray peacoat, leaning against a pillar in all his freckly, gangly glory. If I thought being separated over the holiday break might dull my feelings for him and convince me to accept that we're destined to just be friends, then I was wrong. I move through the screaming, jostling crowds as though his body is the world's strongest magnet, and when he finally looks over and spots me, the grin that splits his face threatens to topple me onto the sticky, dirt-streaked floor.

We do a stiff friend-hug.

"Happy New Year," he says as we break apart.

"Same to you. Ready to go?"

He nods. "For the love of god, please get me out of this place."

I weave my way back out to the street, Erik following closely in my wake. Outside, I hang a left—dodging the same Twilight Zone Cookie Monster as before—and lead him north on Eighth Avenue in the direction of Central Park.

"Beautiful city you have here," says Erik, who just got body-checked by a large man who came barreling out of a dollar slice shop.

"I promise it has its charms."

This plan came together after Erik told Kelvin we were dying to hear his story. Kelvin didn't want to do it in any way that could possibly be recorded, so he suggested we come by his apartment over the holidays. It seemed a little extreme, but Erik said he'd like to come into the city anyway; his family lived pretty far out in Jersey, and it had been a while since he'd made the journey into Manhattan. Our meeting with Kelvin isn't until three o'clock or so—he's going to let us know when he's home from some errands—so we have around an hour to do whatever we want. The weather is freakishly warm for January—probably thanks to climate change, which is depressing, but it means we can wander around the park in the winter sunshine and slowly work our way up to Eighty-Eighth Street.

We walk the seventeen blocks to Columbus Circle, where we successfully cross the roundabout without getting flattened by any cars, buses, or horse-drawn carriages. Finally, we pass through the stone entryway to Central Park, which might as well be a portal to another planet, given how peaceful it is on the paths that wind around thick trees and grassy hills.

"Okay, fine," Eric says as we cross a wooden footbridge with ornate stone railings. "I might have detected a *smidge* of charm."

"I knew you'd come around."

Erik and I make our way north, talking mostly about what we think Kelvin is going to tell us. It's a relief to be able to have this conversation without constantly looking over our shoulders, paranoid that Allenby or one of the Fives might overhear us. We pass a snack kiosk, where Erik orders two hot chocolates. I pull a few crumpled singles out of my wallet, but he waves them away.

"Wanna go sit on that rock?" he asks.

Drinks in hand, we climb to the top of a giant boulder, like the one we found in the glen that time, and make ourselves comfortable on the edge—or we try to, except the stone is surprisingly cold and makes my butt go numb.

Erik sets down his drink and unwinds the scarf from his neck. "Stand up for one sec?" he says, and when I do, he lays the fabric over the spot where I was sitting. "Okay, Storm. Try that."

"You're such a gentleman." I sit back down; it really is an improvement on my nether regions. "Thanks."

"Anything for you."

My chest feels all fluttery as I sip the hot chocolate. It's warm and sweet and perfect, just like this afternoon.

"Hey, Storm?"

"Yeah?"

"We haven't really talked about it, but, um, I'm sorry I was such an awkward idiot that one time in the archives room. I feel like it's kind of been hanging over us, and, um . . ."

Oh no. Have I been acting like I'm upset about it? Does Erik think I've been holding some sort of grudge?

"It's totally fine," I blurt out. "Please. Don't worry about it. It was, like, a million years ago."

"Yeah, but I still think about it a lot. Because I wasn't exactly honest about what I'd been trying to tell you. I thought I'd just majorly freaked you out, so I made up some stupid line about Dungeons and Dragons."

Oh my god, is it happening? After all this uncertainty, is Erik about to tell me he likes me? I want to tell him I like him, too, but only if he says it first. An image of my finger-painted Father's Day card for Caleb pops into my head uninvited, and my chest aches like it happened yesterday. There's nothing more exquisitely painful and embarrassing than setting your feelings free, only to find out the other person doesn't want anything to do with them.

And so, I ask him again, like I did in the archives room. "Erik, what did you want to tell me?"

"Before I pulled on your curl? Like the weirdest person on the planet?"

"Yes. Before that."

"I wanted to say . . ."

Once again, I fail to find out what the answer is, because Erik's ringtone blares from his pocket. He turned it on earlier at my suggestion—*good one, Eva*—because I didn't want to miss Kelvin's update about exactly when we should meet him. Sure enough, his name is on Erik's phone screen. He picks it up.

"Hey, Kelvin . . . We're just in Central Park . . . We're, uh . . ." He looks at me. "Eva, what street would you say we're at? Roughly?"

"Maybe Seventieth?"

"Seventieth," he says into the phone. "Oh . . . Shoot, that doesn't give us much time . . . You need us there in fifteen minutes?"

Fifteen minutes? I mouth at him frantically.

"Okay. See you soon, Kelvin." Erik hangs up. "His plans changed, and he only has until three to meet with us. Can we make it?"

I leap to my feet. "Yes, but we have to run."

Erik does the same. He quickly puts his scarf back on, the knot all askew, and we both down what's left of our drinks. Then we book it, abandoning our all-important conversation before it ever even got off the ground.

When Kelvin Liu opens the door to his fourth-floor walkup, the look on his face says we must be a mess. Erik's cheeks are beet red, and his hair is either plastered to his forehead or sticking up at an odd angle. I can't imagine I look any better after trying to break the land speed record on foot. I feel the dreaded drop of sweat gathering speed as it trickles down my back and eventually pools around the top of my butt. Lovely.

"Er, you guys want some water?"

"Please," Erik gasps.

Kelvin is dressed in jeans and a red zip-up hoodie, and he lives in a tiny studio apartment that probably still costs him a fortune, because New York City. He directs us to the squishy black couch wedged under his lofted bed, and when he's done filling our water glasses, he plops into his desk chair and wheels himself across the floor.

"Thanks for getting here earlier," he says, handing us the cups. "A client wanted to meet with me ASAP, so I had to move some things around."

"No problem," I assure him, even though I just chugged my water in one fell swoop. "What do you do?"

"I'm a freelance app developer."

"That's cool."

"Yeah, now it is," Kelvin replies, "but it wasn't when I got kicked out of Hardwick and lost my college acceptance with, like, a month to go before graduation. My parents and I kept going back and forth about whether I should redo senior year somewhere else, and eventually, I was like, nah, I'm gonna learn to code, and I put myself through one of those boot camps. It worked out okay in the end, but damn, it sucked when it was happening."

"Kelvin, what *did* happen?" Erik asks.

"I really shouldn't be telling you this," Kelvin says, leaning in with his elbows on his knees. He lowers his voice, even though there's no one else around. "I try not to talk about it with anybody, because I'm still convinced Craig Allenby is going to come in and mess my life up again. That guy is scary as hell. I'm only doing this because you're related to Helen."

"You know who Helen is."

"Yup. I found out a lot of stuff Allenby was trying to keep quiet. I was doing this history project on how regular people got swept up in Cold War paranoia, and out of curiosity, I went to the archives room to read the school newspapers from back then. I start reading, and I come across these articles about a nuclear fallout shelter being built at Hardwick. And I'm like, whoa. So, I keep going, and I find out Hardwick made this plan to lock six students in the shelter over spring recess, to test it out or whatnot. And then I find out Craig Allenby was one of the students!"

If I still had any water in my mouth, I would definitely have spit it out.

"Allenby was one of the six?" Erik exclaims.

"Yep. He was. There were three boys and three girls, whose names I can't remember, except for Helen's. I found an obituary that said she died in an accident due to 'structural instabilities' in the shelter." Kelvin holds up air quotes. "It didn't get into any more detail than that.

"So, at this point, I'm like, screw the history project. I want to do a story on this for the *Herald*. I take all the newspapers that mention the shelter, and I bring them to Allenby's office. I spread them out on the desk, and he looks kinda surprised. He asks where I got them—I guess he didn't know about the archives room, because *nobody* does. So, then he says he'd be more than happy to talk about the shelter, as long as I follow the rules and let him approve the story before it goes to print. I'm like, 'What rules? That's literally the opposite of journalism. It's PR.' I thought I wanted to be a reporter at the time, so I'm being pretty aggressive. But I can't crack him. Then, finally, he takes all the newspapers and says he'll look at them and get back to me with a comment. So, I'm like, 'Okay. Fine.' And I leave.

"Well, fast-forward to the next week, when I get called into his office. I assumed he googled 'Journalism 101' and realized he owed me an apology, but instead, he tells me he ran this English paper I wrote through a plagiarism checker, and it 'severely crossed the line'"—he makes air quotes again—"in terms of how much it borrowed from some random college thesis. He wouldn't even show me the thesis he was talking about—he just kept saying, 'Don't insult my intelligence, Kelvin. I think you already know.' And then he expelled me."

His face flushes red with anger as he relives the memory.

I connect the dots in my head. "You didn't plagiarize anything."

"Hell no. But I couldn't prove it!" He closes his eyes and massages his temples. "I cranked out that English paper in the library one night, because I sucked at focusing on homework in my dorm room. I didn't save it or back it up anywhere, like an *idiot*. Honest to god, Allenby's whole plan was so airtight, I sometimes wonder if he *knew* I didn't have another copy of the essay. Like, was there a spy sitting at the computer next to me? It's bizarre."

A chill goes down my spine as I think about the Fives. I'd bet my life one of them spied on Kelvin that night in the library. "So, what I'm hearing is . . . Allenby framed you and punished you, all because you were researching the fallout shelter."

Kelvin nods. "Pretty much."

"But you were only trying to figure out the truth!" Erik objects.

"Yeah, well, whatever the truth is, it's gotta be something that makes Hardwick look pretty damn bad," Kelvin says.

"You never found out what it was?" I ask. "You didn't find any other clues in those newspapers?"

"Nope. Nada. I'm sorry I can't be more helpful, but I can definitely confirm that something *happened* in there, you know? Something more than a 'structural instability.'"

"Kelvin, I'm so sorry that happened to you. It's completely unfair."

"It's infuriating," Erik adds.

"Thanks, y'all," Kelvin replies. "Luckily, I'm doing all right for myself now."

I lean back and rest my head on a couch cushion, because it feels like it might explode from all the new information I'm trying to process. Kelvin just corroborated our conspiracy theory: that there's something about the fallout shelter Dean Allenby doesn't want people to know, and he's using the Fives as informants in his quest to keep it a secret. I wonder who got admitted early to Harvard for spying on Kelvin in the library. God, I just want to expose them and bring them all down.

First, that means finding out the truth. Whatever it is, it's damning enough that he expelled an innocent student simply for getting near it. There's only one plan of action I can think of. "Erik, I think we need to go back into shelter-hunting mode."

Kelvin's face lights up. "Oh! I can definitely help you there."

I bolt upright. "You know where it was? Or where it is?"

"It's possible I know where it *is*," he says. "After Helen was killed, it said in the *Herald* that no one was allowed to go down there indefinitely, due to safety issues with the ceiling or something. I assume there's a world where no one touched it again."

I swallow. "Where is it?"

"Well, that was the funny part," Kelvin muses. "The whole time he was expelling me, we were sitting right on top of it."

"You mean . . ."

"According to the old *Herald* articles, the shelter's in the basement of the administration building. It's basically right underneath Dean Allenby's office."

FOURTEEN

Connie

"Wake up, Connie. You just fainted. It's gonna be okay."

The first thing I see when I open my eyes is Betty leaning over me, her brow knit with concern. For a blissful three seconds, I have absolutely no memory of where I am or how I ended up on a cold concrete floor.

But then someone eases me up to a seated position, hands me a canteen, and says, "Sip." Still dazed, I tip my head back to let the water hit my tongue; when I do, I see Mr. Kraus's face, and it all comes rushing back like a tidal wave.

Everything we've been practicing down here—it's all real. The fear that's hovered over me since the day I was born is about to come true. *Breathe, Connie.*

Mr. Kraus is still watching me. "How do you feel, Ms. Abbott?"

"Like I'm going to throw up."

"Keep drinking." He turns to the rest of the group crouched around us. "It is perfectly normal to feel overwhelmed by the news I just shared with you. But let it out now, because the New Americans need to show power"—he nods at the newest sign on the post—"if we are going to be successful."

Betty rubs my back as I drink from the canteen. I watch as Steve walks over to the wall and carves our newest principle—Power—under Order and Unity. By the time he returns, I've finished the water, and I feel like I'm having a *minor* heart attack, as opposed to a *major* one, which is a sign of improvement, I guess. But I still have so many questions I need answers to: When is the attack going to happen, for starters? And where? If the New Americans know all this in advance, is there anything they can do to stop it?

The others squirm as though they're also near-bursting with questions, but we all know the rules: no speaking out of turn. Now that I've learned we're training for something real—oh god, we're training for something *real*—I feel even less inclined to step out of line. I keep my mouth shut, and so does everyone else.

Mr. Kraus gets to his feet and picks up his briefcase. "I'm going to leave you now to process this information, but there is one more thing I have to tell you before I go. This is perhaps the most important piece of this whole experience.

"Tomorrow, before you're released, I'll be bringing in a high-ranking member of the New Americans to assess how well you've mastered the principles of our party. He'll be evaluating you as a group, so you'll only pass his test if you all are able to demonstrate your unwavering allegiance to our cause. If you succeed, it'll be your job to recruit your friends and family to join the party."

I breathe a small sigh of relief, knowing I can make sure my parents will be safe.

"If you fail," he continues sternly, "I'm afraid to say you'll be kicked out of the New Americans for good. If I were you, I would pass along this information to Ms. Honeyman."

When the door slams behind him, part of me just wants to lie on my back and wait for it all to be over: the test, the attack, the aftermath, *my whole life.* Instead, I'm nearly crushed in a stampede as Craig, Steve, and Bobby rush to the corner where Helen is sitting, and then I'm dragged to my feet by Betty, who wants us to follow along.

"We have to do what the group is doing, *always.*" For the first time in maybe ever, I hear fear in Betty's voice.

When we reach the others, Craig is standing over Helen with his arms crossed. Bobby and Steve are flanking him like sidekicks. "You were wrong, Helen," he says. "You should have listened to me."

"She shouldn't get to be a New American," Steve jeers. "She should have to try to survive on her own."

Helen looks up at them. She doesn't seem scared. "What is it now?"

Craig proceeds to fill her in on everything Mr. Kraus just told us. When he's done explaining, Helen's eyes dart in my direction, and I nod to let her know it's all true. I silently pray that Helen will change her mind and join the cause. Even if she's not a New American to her core, maybe she could just fake it for long enough to nudge us safely into the future.

But then Helen gets up, so she can look the boys in the eye. "You actually believe all this?"

"Yes." Craig is firm.

"You really think a secret society could have that much power?"

"I trust Andy."

"I think you want to *be* Andy. You want to control the world."

Craig scratches the back of his neck. "Whatever, Helen."

She crosses her arms and changes tack. "Fine. Let's say the New Americans *are* the real deal." She looks around at each of us in turn. When she gets to me, it feels like I have two ropes wrapped around my chest, each being pulled in the opposite direction. "You all genuinely want to join them? You want to join a party that makes you rat each other out? And do weird chants? And communicate through hand signals? You want to give up your individuality for the sake of belonging to some special club? Because it feels safer?"

I stare at my feet because I don't want to have to make eye contact with her again. She has a point, and I know it. But I'm too scared to say so.

That's when Betty raises her hands in the air. She's making the New American sign, and she's glaring at Helen the same way as before. Again, I have the strange sensation of being a million miles away from her, even though we're only standing three feet apart.

"I want to be in that club," Betty declares. "I know it seems scary, but so is a friggin' bomb. And if Andy believes in it, then so do I."

Bobby, who's been watching Betty intently, nods his head. "So do I," he says.

"So do I," says Steve.

"So do I," says Craig.

They each make their New American As.

"What about you, Connie?" Helen asks pointedly.

"I . . ." Am fidgeting with the fabric of my dress, to be perfectly honest, and avoiding anyone's gaze. The two ropes pull tighter and tighter, until it feels like the tension might split me down the middle. I don't like to make big decisions, or even small ones, for that matter. That's why I usually let Betty do it for me. The world is too scary to chart my own course; I'd rather hide in the center of a crowd and follow wherever they're going. I respect Helen for speaking up, and I agree with what she's saying, but is now really the time to resist? There's a nuclear attack happening soon, and the future of the world is spinning like a top that's about to fall over. "I do," I mumble, staring at my shoes on the dingy gray floor. "I believe in it."

I hear Helen's voice. "I need some space."

It doesn't seem like an accident when her body knocks into mine on her way to the bathroom, where she slams the door behind her.

Craig goes over and kicks the wall, and for the first time

ever, I hear him curse. "She's going to ruin this for all of us. What the hell do we do?"

"Do you think you could still persuade her?" Bobby asks.

"OBVIOUSLY NOT!" Craig flails his hand helplessly toward the bathroom door.

"I have an idea," Betty says, and all of a sudden, she's the center of attention. She clears her throat and tilts her chin up. "If we know that Helen will never join us, and she's a totally lost cause, maybe we should just make it really clear to the party member that we don't agree with her, and that we super-duper believe in everything Andy's taught us. Which is the truth."

"I like that idea," says Bobby. "We find a way to separate her."

"Like we know she's not one of us, either," Betty adds.

Craig nods slowly, regaining his composure. "Yes . . . yes, that's it. I think that's the only way to win here. The question is, how do we do it, exactly?"

Steve's head swivels back and forth between the cots and the bathroom door. "We could stack the beds up and trap her in the bathroom."

"But then how would we go to the bathroom?" Betty points out.

"And she still needs food and water," I say softly.

Steve grunts. "Fine. You guys come up with a better idea."

"No, Steve, I think you were on the right track." Craig scratches his head. "We just need to think about it for a second."

"What about in there?" asks Bobby.

I sink onto the floor as the boys start dragging cots toward the New American clubhouse. Craig gestures at the structure like an architect describing a new addition he's going to put on a house, and Steve and Bobby nod along like faithful assistants.

Betty crouches beside me and rubs my back. "It's for the best, Connie."

I wish she wouldn't touch me. I wish we could all just get along, and that the world wasn't ending. "I don't have a good feeling about this," I mutter.

Betty says nothing. Her hand keeps tracing the same path up and down my spine.

A few minutes later, Steve marches over to the bathroom door. Whether Helen locked it or not, he yanks it open with one mighty tug and disappears inside.

Panicking, I look over at Craig. His face flinches for a moment, but otherwise, his jaw remains set.

Back in the bathroom, there's a high-pitched scream. Helen. I leap to my feet, but Betty yanks me back down by my sleeve.

"What are they doing to her?"

"I don't think we should ask questions."

Trembling, I stay on the ground. Betty places a hand on my shoulder to keep me still. The next thing I know, there's another scream, and Steve is dragging Helen's fighting body out the door by her hair.

FIFTEEN

Eva

Back at Hardwick, something called lake effect has turned the campus into the *literal arctic*, with snow up to our waists and icicles hanging threateningly above the entrances to every building. Whenever I pass underneath them, my puffy hood pulled up for protection, I remember reading that an icicle would make the best murder weapon, because it melts away as soon as you're done using it.

I linger under an icy death trap outside the dining hall, where I'm waiting for Erik so we can get rolling on our master plan. When his basketball practice was canceled today, he was told it was because of an all-staff meeting happening in the auditorium—which gave us the perfect opportunity to go poke around the basement of the administration building, where Kelvin said the shelter was. We knew we had to jump on it, because when else would we have the place to ourselves, without Allenby or any other teachers prowling around?

I'm nervous, but the funny thing is, I'm even *more* nervous for the second plan I have for today—the one Erik doesn't know about. For the rest of winter break, I itched to know what he'd been trying to tell me on that rock in Central Park, before Kelvin called and spoiled the moment, and we ended up playing Frogger on Amsterdam Avenue. The plan is that later tonight, if I don't wimp out, I'm going to ask if we can pick the conversation back up where we left off. Depending on how that goes—and if I'm feeling *really* brave—I might see if he wants to go with me to the Valentine's Day dance, which I happened to see a flyer for in Ainsley House this morning.

"Hey, Secret Agent Storm."

I jump when Erik materializes beside me. I'd been picturing us walking home from Dungeons and Dragons this evening, his hand sliding into mine as the snowflakes start to fall.

But first things first.

"You ready?" I ask.

"Let's do this."

He joins me in pulling up his hood so no one can see our faces, and we head off on our mission. It helps that the sun sets so early this time of year. We have the gathering darkness on our side.

We slip through the front door of the admin building and uncover our heads so we can see better. I've only been in here once before, on my first day, when Mom and Caleb dragged me in to pick up my room key. I was too overwhelmed to know where I was or what was going on, but now I look around. It has all the marks of an older Hardwick building: uneven wooden floors, wainscoting, and ornate crown moldings with chipping plaster.

"That's Allenby's office." Erik points to a door with a golden plaque in the middle.

"Let's try *not* to end up in there."

"We'll be as fast as possible. Find the shelter, take a bunch of pictures, analyze them later."

"How much time do you think we have?"

"If the meeting was long enough for Coach to cancel practice, we probably have at least thirty minutes."

We creep past Allenby's door, our eyes on the staircase up ahead on the left. There's plenty of light coming from the floor above, but the steps going down disappear into blackness. There's a metal sign on the wall that seems to be calling to us: BASEMENT OFF-LIMITS. We stand shoulder to shoulder at the lip of the top step. "Here goes nothing," Erik says.

The temperature drops by a solid twenty degrees as we descend into the basement, and I'm grateful to have my coat. It feels like walking into a sewer. At the bottom of the steps, Erik and I both hit the flashlight buttons on our phones, and in the feeble light, we encounter our first obstacle: a door.

I jiggle the doorknob. "It's locked."

"Do you have a bobby pin?"

"Do you know how hard it is to pick a lock with a bobby pin? And I don't have one anyway."

"I bet Allenby has a key."

It's our only option. We hurry back up the steps and go to

the door with the golden plaque. I crouch down to peer through the crack; the lights seem to be off. "Maybe I'm paranoid, but I'm just double-checking. There's a zero-percent chance he's in here, right?"

"Zero. I saw him with a bunch of teachers walking toward the arts building."

"Whew. Okay." I take a deep breath and try the knob. It turns all the way. With a light push, the door creaks open onto Dean Allenby's wood-paneled office.

"I'm surprised he left it unlocked." Erik leads me across the rug to the other side of the mahogany desk, where we each open one of the two drawers. Erik's has a stack of manila file folders inside, while mine is divided into compartments for all the odds and ends you'd expect to find in a teacher's desk: pens, pencils, scissors, and an old-school calculator. I pull it out as far as it'll go, and there, next to a box of paper clips, is a metal key ring with two keys attached.

"Let's hope one of these does the trick." I snatch it up, and we both close our drawers. Shutting Allenby's door behind us, we race back across the hallway and down the stairs so we don't waste any more time.

At the locked door, I try the first key. It goes in, but it doesn't turn. "Shoot."

We're going to run out of time just trying to enter the basement. I jam the second key into the lock. It goes in . . . and twists all the way to the left with a satisfying *click*.

Erik squeezes my shoulder.

Which also happens to be satisfying. In its own way.

Our phone flashlights at the ready, we open the door. It leads us into a dark, dank hallway with cinder-block walls and a dusty light bulb hanging from the ceiling. On the floor, there are moldy cardboard boxes and a few old desks and chairs lying on their sides—probably tossed down here for storage and forgotten about.

"Which way, do you think?" Erik asks.

"Wait, *look!* Shine your flashlight over there again." A second ago, I noticed something on the wall. Erik moves the beam a foot to the left, and there, in all its black-and-yellow glory, is a sign that says FALLOUT SHELTER, with an arrow pointing to the left.

"Oh my god!"

"Come on, let's go!"

We race down the corridor, our flashlight beams bouncing up and down. We pause at a wooden door, but it doesn't look right; the shelter would have a sign on it. "Let's check around the corner first," I say. My throat is tight with excitement—I can barely get the words out.

We round the bend and hold out our phones. This new hallway is too long for us to see the end, so we keep on moving. Erik takes the lead. And then, suddenly, he stops in his tracks.

I see it, too.

It's there, up ahead.

A huge metal door with a familiar pinwheel smack-dab in the middle.

SIXTEEN

Connie

Helen resists the whole way to the clubhouse. Or the jail. Whatever we're calling it now. I don't want to know. But her small body is no match for all six feet, five inches of Steve O'Leary, who tosses her into the structure like a ragdoll. From where I'm rooted to the ground—partly from Betty's grip and partly from pure fear—I can't see what's happening, but I hear her groan in pain as she collides with the floor.

Before she can get out, the boys start stacking cots in front of the opening. With startling efficiency—or Order—they dump the mattresses off to the side and pile the metal frames like they're building a barricade.

There's a grunt and a loud clang. Helen must have gotten up and thrown herself against the beds. The barricade doesn't move, but one of the water drums teeters before righting itself again.

What the hell are they doing?

Why don't they remember how easily Betty knocked over one of the pillars?

Another terrifying clang.

The boys throw their weight against the beds.

"We have to stop them, Bets."

"We can't." Her voice cracks.

"We have to stop them."

"Connie, *no*."

"WE HAVE TO."

Again, I leap to my feet, and this time when Betty grabs my sleeve, I wrench it from her grip. I don't care if we fail the test tomorrow, and I don't care what happens after. Someone is going to get seriously hurt, and I can't sit by and watch it happen. I dig down within myself. I dig down so deep, I see light at the other end. And then I find it. My voice. It explodes into the room.

"EVERYONE, STOP RIGHT NOW!"

But no one hears it.

Not even me.

Dread seeps from my stomach as the teetering drum leans way too far inward, then falls into the middle. The initial crash leads to a sickening metal crunch as the beds topple away from the boys, bringing even more drums down with them. It's a cacophony of horror. The New American clubhouse topples like a series of dominoes, with Helen trapped inside. Craig, Bobby, and Steve stand rooted to the floor, their faces pale.

All I can do is scream uselessly at them to save her, my voice disappearing into the deadly void.

SEVENTEEN

Eva

The other key, it turns out, is for the padlock on the outside of the fallout shelter. Once we get it off, it takes both of us pulling with every available muscle to open the door wide enough for each of us to slip inside.

Before we go in, I swing my backpack off my shoulder and pull out the heavy-duty flashlights I brought back from Mom and Caleb's place—the ones Caleb bought after Hurricane Sandy, just in case half the city lost power again. I hand one to Erik. "Now's probably a good time for these."

We turn them on and step through the door. The shelter floor is slick with dust, and Erik has to steady himself against the wall so he doesn't slip. In the beams of light, we make out a huge room filled with shadowy shapes. I can make out rows of narrow beds, like something out of a horror movie. I switch my phone to camera mode and start taking pictures.

"Hey, notice anything about the ceiling?" Erik points his light up.

"Yeah. It seems *not collapsed.*"

To the left, there are towers of water drums like the ones I've seen in photos. To the right, there are shelves lined with cardboard boxes.

"Hey, Storm, look at this."

"What?"

"It's their names."

He shines his light at the wall, at the spot where his hand wiped the dust away when he slipped a few seconds ago. The beam illuminates six names carved into the concrete in spiky lettering:

Steve O'Leary

Craig Allenby

Helen Honeyman

Bobby Tackett

Betty Walker

Connie Abbott

Underneath the names, there are three words that make the hair stand up on the back of my neck. "Order, Unity, Power. Holy shit."

"Isn't that the Fives' motto?"

"Yeah . . . which is weird. Allenby said he started the Fives as a group for high achievers or something. But there must be some connection to the shelter."

"This is really freaking creepy." He moves his beam into the center of the room. "I guess we should keep looking around?"

"Yeah."

"I'll go first. And I'll shuffle my feet to clear off the dust for you. It's slippery as hell."

"What a gentleman you are."

"You know, I do my best."

I follow along in his wake, shining my beam at the floor to make sure I'm stepping in the path he's cleared. It's all gray concrete underneath the dust, until suddenly, the gray turns brown. "Whoa, whoa, whoa. Erik. What's that?"

"Where?"

"Behind you. On the floor."

He spins around, and we both squat to examine the spot on the ground. I'm shocked Erik happened to walk over it, and that I happened to notice it. It really isn't big—it's about the size of a hockey puck, except with irregular, splotchy edges. It looks like the stain I woke up to on my pillow that time I got a nosebleed in the middle of the night.

I swallow hard. "It looks like blood."

"Do you think it's hers?"

"I don't know, but . . ."

"Who else's would it be?"

"Yeah."

For a few seconds, Erik is quiet. He can't seem to take his eyes off the brown stain.

"Are you okay?"

He blinks and rubs his chest. "Yeah. No. I don't know.

Seeing this makes her so much more human. And it pisses me off that they're obviously covering something up."

"I know. We're going to figure it out, I promise."

I take a photo of the stain, and then we get up to explore the rest of the space, which is mostly beds. We also peek inside a room the size of a broom closet with a single water drum and a first aid kit inside. When we open the kit, everything looks untouched—except for maybe the roll of gauze, which has a frayed edge. But there's still plenty of it there.

"Did no one try to help her when she was bleeding?" Erik mumbles.

"Either that or something happened that no first aid kit could possibly handle."

"I think I feel sick."

On the way out, we dust off a table next to the door with an old-fashioned walkie-talkie-looking thing on it. I wonder who they used it to talk to. I snap some more photos, and then I look at the time. According to Erik's estimate, the teachers still won't be back for a little while, but I'd rather be safe than sorry and get out of here as quickly as possible—especially because we still have to put the keys back in Allenby's desk.

I'm searching for the off switch on my super-flashlight when I catch Erik gazing at the carvings in the wall again. He runs his fingers down the list, lingering on Helen's name and lightly tracing some of the letters.

"You know, my grandpa's pretty out of it, but that time I brought up Helen, he did remember this one story about babysitting her when she was like seven. And she sounded pretty cool."

"Oh yeah?"

"Apparently her brother went out and collected a bunch of caterpillars, and he made a little habitat for them in a jar, and Helen didn't approve of keeping the caterpillars all cooped up like that. She kept bugging him and telling him to let them out, but he wouldn't do it. So during dinner, she lied and said she had to go to the bathroom, but instead she stole the jar and smashed it on the driveway to set them free. And she came in with her hands all covered in blood, but she was happy."

"Sounds like she was a rebel."

"Yeah. That's exactly how he described her, actually. And he said everyone always underestimated her because she was this tiny little thing. Also, it was the fifties when he babysat for her, so I think people just underestimated girls in general?"

"Sounds about right."

Our backpacks zipped up, we leave the shelter and seal the door with the padlock. In the light of our phone flashlights, we traipse back the way we came, past the grimy cinder-block walls and long-forgotten storage things.

"You still wanna go to D and D after this?" I ask hopefully, now that plan number one is almost complete.

"Definitely. I think it'll be good to get my mind off this for a bit."

I check the time again—we're still well under the thirty minutes we gave ourselves to look for the shelter. We go through the door at the base of the staircase, and after I close it gently behind us, I lock it with Allenby's key.

"Mission accomplished," Erik says.

"Who's down there?"

At the sound of the voice, every ounce of blood in my body seems to drain through my heels and pool on the floor around me. Erik looks exactly the way I feel, his face slack and ghostly white.

He mouths, *Allenby*.

I mouth a panicked four-letter word back at him.

I don't understand. The entire building is silent as a crypt, except for his footsteps on the wooden floor above. He must have returned from the meeting early for some reason. There's a jingle of keys as he walks closer and closer to where Erik and I are huddled in the darkness. Did he come back to lock his office? Did he realize he left it open? Jesus Christ, the explanation doesn't even matter. There's a missile hurtling toward us, and there's no way to stop it. We're doomed.

And then Erik yanks the keys from my hand.

He whispers, "Promise me you'll solve it."

And before I even know what's happening, before I can try to stop him, he's bounding up the stairs and into the light.

EIGHTEEN

Connie

My brain is broken. Scenes flash by like photos on a slide reel, random and disconnected with big gaps of blackness in between.

Mr. Kraus on his knees, sobbing. It's the first time I've seen a grown-up cry, and it feels like the universe is fraying. "I didn't know—I didn't mean to—it wasn't real—not supposed to happen . . ."

Bobby trying to sift through debris. His eyes wild.

Steve pulling him back. His eyes dead.

Blood seeping out from under the rubble. So much of it. A dark, shiny pool.

Betty trying to hold me. Like, really hold me, with her arms around my torso. "Please let go."

"No."

"Let go."

"No."

"Will you get the hell away from me?"

I don't know how my limbs work, but I'm going to the door. "I'm getting help."

"Wait."

Craig.

His hand on my arm. Too tight.

His face with that competitive look.

"We need to agree it wasn't our fault. It was an accident."

Mr. Kraus wiping his tears and nodding. "An accident—yes—that's what it was. Connie, let me get help. You all stay here. Remember, it was an *accident*."

The five of us left in the room with her body.

Hands in the middle of a circle.

"Don't breathe a word."

"Only we know."

"Only us."

"The five."

NINETEEN

Eva

I stomp through the unlocked door of Luisa's dorm room and flop onto her bed, burying my face in the purple polka-dot duvet and groaning from the deepest, darkest depths of my soul.

I hear the creak of wood that means Luisa has gotten up from her desk, and feel her weight on the mattress as she sits down beside me and pats my curls.

"Thanks," I mumble.

"It's hard to find your head in here, but I'm trying."

If it weren't for my newfound friendship with Luisa, I don't know how I would have gotten through these past two weeks without Erik. After he went and sacrificed himself to Allenby, I stood there in shock and listened as the dean of students dragged him into his office and slammed the door. Light-headed and shaking, I forced my feet to carry me up the stairs and out of the building, fighting the urge to burst into Allenby's office and take the blame, too. But what good would that do? I'd most definitely be kicked out of the Fives, and we'd lose our direct pipeline to inside information. I'd be outed as a spy. Reeling with guilt, I stumbled up the sidewalk and around the edge of the snow-covered quad, ending up at the only place that felt safe to me in that moment: the archives room on the second floor of the library, where Luisa was there early, setting up the maps on the floor. One glance at my face, and she asked me what was wrong. I couldn't help it; I felt like I was going to burst open and my secrets were going to spill onto the floor anyway. I told her everything—*everything*—and she pulled me into a hug and promised not to tell another soul. We were standing like that, my head on her shoulder, when Erik texted to say he'd just been expelled.

"I take it the dinner was . . . not good?" Luisa asks now.

"Absolutely horrible." I roll over and drag myself up to a seated position, take off my boots, and fling them toward the door. Luisa scoots back to lean against her pillows, and I pull my feet up so I can face her, cross-legged. "I could barely bring myself to look at his stupid, evil face. They *all* have stupid, evil faces!"

At this point, there isn't anything remotely alluring about being part of the Fives. I've even faked sick a couple of times to avoid some recent late-night gatherings. But when another dinner at Allenby's appeared on the calendar—the first since Erik's expulsion—Luisa insisted I go. She said I couldn't make them suspicious of me, and that I might pick up more useful information on what's clearly now a decades-long cover-up. And so I went, wearing my ring and chanting "order, unity, power" with the best of them. I felt like I was betraying Erik as I picked at my salmon and pretended to laugh at one of Heather's stories, and I kept having to remind myself that he'd want me to be there. *Promise me you'll solve it*, he said before he raced up the stairs. To solve it, I'd have to keep the target off my back. And to keep the target off my back, I'd have to keep coming to these dinners.

"The whole thing started with Allenby announcing the 'safety issue' he'd been concerned about all year had finally been taken care of. Then, on a totally different note—well, not to me, but to everyone else—he said he'd also taken care of an 'egregious act of stealth.' He's making it seem like Erik was expelled for breaking into his office and going through his desk. Obviously, the real reason is that we were down in the basement!"

She bites her bottom lip and shakes her head. "First that Kelvin guy, and now Erik."

"I know. It's so messed up. Oh! And on the walk back up to campus, Heather starts bragging about how she's *definitely* getting the Spirit Award at graduation, because she was the one who originally reported the safety issue to Allenby."

"She is the *worst*." Luisa pounds her fist into a pillow. "Did I ever tell you about the time we were partnered on an AP history assignment?" (Luisa, I've learned, takes quite a few classes with the grade above us, because she's just that smart.) "We had to identify the regions and time periods of these random ceramic objects, and she didn't do anything. I was, like, *sweating* in the library doing all this detective work, and she was scrolling through Instagram."

"Probably because she knew she couldn't fail."

"That is *so* unfair, while the rest of us are working as hard as humanly possible . . ." She stares at the poster of the periodic table taped to the wall next to her bed. "Speaking of which, I was just putting the finishing touches on my English paper when you came in. You don't mind if I . . ." She breaks eye contact with plutonium (Pu) and nods toward her laptop.

"No. Of course not."

She jumps to her feet, but instead of going straight back to her desk, she stands there and twirls a lock of chestnut-brown hair around her finger. "You should stay and hang out," she says quickly. "It's, um, nice to have some company for a change."

"Luisa, do you spend every Saturday night working?"

"I spend *every* night working," she replies, "unless I have D and D or A/V Club."

"That's pretty amazing."

"Yeah, well, to be honest, it can also be kinda lonely, so if you *do* wanna stick around . . . I can make us some tea"—she gestures to the little red kettle sitting on her shelf—"and you can borrow one of my textbooks if there's anything you have to study for."

I've made it a general life rule that I won't do homework on a Saturday night, but I still want to stay and hang out with Luisa. "I can do some more research on the names from the fallout shelter."

She smiles. "Great. Have you made any progress?"

"No, but I've only tried Facebook so far."

Luisa leaves the room to go fill up the kettle, and I take out my phone to see if I can find a former fallout shelter kid who'll tell me the truth. More than anything, I wish I could text Erik, but his parents confiscated his phone and laptop as soon as he got back to New Jersey. He emailed me the other day from a computer in the library of his new public school, explaining he tried to tell his parents the real reason he was expelled, but they didn't believe a word of what he was saying, and now he was grounded into the next century. We didn't even get to say goodbye before he packed up and left Hardwick, because we didn't want to risk being seen together. Now I have this all-over ache for him, like a layer of me is missing.

I open my browser, because I've already scoured every inch of Facebook. The problem with searching Facebook is it's impossible to know which of the gazillion Steve O'Learys, for instance, is the right one. There are dozens of Bobby Tacketts, and Bob Tacketts, and Robert Tacketts. There are countless Betty Walkers and Elizabeth Walkers and Connie Abbotts and Constance Abbotts—and then there's the possibility that the women got married and changed their last names, so I'm not even searching for them correctly. There's also the possibility that none of these people even *have* Facebook, because they're somewhere in their mid-seventies.

Maybe I'll find them if I get a little more specific in my searching. Some people put their high school on their LinkedIn page, right? I google "Steve O'Leary Hardwick," but all the top search results have to do with some chef named Steve Lear opening a restaurant in Midtown Manhattan called The Hardwick. Next, I try "Connie Abbott Hardwick," but it's a website for a chiropractor named Sheila Hardwick in Abbot, Maine. *Ugh.* I try "Bobby Tackett Hardwick."

Well, this is more interesting. The top result is a 2011 story from Hardwick's alumni magazine: "Hardwick Alumni Make Generous Donation to Arts Building." I click the link, and the next thing I see is a photo of a slightly younger Dean Allenby posing on the quad with one arm around a short, curly-haired man, and the other around a woman with large cat-eye glasses. I scan the first few paragraphs of the story below.

Bobby Tackett '63 and Elizabeth Tackett (née Walker) '63 made a generous donation to Hardwick Preparatory Academy in April that is intended for the renovation of the arts building.

"I have the fondest memories of performing in Hardwick's school plays as a young girl, so it's an honor that my husband and I can help update the facility with the latest and greatest equipment and amenities," said Mrs. Tackett, now a theater professor at Connecticut College.

The renovation is set to begin this summer . . .

Whoa. A lot of things jump out at me here. One: If Elizabeth Tackett's maiden name is Walker, and she also graduated from Hardwick in 1963, she *has* to be Betty Walker. Assuming she is, let's move on to two: If Helen died a violent death in a fallout shelter experiment gone wrong—and these people had to witness it—why are they still so loyal to Hardwick? And three: There is absolutely no way in hell I can safely reach out to Bobby or Betty for answers about the fallout shelter—not if they're still best buds with Allenby and donating heaps of money to the school.

Luisa returns to the room with a kettle full of water. "Any luck?"

"Not really, no." I scroll back up to the picture and glare at their faces, hating the three of them for laughing so carelessly, especially now that I've seen what might be Helen's blood on the shelter floor. And then an unsettling thought pops into my head—a possible answer to one of my questions from before. Maybe Bobby and Betty weren't just innocent witnesses. What if they were directly involved in Helen's death somehow . . . and the reason they're so loyal to Hardwick is because it helps keep their secret safe? Who would ever suspect, or speak ill of, the couple who just donated bajillions of dollars to redo the arts building?

"You look like you're thinking about something. And like you maybe want to do a murder."

"Luisa, I swear to god, I'm going to burn this whole society to the ground." I put down my phone and get up to help her

276

choose which kind of tea we're going to make. "I just have to figure out how."

The days start getting longer, but winter clings to campus like it's hanging on for dear life. Just when the sun comes out and the snow starts to melt, the temperature plummets and we get dumped on again, and it's back to wearing gym pants under my kilt to walk from building to building.

I know Erik's trying to be positive, but I can tell from his emails he's more miserable the longer he spends away from Hardwick. I never knew how much he liked it here, but now that I sense his thinly veiled pain, I'm even angrier at Allenby than I was before, which is saying something.

Hey Storm.

Snuck to the library to "print out my essay," aka email you back. Want to know something weird? They're just starting *The Picture of Dorian Gray*, which means I'm super ahead in English, because I read it over winter break. But it also means I have to relive that entire chapter describing the guy's jewel collection, which is honestly worse than getting expelled.

Kidding. I was trying the whole "dark humor" thing to see if it helped, but it didn't. To answer your question about whether I'm happy here: It's fine, but I miss Hardwick. I know it sounds weird! But other than the shelter stuff, this year was going really well. Like, maybe my best year ever. I feel bad that our D&D crew has to fight the evil dragon without Gordon the elf. Also, they don't have cheeseburger soup in the cafeteria here, and it's extremely problematic.

My parents probably won't give my phone back until I'm 36, so keep emailing me here. (Please! I feel like I got voted off *Survivor* before the merge, and there's no Redemption Island or Edge of Extinction. I need updates on what's happening in the game.)

—Erik

I send him updates on Dungeons and Dragons, and funny things that happen at assembly, and weird things they serve in the dining hall—like "quesadilla stew," which is obviously a not-so-creative repurposing of the previous night's quesadillas. I wish I could tell him I've made some kind of progress in solving the fallout shelter mystery, but the truth is, I have nothing to report, except that Bobby Tackett and Betty Walker once made a hefty donation to renovate the arts building.

Then, one Thursday morning, Candace strolls into the dining hall with a copy of the *Hardwick Herald* in her hand.

"Hot off the presses!" She tosses it onto the table, where it lands on top of Luisa's math homework, and slings her messenger bag over a chair. "Mind watching this stuff while I go make toast?"

"No problem."

As she walks away, Luisa sighs and pushes the *Herald* off to the side. Candace should know better than to interfere with Luisa's homework. Until she got here, we'd been sitting in studious silence: Luisa tearing through trig problems, and me trying to catch up on *Dorian Gray*, which—no offense to Oscar Wilde—is as boring as Erik says it is. He was serious: there's a whole entire chapter describing the contents of a guy's jewel collection. Who has time for that? Come to think of it, I could use a break, so I put down my book and pull the new issue of the *Herald* toward me. A bolded headline on the front page immediately catches my eye.

DEAN ALLENBY TO RECEIVE LIFETIME ACHIEVEMENT AWARD

"You have got to be kidding me."

Luisa looks up and adjusts her glasses. "What is it?"

I read the story in a hushed voice, so there's no chance of any passing Fives overhearing my anger. "Craig Allenby, Dean of Students, will receive a lifetime achievement award next month for his years of valuable contributions to the Hardwick Preparatory Academy community. The dean will be honored with a ceremony in the auditorium on Sunday, March 8, as well as a new campus garden in his name later this spring."

"That jerk is getting an award?" Luisa hisses. "And a *garden?*"

"I know. I'm so angry."

I scan the rest of the story. The next few paragraphs talk about how Allenby was a model Hardwick student back in the fifties and sixties—no mention of the shelter, obviously—and how he returned to campus as a teacher once he graduated college. He's been at the school ever since, rising through the ranks before landing his current leadership role in 2005.

"Whoa, here's something interesting." I start to read aloud again. "Alumni have been invited to return to campus for the weekend's festivities, including members of Dean Allenby's graduating class. Guests can enjoy guided tours of campus, a Saturday speaker series, an early look at the theater department's spring show . . ." When I look up, Luisa and I lock eyes. "You don't think . . ."

"The other four shelter people will come? That's *exactly* what I was thinking." She presses her pointer finger into the newsprint. "Eva, this could be your opportunity to get the real story."

But there's an obvious problem with the plan. "Luisa, if they're coming back for this award ceremony, won't they all be super allegiant to Allenby? It'll be impossible to get them to talk to me—and they also might go and report me."

"Maybe." Luisa drops her voice to a whisper as Candace makes her way back to the table with a small stack of toast wrapped in a napkin. "But it's the best chance you've got."

TWENTY

Eva

I see the first car on Friday afternoon, as I'm treading through the gray slush on my way to math. The black sedan rolls up the hill at a snail's pace, the adults in the front seats swiveling their heads this way and that, taking in the sight of the campus blanketed in snow. Anticipation ripples through my chest. They're here: the alumni are arriving for Dean Allenby's big weekend.

You can tell the school is getting ready to host a bunch of important visitors. Last night, we got a sternly worded email from Mrs. Krakowski ordering us to take whatever was ours from the common area and back to our individual rooms, lest some unsuspecting alumni stroll into Ainsley House "and see our adolescent debris lying around." When I got to breakfast, vases of white flowers had appeared in the center of every table, the small mountain of crumbs had been cleared from the bottom of the toaster, and there were signs in silver frames announcing what was being served at each food station. Everyone seemed to be gushing about their plans for the weekend, with Friday night curfew lifted and Saturday classes canceled.

At formal assembly, when I sat down next to Luisa, she jutted her chin with extreme disdain toward the navy-blue banner strung up over the stage, which I'd somehow missed when I first walked in. When I looked at it, I groaned. "Tell me that's not real."

The banner said "HARDWICK HERO" in white block letters, and in the middle of "HARDWICK" and "HERO," there was a blown-up photo of Dean Allenby's smiling face. Like he was goddamn Mother Teresa.

"Oh, it's real," Luisa replied. "Last night at A/V Club, I had to practice aiming the spotlight at it. I got assigned to work the award ceremony on Sunday, which sucks, but I didn't have a choice. There's gonna be some slideshow, and they said we had 'no room for error.' I'm the best at working the video projector, so . . ."

"So . . . any chance you can rig something so the banner falls on his head?"

She laughed. "Yeah, I'll see what I can do."

From my desk in math class, I watch through the window as the cars make their slow procession up the main road. Mr. Richterman is in the midst of explaining last night's home-work, and I know I should be paying attention, but honestly, how am I supposed to focus on SOHCAHTOA when someone who knows what happened to Helen Honeyman might be roll-ing up the hill in that silver SUV? Or that green minivan? The truth feels closer than ever before, and it's up to me to find it before it disappears again. But how? How am I going to find who I'm looking for, and how am I going to persuade them to talk to me?

A tiny ball of paper skitters across the windowsill, bumps into my forearm, and comes to a stop. *Not now, Jenny. I'm too busy thinking.* I force a smile at her reflection and transfer the note to my lap, hoping it's not an invitation to skip class with her. I really don't feel like watching Hulu in her dorm room.

V ALUMNI PARTY OFF CAMPUS 2NITE.
MEET STUDENT LOT 8:30.

Whoa. A party with Fives alumni?

Yes.

Yes.

With trembling fingers, I write a check mark under Jenny's message, crumple up the paper, and flick it back to her. She opens it and gives me an affirming nod in the window.

For the rest of the afternoon my heart thuds like a ticking time bomb. I obviously don't know anything for sure, but I *feel like* if the other four shelter names are coming back to campus for the weekend, then this gathering is the best place to find them. The Fives and the fallout shelter are obviously connected: Dean Allenby is part of both, and it sure as hell can't be a coincidence that I found the words Order, Unity, and Power carved into a wall down there.

283

Of course, if I *do* find Bobby, Betty, Steve, or Connie, the next question is whether I can convince them to admit the truth, and not get myself expelled in the process.

At dinner, I practically inhale my food and hurry back to Ainsley House to put together an outfit for tonight: something that screams, "I need you to tell me the school's darkest secrets," but also, "I'm very friendly and innocent and have no ulterior motives beyond making polite conversation, I promise!" I end up going with a long-sleeved navy-blue dress over tights, and because it's freezing out, I wrap my neck with the matching blue Hardwick scarf Jenny and Niah got me for my birthday in December.

On the way out the door, I pause at the mirror and swipe on the dark red lipstick Ella gave me for Christmas, which I hadn't been expecting. It was sweet, actually: she said she showed my photo to the guy at Sephora, and he helped her pick out the right color. They chose well; the shade makes me feel kind of powerful, even though I'm really freaking nervous. I can't blow this chance. I flip up my hood and march through the cold darkness to the student parking lot, picturing myself as a spy about to infiltrate an enemy fortress.

"There it is," Heather says, tapping her long nails against the passenger-side window of the Uber. For the past twenty minutes, I've been squeezed in the back between Jenny and Niah, worried they could feel my heart pounding. I shift in my seat so I can peer through the glass, and I see it.

The inn looks like a castle. Literally. Nestled among the evergreens and lit up by dozens of lamps staggered around the property, it's a large stone building with turrets, pointy spires, and a giant wooden door that looks like it could keep out an army. Through the windows on the ground floor of the largest turret, I see people milling around in the soft golden light.

Niah claps her hands as we walk up the driveway. "Let's have a good night, ladies."

"*Hell* yeah," Jenny says.

"Hey!" shouts a voice from behind. I'm so on edge, it makes me jump. "You guys gonna wait for us, or what?"

We turn around to find Jackson, Xavier, and Raven climbing out of another car. Jenny laughs and waves them over, and we walk up the wide stone steps as a unit. Little do they know I'm not one of them. Not really. I'm going to have to figure out how to detach myself as soon as we get inside, so I can try to track down my targets.

An attendant opens the door for us. "You're with the Hardwick party?"

"Yes," Heather replies coolly.

"You'll be in the parlor. Straight ahead and up the small set of stairs to your right. Enjoy."

Jackson makes an embarrassing whooping sound.

The lobby has bloodred carpeting, wood-paneled walls, and a moose's head mounted over the check-in desk. My stomach churns. *Please, god, if you exist and you happen to be free right now, do not let that moose be an omen.*

We check our coats, but the inn is drafty and cold, so I keep my Hardwick scarf on. Plus, an extra dose of school spirit can't hurt if I'm trying to get Fives to open up to me. The first person I see at the top of the stairs is Simon Banbury, standing next to a large wooden post with decorative snowshoes nailed to it. The woman beside him must be his mom, because she has the same blond hair, same pointy nose, and same sense of style that resembles someone who just stepped off a sailboat. The two of them are deep in conversation with a couple whose backs are toward us, but judging by their gray hair, they look like the right age of the people I'm searching for.

"I'm gonna go say hi to Simon," I announce to the group. Thankfully, no one follows.

"Hey, Simon."

"Eva!" He throws himself at me, wrapping his arms around my neck. The overblown affection takes me by surprise, but then I realize he must want to show his mom he's part of the gang. When he lets go, I pat him on the back a couple of times. He announces proudly, "Mom, this is Eva, one of the other recruits this year. Eva, this is my mom."

"It's nice to meet you, Mrs. Banbury."

"It's nice to meet *you*, Eva. Simon told me all about your night in the woods."

As I try to come up with a witty reply—something that makes Simon sound a lot braver than he actually was—I catch a glimpse of the older couple standing next to us, smiling as though waiting to be introduced. My words get caught in my throat, and I completely forget what I was about to say to Mrs. Banbury. The couple has aged a bit since the 2011 photo, but there's no mistaking the man with gray curls and the woman with cat-eye glasses.

Mrs. Banbury puts a hand on the man's arm. "Eva, this is Bobby and Betty Tackett. They're both former Fives."

Oh, I know who you are. I shake both their hands, trying to remember how to smile like a normal human.

"Wow. It's really nice to meet you. When were you guys at Hardwick?"

"The fifties and sixties," Betty says.

"Basically, the Stone Age," Bobby adds. Everyone laughs politely, which gives me time to think about my next move.

"What was it like back then?"

"Well, the campus has changed quite a bit," Bobby answers. "It's wonderful to see what they've done with the athletics building, and of course, the theater is completely different than when Bets used to perform there. I don't know if you know this, but Betty and I helped Hardwick with a massive renovation a few years back . . ."

While Bobby and Betty talk about the arts building, Mrs. Banbury waves to some friends who just walked in, and pulls Simon away to go and greet them. Now it's just the three of us. And before we get interrupted, I need to see if I can learn anything useful.

"I think everyone's really grateful for your generous dona-tion," I tell them. They both grin, and Betty rubs her husband's back. Now's my chance to change the topic. "So . . . have you two been together since Hardwick?"

"Since our senior year," Betty replies.

"Wow! That's a long time."

"Don't I know it," she jokes.

"Did you meet through Fives stuff?"

"You're talking to two founding members right here, along with your wonderful dean of students," Bobby says. All of a sudden, the hand that was rubbing his back is squeezing his shoulder. Betty's still smiling, but there's something pinched about her expression. Bobby shrugs, and she takes her hand away. "I'm not sure if you've heard the story," he says pointedly, "but the Fives started when a group of ambitious students got together and decided we wanted to help each other go farther in life. We all had different talents—Betty here is a wonder-ful actor—and we figured we could pool our resources and share our connections. We were like one of those final clubs at Harvard, except in high school!"

"How long have *you* been at Hardwick, dear?" Betty asks.

Clink, clink, clink. Over by the windows, Dean Allenby is standing on a coffee table and tapping a knife against his flute of champagne. A hush falls over the room, and Betty takes the opportunity to wave goodbye, seize Bobby by the upper arm, and steer him toward the front of the crowd. I sigh and lean against the wooden post with the snowshoes. They weren't going to tell me anything about the fallout shelter.

That being said, it wasn't a totally useless conversation. First of all, I learned that three students from the shelter went on to found the Fives. Interesting. And when Bobby first brought up the origins of the secret society, I could tell by the look on his wife's face that it was potentially dangerous information. (Betty isn't *that* good of an actor.) I just wish I knew what any of it meant.

With everyone's eyes on Allenby as he makes his welcome speech, I take a moment to scan the crowd. Generations of Fives stare adoringly up at their leader. They smile when he smiles and laugh when he laughs . . . everyone except for an older woman standing alone near another wooden post, a few feet behind the rest of the group. She has long gray hair that falls halfway down her back, and she's still wearing her wool coat, as though she hasn't fully committed to staying. She listens to the dean with her arms crossed, her lips pressed tightly together, and a deep crease between her eyebrows.

When Allenby's speech ends with a lively chorus of "ORDER! UNITY! POWER!"—and everyone in the room raises their glasses in triumph—the gray-haired woman closes her eyes, shakes her head, and holds on to the post for support.

Something tells me I need to go talk to her.

Before we get separated by the wave of people shuffling to the bar to refill their drinks, I dart across the carpet, then slow as I make my approach, worried she could leave at any moment. I give her a small wave before I say anything. She looks at me curiously, like she's trying to place me, and smiles weakly.

"Oh—you don't know me!" I blurt out. "I was just coming to say hello, because we were both, um, standing alone."

"Oh. Hello."

"I'm Eva."

"I'm—"

"Connie FREAKING Abbott!" Betty sidesteps her way through the crowd, waving her arms in the air. She looks ridiculous, and the gray-haired woman—who must be *that* Connie Abbott, oh my god—looks tremendously uncomfortable. I lunge backward to let Betty through and watch as they reunite, these two women who survived the shelter experiment together. Betty wraps Connie in a hug, but Connie stands there motionless, stiff as the wooden post. Betty seems to realize she isn't being hugged back, so she drops her arms and pretends to adjust her sweater.

As Bobby joins them, I take another step back—close enough that I can still hear their conversation, but far enough that they won't realize I'm eavesdropping. I lean against a high top and act like I'm super engrossed in something on my phone.

"It's been ages," Bobby says. "We haven't seen you since . . . when? Jeez, has it been since our wedding?"

"I think so," Connie answers.

"Well, how are you?" Betty asks, her voice higher-pitched than when we talked before. "Are you married? Kids? Grandkids? Where are you living these days?"

"I'm married with a daughter and two grandkids. I was a

290

costume designer in Manhattan for a long time, but now my husband and I are retired and living up in Maine."

"A costume designer!" Betty claps. "You were always so good at that. I remember you working backstage with that old lady who screamed at everyone."

"And Maine is beautiful," Bobby adds. "How'd you get here? Did you fly?"

"Drove," Connie replies.

"Wow, that's gotta be, what? Five hours?"

"Seven."

"Jeez."

"Speaking of driving," Betty says, "did you hear about Steve? I don't know what Hardwick news makes its way up to Maine."

"Steve O'Leary? No," Connie says.

"Oh." Betty seems to pause for dramatic effect. "He passed away in a car accident a couple of years ago, on his way home from the bar. It was winter—this kind of weather—and he skidded off the road and hit a tree. It was so sad—and his poor wife. Did you know he married Kathleen Whitby from when we were—"

"My god, is that *Connie Abbott?*"

I look up from my phone to see Dean Allenby striding over to the awkward threesome, and Connie shrinking farther into her coat like a turtle retreating into its shell.

"Hello, Craig." Her voice wavers.

I keep watching as Allenby claps a hand onto Connie's

shoulder, the force making her knees wobble. "What a treat it is to see you again! I didn't think it would happen. You look great, Connie. Really great."

"Thanks."

"Well, thank *you*, for coming all this way to support me. It means a heck of a lot."

Then I realize Connie's legs are still shaking. She wriggles out from Allenby's grip, tucks her hair behind her ears, and says, "I'm going to grab a drink. Would anyone like anything?"

Allenby drains the rest of his glass. "I'll take another champagne, please."

Connie nods and shuffles toward the bar, walking past me on her way. She's biting her bottom lip so hard that the skin is turning white. I give it a second, so it doesn't look like I'm following her, and then I do exactly that. I wander over to the bar and stand about two feet away from her, my chest against the ledge and my back to the rest of the room. She doesn't seem to realize I'm there; she's searching her wallet for small bills to leave the bartender, but her trembling fingers are making it difficult. She lets out a long, low sigh.

"Connie!" Allenby calls from across the room. She gasps and looks over her shoulder. "Make sure he gives me the Veuve and not the Moët? Thanks so much."

She nods, turns back around, and quietly mutters, *"Ass-hole."*

My respect for Connie soars to the moon.

The bartender brings her a flute of champagne. "I'm so

sorry," she says, twirling the stem of the glass, "but what kind of champagne is this?"

"It's the Moët."

"Perfect."

"And you also wanted . . ."

"A glass of the Malbec, please."

"That'll be just a minute." He nods and disappears.

Connie twirls the champagne flute, and I take a deep breath. I check to make sure there's no one in hearing range, and then I slide another foot toward her. There's no turning back once I show her my cards, but I feel like I'm safe; she just called Allenby an asshole.

I clear my throat. "Connie?"

She jumps. "Oh, hello. I'm so sorry. Your name was . . ."

"Eva." I keep my eyes on the shelves of liquor behind the bar, so it doesn't look like we're talking to each other. I need to get to my point quickly, because that bartender could be back at any moment. "I want to talk to you. I know about the fallout shelter."

Silence.

"I know something bad happened, and I know Allenby's covering it up."

Silence.

Silence.

Silence.

And then, finally, "How do you know about that?" she whispers, her voice laced with fear.

I shift even closer and drop my voice as low as it'll go. "Because my best friend at Hardwick is related to Helen Honeyman, and we've been trying to find out what really happened to her. We found the shelter, but my friend got caught, and Allenby expelled him."

"No."

"Yes."

"You're telling me he's punishing Helen's family?"

"*Yes.*"

"I am going to scream."

I was right. Connie's on my side. But now what? The bartender reemerges with the glass of red wine. He sets it down in front of Connie, and Connie hands him a generous tip. As he walks away, she whispers, "Meet me in the bathroom in five minutes." Then she picks up the glasses and shuffles back over to the group.

I go straight down the steps and follow the signs to the bathroom. It's one of those fancy restrooms with a plush seating area, so I lower myself onto an ottoman to wait for Connie. I fire off an email to Erik, even though he won't get it until he's back at school on Monday. I send a text to Luisa. Then I fidget with my scarf, my eyes glued to the door.

It bursts open. Heather struts in. The absolute last person I want to see right now, other than Allenby himself. She frowns. "What are you doing in here?"

Oh no. It *does* look weird that I'm perched on an ottoman alone, and not doing my makeup or anything. "Um, my mom needed to call me about something." I roll my eyes for added effect. Heather cocks a slender blond eyebrow, then proceeds toward the stalls. What am I supposed to do now? I have to follow through on my lie. Thinking fast, I go to the phone menu where you can test different ringtones and press one at random. Then I hold the phone to my ear and start up a conversation with no one.

"Hey, Mom . . . I'm good, how are you? What did you want to talk about? . . . Oh jeez, really? Caleb has the flu?"

The door opens again, and this time, it's Connie. She opens her mouth to speak, but I shake my head furiously and jab my finger at the stalls. Meanwhile, I have to keep up my fake conversation. "Oh jeez, Mom. It's never good when it's coming out both ends . . . Well, I'm sure you guys will go to Miami some other time . . ."

The toilet flushes, and Connie seems to understand the panicked look on my face. She lowers herself onto the couch opposite me and busies herself sorting through her purse. Meanwhile, Heather washes and dries her hands, smooths down the sides of her bob, and then—thank god—makes for the door. When she passes me, she mouths, *I'll see you out there.* I give her a thumbs-up, point to the phone, and roll my eyes one more time.

As soon as the door closes behind her, I put down my phone and sigh with relief. Connie procures a sewing kit from her bag and points to the end of my Hardwick scarf. "I can fix that for you."

I look down. In my panic about Heather, I didn't even

realize I pulled a loose string that made the whole hem fall apart. "Oh, thanks. That would be great."

She opens the case and threads a needle. Her fingers are no longer trembling like they were in the other room. She examines the edge of the scarf, and then in one swift movement, plunges the needle into the fabric. "I'm glad you found me," she says. "If you hadn't told me about your friend, I might have lost my nerve to go through with it."

"To go through with what?"

She looks up from her task, and the two of us lock eyes. "Eva," she says, "what happened in the fallout shelter is the reason I'm here."

TWENTY-ONE

Eva

"Well? Are you ready to do this?"

In the silvery morning sunlight, Connie jams her hands into her pockets and stamps her boots on the snowy pavement. "I think so. Maybe. I don't know."

It's strange to see a woman in her seventies so nervous to speak to another adult. I'm fired up with energy, ready to take on the world, but her body language is telling an opposite story. This isn't going to work. We need to be pillars of strength if we're going to pull this off.

I point to a bench at the edge of the parking lot, on the fringe of the trees. "Do you want to go sit down for a minute?"

She nods.

We crunch through the snow and sit side by side on the cold wooden planks, near where Heather passed me a candle and welcomed me to the Fives. It snowed again overnight, sprinkling a fresh coat of powder over the campus. Across the road, an energetic senior walking backward steers a group of alumni around the quad, her bubbly voice audible but too far away to make out the words.

"This is what I told you about." Connie sighs and stares at her feet. "He has this weird power over me. It used to be that I wanted to impress him, but now it's that I'm terrified to speak up against him." She puts her face in her hands. "It happened in 1962."

"Connie, look at me." She looks at me. Her eyes are sad, and the corners of her mouth are wilting. "I get why it's scary. I was sucked under their spell, too. But remember how you felt last night, when I told you about Erik. And remember how you felt when you heard about his lifetime-*freaking*-achievement award. You drove seven hours by yourself for a reason."

"I know." She shakes her head and gazes in the direction of the administration building. "I couldn't stay silent anymore. I just couldn't. I saw the tweet and I'm telling you: I went out the back door, found the biggest rock I could, and hurled it into the ocean."

I press the heels of my palms into my knees. Now that I know the whole story—Andy Kraus, the New Americans, the clubhouse-turned-jail that collapsed onto Helen—my drive is even stronger to bring this whole cover-up crashing to the ground. I am not the girl who jumped off a cliff in the dark; I am Xena the freaking Warrior Princess, swinging my sword and taking no prisoners. I am going to end this cycle so no one else goes down for resisting Craig Allenby. "I've been dying to expose him, but I can't do it without you," I tell Connie. "He'll just expel me, and then if I try to go public, he'll say I'm lying. You know it's true. I need you as a firsthand witness."

"It's true," Connie admits. "It's true."

"He's having open office hours for the next hour. It's the only time we're going to get him on his own." I cross my arms. "And if we don't do it this weekend, think of how smug he's going to be when he accepts his award tomorrow."

A cold gust of wind sends loose powder swirling around us, but Connie doesn't seem to feel it. She narrows her eyes. "Craig won head boy by a landslide after the shelter. I *know* what that smug face looks like, and I don't want to see it again." She makes two fists and gets to her feet. "Come on. Let's do this before I chicken out."

I leap to my feet and follow her through the snow, our boots leaving a trail of deep footprints. Together we march toward Allenby's office, ready to free the secrets buried beneath it.

"Is your technology ready to go?"

I tap my screen and show Connie the Voice Memos app. "I'll hit the record button as soon as we go in."

"You think it'll pick everything up?"

"It should. I'll keep my phone in my hand the whole time."

She nods and leads the way into the administration building. Up ahead on the right, a middle-aged couple stands in the dean's doorway, trapped in one of those long goodbyes. There's no one else waiting on the bench outside, which means Connie and I can go in next. We pause just inside the front door, out of the couple's earshot.

"Oh my," she says softly, her eyes darting around the main hallway. "This place hasn't changed a bit. I remember it as if it were yesterday, following that *fool* down those stairs over there."

"I forgot to ask you what happened to him—to Mr. Kraus."

"Well, I told you he was able to persuade that lazy detective assigned to the case that the whole thing was an accident, right?"

"Yeah. Sounds like he was good at persuading people."

"After that, he resigned and went to work for his father or something. All the kids were crushed, and I remember *hating* that I couldn't tell anyone the real story. I think Helen was the only one, besides me, who knew he was bad from the start."

"How did you know?" I whisper.

"Hmm." She rubs her chin. "He was always sort of a show-off, but I think it was something more than that."

The couple waves and says goodbye, loudly this time.

"I think," Connie says, "it was the way everyone fed off his approval. I saw how my friends became totally different people when they were around him. You know, I've come to realize, the best people in life . . . you don't have to worry about whether they like you or not."

Just like that, I see the people and places in my life laid out on a hand-drawn map. On one side with dark caves and gnarled trees, there's Mom and Caleb, the Fives, Dean Allenby; on the other side, an orange glen at golden hour, there's Erik, Luisa, cross-country, D&D. There's maybe even room for Ella, if we can find a way to carve out our own relationship. While

I was at the Fives party last night, she actually tried to Face-Time me—which rarely happens—but by the time I noticed her missed call, it was too late to try her back. I'm going to find time to do that in the next few days.

"You don't have to worry about whether they like you or not," I repeat. "You just know."

"Yes. You just know."

Allenby's visitors finally make their exit, happily chatting about lunch options as they weave around us in the hall. I follow Connie toward his office. I see her shoulders rise and fall with one last deep breath before she raises her fist and raps on his doorframe. "Is that Connie Abbott?" he asks in a booming voice. She takes a step into the room. I slide in after her, but first, I hit the record button.

"And Eva Storm?" Allenby looks surprised to see me. His grin flickers for a second before returning to full wattage. He leans back in his desk chair and folds his hands behind his head. "This is interesting. Did the two of you meet last night?"

"We did," Connie says.

There's an awkward pause in which Connie and I teeter on the edge of Allenby's carpet. Then he waves his hand at us. "Come in! Please. Grab seats. Is this your first time in my office? Ms. Storm, you must have been here before, right?"

My stomach flip-flops, but he can't have meant that seriously. He doesn't know I was in here with Erik on the day my friend got expelled.

Her face calm, Connie shuts the wooden door with a creak.

"Oh, I should leave it open in case other folks come by," Allenby says. "You don't have to close it."

"Actually, we do," Connie says.

Allenby's grin flickers again. This time, the final product looks forced; it doesn't meet his eyes. He unclasps his hands and folds them on top of his desk instead. "Everything okay, ladies?"

I follow Connie's lead and take a seat in one of the two wooden chairs facing Allenby. "No," she says, "it is not."

I guess we're getting straight to the point.

"C-Craig," she continues, shaking off her slight stutter, "I know what you've been up to. You've been unfairly punishing and rewarding students so you can protect Hardwick and keep what happened down there a secret, and it needs to end." She lays her palm on the surface of his desk and leans forward. "You need to tell the truth already, and let Eva's friend come back to school. It's gone too far."

Allenby crosses his arms and leans back again. Now his face is expressionless, but obviously, whatever's coming isn't *good*. "I don't know what you're talking about."

His words have no inflection.

Connie's nostrils flare like a dragon about to breathe fire. "Fine then. I suppose I'll remind you." She straightens her posture and tucks her hair behind her ears, and I know this is the speech she's been waiting to make for who knows how long: years, or even decades. "In the spring of 1962, a twenty-four-year-old who wanted to be a famous researcher like Stanley

Milgram ran an incredibly ill-conceived psychological experiment on us. He wanted to see how easily he could make us loyal to some stupid cause in the face of mortal peril, and guess what? We all fell for it, except for Helen. She didn't die in whatever accident Mr. Kraus made up; she died because we were weak and easy to control and terrified of going against the group. That's the truth you've been hiding all this time, and it makes me sick to my stomach to see you with your secret society of spies, expelling people left and right. You're using the exact same tactics he used on us. The same *fucking* tactics that made us kill her, Craig!"

"Now, that's enough!" Allenby slams his palm on the desk, rattling his cup of Hardwick pens. "I don't want to hear it."

"Because I'm wrong?" she fires back. "Or because I'm a hundred percent right, and you're ashamed to admit it?"

Allenby clenches his jaw and squints his eyes. A muscle twitches in his jaw.

"Order, unity, power," she says. "It's a weapon, and you're still using it. Admit it."

"I—"

"Admit it, Craig!"

"Fine!" he screams. "Fine. But for the record, we were following orders. We did what we had to do."

Connie must have used up all her firepower. She slumps forward, puts her face in her hands, and sobs. I glance at my lap to make sure the Voice Memo app's still working; I want to have a record, just in case he tries to pretend the conversation never happened. I stealthily tap the screen, and I'm relieved to see the timer ticking away, the red sound wave rolling along.

It's almost as if my phone knows I'm staring at it. It rings with one of those annoying "potential spam" calls, which I immediately decline before looking up again.

Connie lifts herself up and wipes her eyes with the back of her hand. She sniffs and blinks a couple of times. "You'll take responsibility, then? You'll tell the truth about what happened and end all this Fives nonsense?" She looks hopeful, the way she shifts to the edge of her seat. "Please, Craig." She touches the desk. "I know how much Hardwick has always meant to you, but this is wrong. Let's make it right, even if we're way too late."

"I'm afraid you misunderstood," Allenby says, and Connie retracts her hand. "I admitted your version of events was accurate." He drums his fingers on the desktop. "But you can't possibly think I would go and make that public. Do you know how bad that would look for Hardwick? Do you know how bad it would look for *us*?"

Connie's face falls. "Are you serious?"

"Of course I'm serious, Connie. I care about you."

"Oh, really?"

"Yes! I do."

"Like you cared about Helen?"

"Stop this nonsense," he says dismissively. "You should be thanking me. You know what this school means to me, and it's a dream I've been able to spend my life here, but at times I've barely been able to enjoy it because I've been so busy guarding this secret—making sure no one knew what happened in that basement—so you four could live your normal lives in peace."

"You think any of us have lived in peace since that experiment?" Exasperated, she waves a hand out to the side. "Look at Steve."

"Don't you blame me for his drinking."

"I'm not. I'm just saying you haven't done us some great favor. We should have told the truth from the start."

He mutters something under his breath that sounds a lot like "ungrateful bitch."

Shaking with defiance, I stand up. "Connie, let's go. It doesn't matter what he says now. We can just go public." *We got the confession.*

Connie stands up, too. I watch Allenby, waiting for his reaction, but it's not what I expected.

Looking strangely calm for someone who recently made a pretty serious confession, the dean raises his pointer finger. He might as well be checking the direction of the wind. "Wait just one moment, ladies." There's a touch of syrup in his voice, which makes my alarm bells go off. "Before you go off and tell whomever you plan to tell, there's something I think you'll want to know. You in particular, Ms. Storm."

Huh? What could he possibly be talking about? I look at Connie, whose eyes are wide and still puffy at the same time. She doesn't move; she seems to be waiting on me to make the call. I give myself a millisecond to think about it. If I'm going to take on the dean, I can't go in blind. I want to know every bit of what I'm up against. I drag the chair toward me and take my seat again. Connie does the same.

On the other side of the desk, sitting like a king on his throne, Allenby strokes his chin and surveys me. "You say it doesn't matter what I do now, because I already confessed," he muses. "Well, I say it *does* matter quite a bit, because it just so happens, Ms. Storm, that I have something to show you."

He types something on his keyboard and clicks around on his screen. My face getting hotter, I stare at his thumb resting on the side of his mouse. I won't let him see me panic. I will channel all my hatred into the one cuticle at the base of his otherwise manicured nail.

"Ah," he says, "here it is." He spins the monitor around so we both can see the grainy gray-and-white image blown up on the screen. It looks like security camera footage from—oh no. Bad, bad, bad. Please make it go away.

"This footage is from the hallway outside my office," Allenby boasts.

Hearing him state the obvious makes it even worse. Like getting slapped in the face and then punched in the stomach. The blood starts to drain from my head, the same as it did when Erik and I heard Allenby's angry voice from the base of the stairs.

"After I caught Erik Ellis trespassing in the basement," Allenby says, "I put a request in for the building security footage, just to see if he'd *really* acted alone, like he said. Our security company was in the midst of changing owners, and it took forever to process the order, but the tape finally came in this morning."

He hits the space bar to make it play, not that I needed the visual to know what was coming. Feeling light-headed, I watch from above as a lanky boy and curly-haired girl enter the hall. They—we—disappear past the bottom edge of the screen for a while, then reappear and enter Allenby's office. Shortly after, we slip out the door and race toward the stairs.

"It's obviously you," Allenby says, rewinding the video and pausing at a frame where my face is clearly visible.

"What is this?" asks Connie.

"It was the day we found the shelter," I tell her. There's no point in denying it. "At least this proves I've been down there. I've seen your names scratched into the wall, and the words 'Order,' 'Unity,' and 'Power.' I've even seen her blood. It stained the floor." Which reminds me—I turn back to Allenby. "We took photos," I inform him. "Loads of them. I know you've kept people from going down there on purpose, but we have proof of what's inside."

"Well, I can promise that if you ever think about sharing any of them, I'll make sure you go the same way as your friend Mr. Ellis," he fires back. "And if that doesn't sound so bad, I'd like to remind you I know a lot of people in academia, and I have sway at most halfway decent colleges in the country. I also have generations of Fives in very high places in every industry you could imagine, all of whom owe me favors, no questions asked."

The meaning of his threat sinks in like icy water. If we go public, he wouldn't just expel me from Hardwick; he'd try to prevent me from succeeding for the rest of my life.

Connie balks at him. "Craig . . ."

"I'm sorry, Connie, but it's what I have to do!" He smacks the table again, and we both jump. A vein pulses right above his temple, his head turning redder by the second. "Try to see it from my perspective for just one second," Allenby pleads. "It would become a huge story. We would be in full crisis mode. Alumni would pull their donations. Enrollment would drop. I can't let that happen to Hardwick. Not to mention the authorities would likely get involved, and no one wants that."

"No, Craig, *you* don't want that," Connie says. "Because you know you're responsible!"

"Maybe you've forgotten you were there, too. Who's to say *you* didn't put her in that clubhouse?"

A wave of horror passes over Connie's face.

"And you know Betty and Bobby will back up anything I say," he adds.

"Why are you doing this?" she pleads. "I don't understand. Why don't you feel the guilt I've been living with for the past sixty years?"

Allenby pauses for a beat, and when he speaks again, his voice is softer and more intense at the same time. "It's simple," he says. "This school is everything to me. You guys all had your nice, perfect families and whatnot, but I had Hardwick. It was home."

Each of us looks back and forth between the other two people, waiting for someone else to make the next move. At least ten seconds go by, Allenby's heavy breathing the only sound in the room. I'm all out of ammo; I guess we all are. I make eye contact with Connie, and we both stand up to leave at the same time.

In the vestibule between the two sets of front doors, I go to hit the end button on the recording app—and my breathing stops.

"Connie." My throat feels strangled. "Connie, it isn't running anymore. It was recording earlier, but now it's not."

"What?" She puts her hand on my back and we both look helplessly down at the phone. "When did it stop?"

I look over my shoulder to make sure Allenby's still in his office, and then I press play on the saved recording and fast-forward until the very end. A tinny version of Connie's voice echoes around the small space; it's when she's making her big speech about what really happened in the shelter. Then Allenby admits it's all true—thank god we got that, at least—and the recording abruptly ends.

"I got a spam call," I suddenly remember. My stomach is somewhere around my feet. "I declined it, but it must have shut off the recording."

Connie moves her hand in circles on my back. "At least we got his confession."

"But we didn't get the part where he threatened us," I groan. "Oh god, I'm so sorry, Connie. I didn't know."

"Hey. *Hey.* Come on. Let's get something to eat and figure this out."

We drift out of the building like empty husks of humans. The sun is gone, covered by clouds; now everything looks gray. As my mind tries to process everything that just happened, I numbly follow Connie back across campus to her car. I feel confused, battle-weary; frustrated to be locked in a stalemate with Dean Allenby, especially knowing our position would have been stronger if my recording app hadn't shut off.

As I mull it over, a phrase returns to me from one of the Netflix Cold War documentaries I watched. As America and the Soviet Union built up their nuclear arsenals, both were scared to attack because of how the other might respond. The same general principle applies now: if we go public, Allenby will expel me, get me blacklisted at a bunch of colleges, and try to frame Connie for Helen's death—and vice versa.

"You know what this is?" I mumble.

"What?" she asks.

"It's mutually assured destruction."

TWENTY-TWO

Eva

We drive in silence, my thoughts racing. Connie drives with
her shoulders hunched up to her ears. The reality of what we're
up against gets heavier with each passing second, and by the
time we pull up in front of a pea-sized diner called Matilda's,
I feel like I'm lugging around a sixteen-pound bowling ball in
my stomach.

Connie must feel a gazillion times worse. She finally
divulged the painful secret she'd been carrying around her
whole life, only to have Dean Allenby squash it like a fly.

The diner has floral wallpaper and framed needlepoints of
kittens and sunflowers. A bubbly waitress says, "Morning, y'all!
Welcome to Matilda's!" and seats us by a window with lacy
pink curtains. The vibe is so *off* compared to how I'm feeling right now that I actually burst out laughing as soon as the
woman leaves us with our laminated menus—either that, or
I'm slowly unraveling at the seams. Whatever the case, Connie
starts laughing, too, and eventually we both have to hold our

menus over our faces to avoid the glances from people at neighboring tables. When the waitress returns to take our orders, Connie and I are wiping tears from our eyes.

"You two look like you're having fun," she says brightly.

"Nothing like a good cathartic laugh-cry," I reply.

As we eat our pancakes, I ask Connie about her life since Hardwick; I think we both need to give our brains a break before we make our way back to discussing Dean Allenby. She tells me how she went to Barnard College to get a liberal arts degree, and it was there she met her husband, Arthur, a shy biology student at Columbia. At Barnard, she got a job sewing costumes for the theater department, and one day, a professor introduced her to a friend who did costume work on Broadway. The friend offered Connie an apprenticeship, and that's how she began her career as a New York City costume designer.

"I loved my job," she says. "But part of the reason I wanted to sew all the time was that it forced me to focus on the present moment. My thoughts couldn't stray to the things that made me feel scared or guilty."

"Did you ever tell anyone about the shelter?"

"No one."

"Not even Arthur?"

She shakes her head. "Not until the other week, when I decided to drive out here. I worked out this plan that I would come and confront Allenby on my own—or even with one of the others, if they were willing to join me. You should have seen Arthur's face. He just couldn't believe it—he was stunned.

And I still haven't told my daughter, Julie. I kept the whole thing locked away; I was always too scared to break my promise to Craig. I think in my head, I told myself, *if you ever speak out, you'll end up like Helen.*"

I swallow my last bite of pancake and set down my fork. It's time to figure out what our next move is—if anything. "I just *hate* that he has so much power over us," I say.

"I do too," she replies wistfully. "I've spent the past sixty years carrying around a secret, even with my own family. On the day I got married . . . the day Julie was born . . . the day *Julie* got married . . . it was still there. Eating at me. Which is why I almost lost it when Craig said I should thank him! Can you imagine?"

"Then we have to do something," I say matter-of-factly. "We can't back down."

"I don't want to back down." She picks up her paper napkin and crumples it into a ball. "I . . . I think *I'm* ready to navigate whatever he tries to throw at me." She passes the wad of paper back and forth from hand to hand. "But you . . . you're still so young, Eva. Your whole education is on the line. I don't want to force you to risk it . . ."

At some point while we were eating, the clouds shifted to make room for the sun again. Now a mottled beam of light shines through the lacy curtains onto our table. The waitress circles back to take our plates, and then I lean forward on my elbows, my fingers pressed against my temples. I've thought about it enough, and I feel like I finally have clarity on what we need to do. "Helen *died* because she resisted," I point out. "No matter what he tries to pull, we have a whole lot less to lose. We have no excuse."

"You mean you want to keep fighting?" Connie asks.

"Yes. Absolutely."

She smiles in a way that looks like she's holding back tears. "So do I."

"Good. And I think I have an idea." Connie raises her eyebrows, and we both lean in to the center of the table. I bite my lip, and then I say, "We need to go back to campus and talk to my friend Luisa."

TWENTY-THREE

Eva

My body feels like one giant pounding heart as Connie and I join the mass of people filing into the arts building on Sunday afternoon. I can feel my own pulse in my face, my chest, my stomach, my knees.

"How are you not almost throwing up right now?" I whisper to Connie, who seems to be walking easily with her chin held high. Her posture has changed dramatically since the first time I saw her on Friday night, when she was pulling her coat around herself like a shell. Now she might as well be walking into the arts building to accept her *own* award.

"I woke up feeling so clear about everything," she says. "As soon as we had a plan, it was as if a great big weight was lifted."

In the lobby, there's confusion about which way people are supposed to go. To make room for the returning alumni in the first handful of rows, the ninth through twelfth graders are being sent up to the mezzanine—courtesy of Ms. Pell, who's standing on a chair, barking and waving her arms around like an air traffic controller.

"It looks like we have to split up," I say.

Connie squeezes my shoulder. "It's going to be okay. I'm completely ready."

"I—I think I'm ready," I stammer.

"And Luisa, she's ready?"

I nod. For the first time in her Hardwick career, Luisa spent a Saturday night *not* doing homework. Instead, she and I were sharing my desk chair and passing my laptop back and forth, assembling all the materials and figuring out the logistics of how the plan would actually work. At the end of the night— bleary-eyed with exhaustion and surrounded by a graveyard of silver Hershey's Kisses wrappers—we dragged everything onto a thumb drive, which Luisa happily slipped into an inside pocket of her backpack. "I'm doing this for Erik, and for all the kids who actually work their asses off," she murmured before hugging me goodbye and heading two floors down to her room.

I walk up the stairs alone in the middle of a crowd, but I know I have Connie down below and Luisa up in the booth, both of them on my side. And I have Erik, at home in New Jersey, who's going to fall off his damn chair when he checks his school email tomorrow.

Stepping out into the second level of the crowded auditorium makes me go dizzy for a second, so I sink into the nearest empty aisle seat. The buzzing of hundreds of voices takes me back to middle school, when they still forced us to be in the school plays, and you could hear the chatter on the other side of the curtains growing louder and louder as the seats filled up with parents. Eventually the curtains flew open, and you were totally blinded by the lights, but you had no choice but to press on.

I crane my neck and find Connie in the center of the second row. There's no turning back now. We have to press on.

"Hey."

I flinch with surprise when Simon Banbury materializes at my side. Smiling politely like we don't really know each other— like he didn't just introduce me to his mom on Friday—I stand up so he can squeeze past and plop into the seat next to me. I wonder if Allenby told the other Fives about my transgressions. But no—how could he have? That would mean telling them the full story of the shelter they're not allowed to talk about, and there's no way he'd ever do that. What if more of them turned against him when they found out the full dark truth behind their Wall Street internships? I scan the mezzanine for other Fives: Jackson tugs on the braid of the girl in front of him, then cackles as she turns around and swats his hand away; Jenny slouches with her elbow up on the back of her chair, her other hand scrolling on her phone, even though we're not supposed to have them out in here; Heather smiles coolly at something a friend just whispered in her ear.

They won't believe what's about to happen.

The lights dim, and a hush falls over the auditorium as the headmaster, head girl, and head boy stride onto the stage and take their places at three of the four folding chairs set up behind the podium, and underneath the horrible "HARDWICK HERO" banner.

The headmaster, Mrs. Suresh, steps up to the microphone and smiles warmly at the crowd. I haven't had much interaction with her outside of her announcements at assembly, but my impression is that she's calm and in control at all times. "Good morning, students, faculty, and members of the Hardwick Preparatory Academy community," she says. "And a special welcome to our returning alumni. Thank you for being brave enough to experience *another* Hardwick winter after you thought you were out of here for good."

There's polite laughter.

Mrs. Suresh continues, "We're here today to honor a man who's dedicated his life to making Hardwick a better place for students. And I can say personally that when I joined Hardwick last year, he made me feel very welcome and helped make the transition as smooth as possible. So please join me in welcoming to the stage the recipient of a Hardwick Lifetime Achievement Award, Dean of Students Craig Allenby!"

A round of applause breaks out as Allenby, waving, half jogs onto the stage like a celebrity on a late-night show. He shakes hands with the three people onstage, grinning from ear to ear.

Mrs. Suresh goes back to the microphone. "I've invited our head girl and head boy, Stacey Evans and Joseph Okoro, to each say a few words on behalf of the student body. Then we have a wonderful video presentation from our friends in the A/V Club, which I'm told features some *excellent* old photos of your dean of students. Don't worry, Craig—I'm sure you haven't aged a day."

Allenby throws back his head with laughter.

"Stacey," says Mrs. Suresh, "would you like to get us started?"

I barely hear a word of Stacey's and Joseph's speeches, which are each a few minutes long and punctuated by bursts of laughter. All I can do is stare at my watch, the tiny silver second hand ticking closer and closer to showtime.

Eventually, Joseph is thanking the crowd and accepting another hearty handshake from Allenby.

Then, with a smooth mechanical whir, the projector screen descends from the ceiling. I catch sight of the back of Connie's head one last time before the footage starts to play.

The presentation opens as initially planned. There's an old-fashioned movie countdown—six, five, four, three, two, one—and then a title that says: "Our Hardwick Hero Through the Ages."

"Yesterday" by the Beatles starts to play.

The slideshow begins with black-and-white photos from Allenby's earliest days at the school. There are *awww*s from the audience as his younger face flashes across the screen, and muffled laughs at some of the wacky sixties hairstyles. Any second now . . .

The music abruptly cuts out, and the photos go away.

319

A few people twist in their seats and look up at the booth, as though maybe there's a technical difficulty. Clearly, they don't know Luisa Luna very well.

Then the new words appear on the screen—the ones Luisa and I typed on my laptop last night: "Do You Really Know Your Hardwick Hero?"

"Yesterday" starts to play again from the beginning, but it's a hell of a lot eerier as it becomes the backdrop to the story I typed on the next slide: "In 1962, Hardwick sent a small group of students underground to test a nuclear fallout shelter. Six went down, but only five survived . . ."

The audience is abuzz. There's a crash onstage, and I can just detect the outline of Allenby knocking his chair over as he leaps to his feet in a panic. He starts to scream, but his voice is immediately drowned out by the audio that blares from the speakers: the portion of our meeting with Allenby I *did* manage to record.

"In the spring of 1962, a twenty-four-year-old who wanted to be a famous researcher like Stanley Milgram ran an incredibly ill-conceived psychological experiment on us," Connie's voice booms. "He wanted to see how easily he could make us loyal to some stupid cause in the face of mortal peril, and guess what? We all fell for it, except for Helen. She didn't die in whatever accident Mr. Kraus made up; she died because we were weak and easy to control and terrified of going against the group. That's the truth you've been hiding all this time, and it makes me sick to my stomach to see you with your secret

320

society of spies, expelling people left and right. You're using the exact same tactics he used on us. The same fucking tactics that made us kill her, Craig!"

As her voice echoes around the space, a series of incriminating images appears on the screen. Photos of the door of the fallout shelter; the names scratched into the wall; the words order, unity, and power carved beneath them; the bloodstain on the floor. Photos of my golden Fives ring; my Fivesgiving invitation; the set of rules I received when I passed my first initiation.

From what I can see of the stage, Allenby is in total panic mode. He's on the verge of injuring himself as he jumps up and down trying to grasp the projector screen, which is still a solid three feet out of his reach. Mrs. Suresh, Stacey, and Joseph stand off to the side, frozen. The mezzanine's too dark for me to find the other Fives, but when I steal a glance to my right, Simon is staring straight ahead, his eyes wide and his lips slightly parted.

Then, in what can only be a stroke of Luisa's genius, the lights come up on a disheveled Allenby panting center stage— right as his own voice erupts from the speakers:

"Fine. But for the record, we were following orders. We did what we had to do."

The final deadly blow.

Allenby shields his eyes. While hundreds of people stare at him, whispering, the dean of students opens and closes his mouth like a goldfish. He wasn't expecting this: neither the rigged presentation—obviously—nor the fact that Connie and I would keep fighting.

The hand that was covering his eyes clenches into a fist, and his face turns a dangerous shade of red. "It's all lies!" he yells at the crowd. "Who did this? I demand to know who did this!"

He's faking. He has to be.

"YOU KNOW WHO DID THIS!"

Connie's voice explodes into the room—not from the speakers this time, but from the middle of the second row. Everyone gasps and stares as she jabs her finger at Allenby. "It was you. You did all of it."

"Ridiculous." He looks frantically at Mrs. Suresh, whose hand is pressed to her chest. "You can't possibly believe this, Nadia. I—it's all nonsense." He's sputtering now. "I—I don't even know who this woman is."

"You know exactly who I am!" Connie fires back. "My name is carved on that wall, too! I saw everything you did in that shelter, and I know how you've covered it up!"

"I haven't covered up a damn thing!"

"You *have*—and you *admitted* it! Everyone just heard the tape, Craig, so you can give up the act!"

"The person on that tape wasn't me," he growls.

"It *was* you!"

"Prove it."

I've been waiting for the right time to jump in. It has to be now. Connie's in need of reinforcements. Gripping my armrests, I vault myself to standing and scream down from the balcony.

322

"IT *WAS* YOU, AND I *KNOW* IT WAS YOU BECAUSE I WAS THERE, AND I RECORDED IT!"

Another round of gasps. Now everyone's eyes are on me.

I notice Heather a few rows down; her expression isn't the murderous death stare I expected, but rather a mingling of shock and concern that softens her whole face. She must not have known the reason we couldn't talk about the shelter. She probably never asked. The perks of being a Five were too appealing to put them in jeopardy.

Before a furious-looking Allenby has a chance to respond, Mrs. Suresh puts one hand on his back, the other on his shoulder, and shepherds him into the wings, out of sight. A few seconds later, she marches back to the podium and tells everyone to leave the auditorium in an orderly fashion.

I sink into my seat, trembling, as everyone else stands. It's over. It went exactly according to plan. I know I should feel proud, and I do, but I'm also shaking under the weight of what we just pulled off.

"Hey," says Simon, resting a hand on my shoulder. He's the only other person who hasn't gotten up to leave. "That was . . . amazing."

"Really?" I'm surprised. "I thought you were going to be sad. You love the Fives more than anyone on earth."

"Not if that horrible story is the reason we exist! Thanks, but no thanks."

"Wow. Who knew Simon Banbury could be converted so easily?"

"Well . . ." He bites his upper lip. "Let's just say those two initiations did part of the job. Especially the second one."

I roll my eyes at the memory of us crawling around on our hands and knees in the woods. "God. Why the hell did we *do* that?"

Simon shrugs. "No clue."

TWENTY-FOUR

Eva

There's nowhere to hide in the one-room Amtrak station in Rome, New York. The old-fashioned wooden benches are packed with Hardwick kids heading home for spring break—kids who keep not-so-subtly dipping out of their conversations to peer at the girl at the top of the stairs leading up to the platform. I thought it was a smart move to wait for the train up here, out of the fray, but I think I actually made myself even more noticeable. All anyone has to do is look up to find the girl who dropped a bomb on Allenby's award ceremony and turned the campus into a crime scene.

When the award ceremony ended, I had no idea what would happen next. Part of me worried Mrs. Suresh would take Allenby's side, since she was relatively new and might not want a scandal on her hands. Instead, Connie, Luisa, and I stood outside the arts building long enough to see the headmaster practically frog-march the dean of students out the door and

325

across the quad, her eyes focused like laser beams on the administration building off in the distance.

Mrs. Suresh ended up calling the police, and by Monday, it looked like they were filming an episode of *Law & Order* around the fallout shelter. Walking to the dining hall after math class, Luisa and I spotted a parked police van that said Crime Scene Unit, and nearby, two stern-looking women in trench coats who could only be detectives. At dinner that night, Candace—who couldn't wait to cover the story for the *Hardwick Herald*—said she'd seen officers leaving the administration building carrying brown paper bags marked "Evidence."

I wondered what remained of the Fives, or if they'd even continue to exist in the future. Needless to say, I was pretty sure I'd already been stricken from the group chat. Not far away from our table in the dining hall, Heather, Alyson, Jackson, and Jenny were sitting with their heads together. I tried not to notice them peering in my direction every few minutes, but eventually it got so distracting that I stood up, smiled, and gave them a big wave. Heather scowled and turned back to her salad.

When I went to clear my dishes, it happened to just be me and Jenny in the alcove with the conveyor belt that leads to the kitchen. I could see her eyes calculating if there was enough room to squeeze by and not say anything.

There wasn't.

"Hey, Jenny."

"Oh. Hey."

"Uh, should we talk?"

She picked at her thumbnail, chipping the pale pink polish. Tiny flakes drifted to the floor. "Look, Eva . . . I'm in a really tough position . . . People are kind of pissed off . . ."

"Don't they want to know the truth about what they're helping cover up?" I asked. Even Heather had looked concerned when she turned to face me in the auditorium.

"Well, I'm sure they do, but . . ." Jenny moved on to her other thumbnail. "I think it was more the *way* you went about it. It was kind of aggressive."

"But there was no other way to do it! We tried to talk to Allenby privately, and he threatened us, so we had to go bigger."

Jenny held up her hands. "I'm sorry, Eva! I'm just telling you how everyone feels."

"Well, how do *you* feel?"

She made weird shapes with her closed lips. They were a bright fuchsia, and I was transported back to our very first hangout in the glen, when a text from Heather abruptly yanked her away.

She shrugged. "I dunno, dude. I should probably get back to them. I'm sorry."

"Okay."

I stepped to the side. She smiled weakly and walked past me. Same as that September afternoon, I watched her hurry back to them, backpack bouncing heavily against her side—not quite running, but almost. I flashed a peace sign at her back. A last goodbye.

Then I returned to sit with Candace and Luisa—strangely,

327

feeling lighter than I did before.

That night, an emailed statement went out to the Hardwick community that police had officially opened an investigation. It also said Craig Allenby had stepped down from his post—I imagined "stepped down" was the nice way to put it—and Ms. Pell would be taking his place in the interim.

As I was reading, the phone rang.

It was Connie.

She said the police were bringing her in for questioning, and she suspected Allenby, Betty, and Bobby had been called in, too. She planned to tell them the whole truth, no matter what it could mean for her in the future.

"I'm not afraid," she said calmly. "Not this time."

The following afternoon—Tuesday—Mrs. Suresh pulled me out of English class to thank me for coming forward, and to let me know she was there for me if I ever needed anything. All I had to do was come find her.

"Well," I began, "there is *one* thing I wanted to talk about . . ."

I didn't even have to finish explaining myself. Mrs. Suresh put a comforting hand on my arm and said, "Don't worry, Eva. It's already on my list."

A few hours later, we were sitting on the floor of the archives room playing Dungeons and Dragons: me, Luisa, Candace, Hassan, and Max. We were midway through battling a small army of ash zombies when I got the call that made tears spring to my eyes.

The name on my lock screen. It was Erik.

"Storm," he said breathlessly the moment I picked up. My heart leapt; I'd missed hearing his voice. "Mrs. Suresh just called my parents. She told them everything that happened."

Erik paused.

I held my breath.

"It looks like I'm coming back to Hardwick."

For now, things are as good as they could possibly be, but I could still use a break from the raised eyebrows that have trailed me nonstop over the past week. I typically don't mind being the center of attention, but it's getting kind of exhausting to forcibly wave at every single person trying to sneak a glance at the girl who helped bring down Craig Allenby. I pick up my duffel bag and shoulder my way through the door, even though it's bound to be pretty tundra-like out on the platform.

Ugh—yep. As soon as I step outside, an icy breeze sends my hair whipping across my face. I go around the corner, plop my bag on the ground, and sit with my back against the brick wall and my knees drawn up to my chest for warmth. If I could handle the past seven days, I can *definitely* manage the next ten minutes.

That's when I remember: I never returned Ella's FaceTime from last weekend. I got so caught up in everything else, I completely forgot she'd tried to reach me. With one hand, I hold my curls out of my face, and with the other, I take out my phone and tap her name in my contact list.

"Hey!" she says brightly, from what looks like her bedroom. Ella got the Caleb genes, physically speaking; she's fair-skinned with pin-straight blond hair that falls neatly to her shoulders. It's hard to believe we're related, let alone half sisters.

"Hey, you. Sorry it took so long to call you back. I . . ."

"It's okay. Mom got the email from your school about the police investigation. Holy *crap*. What's the deal with that?"

"Uh, well, I actually . . . sort of . . . started it?" Ella gapes at me. "I'll tell you the whole story when I get home. There's not enough time before I get on the train."

"Jesus, Eva! But you're okay?"

"Yeah. I'm totally fine."

"Good."

There's a bit of an awkward pause. I don't want to ask Ella *why* she called last Friday, because it would imply that we don't talk unless we have a specific reason to do so. But . . . that's also been the truth for us. We keep each other at a safe distance, controlled by the dark forces of Mom and Caleb.

"You're probably wondering why I called the other day," she says.

"Well . . . yeah," I admit.

She looks somewhere off-camera and takes a deep breath. "I got grounded for the rest of the year."

"What?" Ella, *grounded*? It's so unlike her, I figure she must be joking.

"I'm not joking," she says, reading my mind. "I'm not allowed to leave the house unless it's for school or other 'essentials,' like the dentist, or whatever. I can't see my friends, or Benji, or do anything fun."

"Ella, what the hell happened?"

"I'm so mad at myself."

"What did you do?"

"Mom skipped her workout class and came home *way* earlier than expected, and she walked in on Benji and me making out on the couch." Then she diverts her gaze downward and mumbles something unintelligible.

"I can't hear you, Ella."

"We were . . ." She looks up helplessly and leans into the phone. *"Not wearing shirts."*

I can't help it. I burst out laughing. "Well, I'm happy to hear you guys are still going strong!"

"Ha-ha-ha." She rolls her eyes. But instead of meeting my gaze again, she stares off into the distance and doesn't say anything else. Her bottom lip trembles.

"Ella?"

All of a sudden, tears splash down her cheeks. "You laugh, but Mom freaked. She thought we were about to, like, do it, which we *so were not*—we're not even remotely ready for that. She basically chased Benji out of the house, and then she sat me down and went on this screaming rant. She said I was acting like a tramp, and I was going to embarrass the family."

"Mom called you a *tramp*? Who even says that word? And to their own kid?"

"But what if I really embarrassed her?"

"This makes me so mad. *Of course* all she cares about is 'embarrassing the family.' That's all she's ever cared about—is having her perfect little family. Why do you think she sent me to Hardwick?"

Ella continues to cry. "I know. Like, logically I'm aware of what you're saying—that our relationship is totally conditional on me getting good grades and stuff. But . . ." Now she's really crying. I want to reach through the phone and hug her. She wipes her eyes and nose with the back of her free hand. "I'm just so scared of disappointing her."

"Well, greetings from the other side of disappointing Mom." I give her a cheesy wave. "I did it and lived to tell the tale."

"I know, and . . ." Ella looks like she's holding back more tears. "I'm sorry I haven't been there for you more. You're my cool older sister, and I want us to do stuff together. I always have. And I promise I'm not just saying this because I need someone in the family to like me again," she adds with a wet-sounding laugh.

"I know you're not," I assure her.

She lets out a big sigh and in a smaller voice, she asks, "Do you think Mom is going to hate me forever?"

It kills me to see the fear in her eyes. "No. Because from here on out, I vow to continue making myself her least-favorite daughter."

"Eva, *stop.*"

"I'm serious!"

From around the corner, I hear the door burst open and the sound of other people's conversations spilling out onto the platform.

"Hey, Ella, my train's almost here." I tilt the phone so she can see the lights approaching way off down the track. "Let's keep talking when I'm back, okay? Even though you're grounded, I assume you can still hang out with your sister?"

It just slipped out. Not half sister. *Your sister.*

Ella sniffs, wipes her eyes again, and smiles. "Yeah. Sounds good."

"She's home!"

I hear her voice before I even set foot in the apartment, when I'm still turning my key in the lock. I open the door, and there she is, standing in her Pilates gear with her sinewy arms outstretched, like she just couldn't wait for me to get here.

"Hey, Mom."

Caleb wanders into the foyer, too, smiling sheepishly. "Welcome home, kiddo," he says, lifting my duffel bag from my shoulder so Mom can wrap me tightly in a hug. I stand there stiffly, in shock, my brain racing to figure out how to respond to these strange new greetings. Mom squealing at my arrival and pouncing on me? Caleb calling me kiddo?

Mom pulls back so she can get a good look at me. I can feel her long nails through the sleeves of my puffy jacket. She releases one of my arms and tucks a stray curl behind my ear. "You look beautiful, honey. It's so good to have you back. Why don't you go freshen up, and I'll take you out for dinner?" she asks sweetly. "I got the email from your school—it sounds like you've been having quite the semester! You can tell me all about it."

There was a time when I would have said yes without even thinking about it. I would have thrown myself at her and clung to her for as long as I could, before she inevitably shook me off again.

But I'm not that person anymore. I think about what Connie said: that the best people in life, you don't have to worry about whether they like you or not. You just know. And standing here, staring at Mom's megawatt grin, I know she's only being this nice to me because she needs me to be her new "good" daughter. The one who wasn't caught shirtless on the couch with Benji.

Well, I'm not going to jump to be friendly with her just because *she* decides she wants me again.

"Thanks, but I can't today." I wriggle out of her grip and take a step back.

As Mom stands there looking confused, her manicured fingers grasping at the air, I squeeze past Caleb and go down the hall to find Ella.

TWENTY-FIVE

Eva

Port Authority.

We meet again.

On my way into the building, I politely (as possible) turn down tickets to a *Sex and the City* bus tour offered by an overenthusiastic woman in a pink feather boa who tries to put another one around my neck. Just when I'm finally free of her, an off-brand Elmo leaps in front of me and asks in a thick Brooklyn accent if I want to take a picture.

"*NO!*" I exclaim, dodging his flailing red arms. All I want to do is get inside and find Erik, whose bus from New Jersey arrived a few minutes ago.

His parents finally ungrounded him after they talked to Mrs. Suresh, and they learned he was telling the truth the whole time. They felt so bad for not believing him, they bought him two tickets to see *Hamilton*. The latter *definitely* didn't make up for the former, but hey, *Hamilton* tickets are *Hamilton* tickets.

Erik called to invite me last Friday, when I got home for spring break.

I'm pretty sure he called it a "date."

When I see him leaning against the same pillar as last time, his hands in the pockets of his peacoat and his elbows flapping sort of nervously, it's even better than when he called to tell me he was coming back to Hardwick.

He's here.

He's real.

He's smiling at me, huge and bright.

The next thing I know, I'm sprinting across the unsettlingly sticky floor. I don't care—I'm letting my brain imagine everything that's about to happen: I'm going to hug him; my cheek is going to touch his neck; I'm going to hold both his hands at the same time; I'm going to tilt my face toward his. My mind is blissfully free of alarm bells. My thoughts aren't getting ahead of me, because with Erik, I just *know*.

"Storm," he says, closing the distance between us.

"Ellis."

And then our bodies are together, every cut-short conversation finished in the way I bury my face in his neck, the way he knots his hand in the back of my hair.

There's a mortifying moment when I realize we're about to have our first kiss in the Port Authority Bus Terminal, next to the glaring neon lights of a Jamba Juice and a rat dragging a french fry across the floor.

But the funny thing is, when it finally happens—when our lips meet and my brain explodes like a firework—I simply can't think about anything else but us.

TWENTY-SIX

Eva, the last Tuesday evening of the school year

The whole group agrees: we can't play Dungeons and Dragons in the archives room—not when it's this warm outside and the air smells like freshly cut grass and the sun will be up until curfew.

Luisa quickly puts the maps and dice back in the box, tucks the whole thing under her arm, and leads the way down the library's carpeted staircase. Along the way, a few people look up from their homework and call out "congratulations!" when they see her go by. Luisa—eternally deferential to the laws of the library, especially now that she's our next head girl—silently smiles and waves back at them. She won the election by a landslide. When word got out that she was the one in the tech booth during Allenby's award ceremony, there was no question that everyone would put her name down on their ballot.

Of course, anyone who'd ever been in class with her knew she'd always deserved it.

We walk out into the golden evening. After making it

through my first Central New York winter, I'm still not over how good it feels to wear knee socks under my kilt again, instead of trudging around in sweatpants, the bottoms getting crusted with ice. At the bottom of the stone steps, we instinctively turn right; apparently, the six of us had the same destination in mind, without anyone having to say it out loud.

The rose-woven archway leads to a gently sloping lawn, surrounded by flowers on three sides and the glen on the other. Luisa, Candace, Hassan, and Max plop down on the grass to set up the game. Meanwhile, Erik slides his fingers through mine and says, "Fancy taking a turn about the garden?"

As soon as the words escape his lips, I snort with laughter, and he furrows his brow. "Oh no. I did the thing where I sounded like a medieval knight again."

"It's okay. I always enjoy it."

We wander along the bed of multicolored blooms: creamy hydrangeas, bright pink azaleas, yellow daffodils, and other things I don't know the names of. Erik points to the center of a purple flower, where a pair of bumblebees seems to be collecting pollen, or doing whatever it is that bumblebees do.

"There's two of them," he says with a smile.

I stand on my tiptoes to kiss him, which still feels like magic, even though I do it all the time now.

I can't believe it's already been a few months since spring break. On the walk back to Port Authority after our *Hamilton* date, I just blurted it out: "So, you're cool with being my boyfriend, right?"

"Um, *yes*," he said emphatically, before yanking me out of the way of a fast-moving New York City pedicab. He held me against his chest for a few beats longer than necessary. "I've been cool with it since I first met you."

Now, we cross the lawn to walk back up the other side. "Can you believe they were going to dedicate this place to *Allenby*?" I mutter.

Erik shakes his head as we come to a stop at a shiny bronze plaque nestled among the flowers.

THIS GARDEN IS DEDICATED TO

THE MEMORY OF HELEN HONEYMAN

(1947–1962)

The dedication ceremony happened the other weekend. It was a small group, including Connie and her husband, Arthur, and a handful of Erik's family members. (His grandfather was a delight, while his parents still couldn't stop apologizing— which, fair.)

We gathered around the plaque, and Connie made a short speech, her voice clear and measured. She talked about growing up in the shadow of the bomb and the Cold War paranoia that provided a backdrop to Andy Kraus's twisted experiment.

"Back in those days, everyone was terrified of this looming, amorphous threat from afar," she said at one point. "I think we failed to see the evil lurking right here, all around us."

A heaviness settled on my shoulders, and judging by the sorrowful looks on everyone's faces, it was clear I wasn't alone.

But for the most part, we were happy that day—and relieved. The news had just come out: authorities had charged Craig Allenby with criminal negligence for Helen's death, as well as extortion in relation to the decades-long cover-up. ("It means he got money out of people by threatening them," Luisa patiently explained.)

Connie was let off the hook for cooperating with the investigation, as were Betty and Bobby. If Allenby tried to persuade them to throw her under the bus, it didn't work—once police got involved, the two weren't as loyal to him as he'd once believed.

In the end, the former dean of students was the only one who continued to spin lies, and the detectives saw right through it.

His trial would begin at the end of June.

"Xena! Gordon! Get over here!" With a wave of his arm, Hassan beckons us to their spot on the grass.

We walk over and join the group, where Hassan hands out our character sheets and Max tosses each of us a black velvet pouch. I tug at the opening and shake the dice into my palm, excited to embark on the next leg of our strange and hilarious campaign.

It happens again. When I'm as content as I am right now, my brain always takes me back to jumping off that cliff in the darkness. I used to think friendship meant hurling your naked body off a ledge and praying you survived, but actually, it's like wearing a parachute and gently drifting to the ground. It's this, all around me. It's Erik's knee resting against mine; the way he reaches to pluck a ladybug out of my hair. It's sitting with friends on a warm summer evening and laughing so hard your stomach hurts.

Without even having to try.

Acknowledgments

When I was a student at Hamilton College, I heard that during the Cold War, our school had created some kind of nuclear fallout shelter underneath the campus. I became obsessed with trying to find it, occasionally recruiting friends (as well as my then-boyfriend/now-husband, Tim) to explore musty old basements with me. Sadly, I never found the mythical shelter, but publishing this book has more than made up for it. I am forever grateful to everyone who helped bring *Don't Breathe a Word* to life.

Catherine Wallace, thank you for believing in this idea. I am so lucky to work with an editor as wise, imaginative, and kind as you (not to mention who also appreciates a little Plutonium Easter egg). Your feedback consistently inspires me and helps me grow as a writer.

Danielle Burby, thank you for that magical dinner in Astoria in the summer of 2019, where we talked about students being locked in a fallout shelter and 1960s sociological experiments. You are a spectacular brainstorming partner, agent, and—above all else—friend.

Thank you to everyone at HarperTeen who helped create this book and share it with the world. Corina Lupp, Alison Klapthor, Shannon Cox, Aubrey Churchward, Shona McCarthy, Mark Rifkin, Erin Wallace: I am so grateful for your hard work. Jessica Cruickshank, thank you for the stunning cover design—I still can't stop staring at it!

Thank you to the Tides of Chaos, and especially our dungeon master, Rem Myers, for teaching me everything I know about the wonderful world of Dungeons & Dragons. Our ongoing quest to defeat Strahd has been a bright spot in the past year. (I hope we've deployed the demon barrel by the time this book comes out!)

Because of the pandemic, it's almost been a year since I've seen all the people I love in Toronto. To my parents, grandparents, aunts, uncles, cousins, and friends, I miss you so much and can't wait to hug you. Thank you for tuning into many a virtual book event this year—I can feel all your love and support from afar. A special thank-you to my mom, Lisa, who read this book many times in many forms and worried about Eva's well-being each time, and to my dad, David, my most dedicated and enthusiastic hype man.

Tim, thank you for being my teammate in life, love, and quarantine. You are the very best thing I found at Hamilton. My love for you is too big for words.

And finally, thank you, reader, for picking up this book.